# THE WINGED FORM
## Aesthetical Essays on Hindustani Rhythm

BY THE SAME AUTHOR

*Studies in the Metaphysics of Bradley*
George Allen & Unwin, London
and Humanities Press, New York, 1967
(Muirhead Library)

*Aesthetical Essays*
Chanakya Publications, Delhi, 1981

*Ever Unto God: Essays on Gandhi and Religion*
Indian Council of Philosophical Research, New Delhi, 1988

*Swinging Syllables: Aesthetics of Kathak Dance*
Sangeet Natak Akademi, New Delhi, 1991

*Art and Philosophy: Seven Aestheticians*
Indian Council of Philosophical Research, New Delhi, 1994

*Hindustani Sangeet and a Philosopher of Art:*
*Music, Rhythm, and Kathak Dance*
*vis-à-vis Aesthetics of Susanne K. Langer*
D.K. Printworld (P) Ltd., New Delhi, 2001

*Hindustani Music and Aesthetics Today: A Selective Study*
Sangeet Natak Akademi
and Hope India Publications, Gurgaon, 2009

*Avenues to Beauty: Eight Essays in Aesthetics*
Sangeet Natak Akademi
and D.K. Printworld (P) Ltd., New Delhi, 2009

*Hindustani Sangeet: Some Perspectives, Some Performers*
Sangeet Natak Akademi
and D.K. Printworld (P) Ltd., New Delhi, 2010

*Aesthetics: Approaches, Concepts and Problems*
Sangeet Natak Akademi
and D.K. Printworld (P) Ltd., New Delhi, 2010

# THE WINGED FORM

## Aesthetical Essays on Hindustani Rhythm

S.K. Saxena
Formerly Professor of Philosophy
University of Delhi

Sangeet Natak Akademi
New Delhi

DK PRINTWORLD
Publishers of Indian Traditions

**Cataloguing in Publication Data — DK**
[Courtesy: D.K. Agencies (P) Ltd. <docinfo@dkagencies.com>]

**Saxena, Sushil Kumar.**
The winged form : aesthetical essays on Hindustani rhythm/ S.K. Saxena.
p. cm.
Includes bibliographical references and index.
ISBN 13: 9788124606339

1. Hindustani music — Philosophy and aesthetics. 2. Musical meter and rhythm. I. Title.

DDC 780.954 23

ISBN 13: 978-81-246-0633-9 ISBN 10: 81-246-0633-1
First published in 1979
Second revised edition, 2012


*Published by*
Sangeet Natak Akademi
National Academy of Music, Dance and Drama, India
Rabindra Bhavan, Feroze Shah Road
New Delhi - 110 001
*Phones* : (011) 2338 7246; 2338 7248; *Fax* : (011) 2338 2659
*email* : mail@sangeetnatak.gov.in

*and*

D.K. Printworld (P) Ltd.
*Regd. office* : '*Vedaśrī,*' F-395, Sudarshan Park
(Metro Station: Ramesh Nagar)
New Delhi - 110 015
*Phones* : (011) 2545 3975; 2546 6019; *Fax* : (011) 2546 5926
*email* : indology@dkprintworld.com
*Web* : www.dkprintworld.com

Printed by: D.K. Printworld (P) Ltd., New Delhi.

To the memory of
my brother
**Prof. Sudhir Kumar Saxena**

for the symmetry
of his bāja
and his lifelong devotion as a teacher
of tablā-rhythm

# Preface

LITTLE aesthetical notice has been taken so far of rhythm in Hindustani (or north Indian) music. The book is a modest attempt to meet just this clear need.

Many of the essays that make this book have already appeared in journals devoted to philosophy and the arts. But I have at places re-written some of these for the present volume; and in doing so I have drawn not only on my essays: "Essentials of Hindustani Music" (*Diogene*, Paris, 1964), "Kant, Aesthetical Theory and some Indian Art" (*Kant Studien*, Germany, 1978) but on my numerous articles and *reviews* contributed — the last, as a music critic — to the *The Hindustan Times*, New Delhi, more than 55 years ago.

Three of the essays here presented are from different issues of *Sangeet Natak*, the journal of Sangeet Natak Akademi, New Delhi, then edited by Mrs. Uma Anand. The fact that this national body has now agreed to bring out a revised edition of the work is an honour to me, and I gratefully acknowledge it.

My approach in this work is all along that of *philosophical* aesthetics as it is done today, that is, as linguistic analysis and as phenomenology. But in accordance with the Indian view that the single word *sangeet* covers rhythm, music and dance, I have also taken care to include two essays on the linkages of rhythm with our classical singing and Kathak dance. Perhaps, where I speak of the structure of *sthāyī* from the viewpoint of its approach to the *Sama* (Chapter 8), some insight may also be had into the art of making music.

My concern here is not only with individual concepts and problems, but with wider questions of the status of Hindustani rhythm as an independent art, and of its relevance to some modern theories of art, both as illustration and as a challenge. This explains why I begin with the essay, "Aesthetic Theory and Hindustani Rhythm" contributed to *The British Journal of Aesthetics*, and presented, very differently, to the World Philosophy Conference at the University of Delhi, on 2 January 1976. At the same time, I have all along kept in mind the details of practical rhythm as well. This in fact explains why, along with other ways of keeping close to fact, the syllables of rhythm too have been freely provided. Further, at the instance of Dr. Ranjan K. Ghosh, an old student of mine and now an established aesthetician himself, I have put each syllable in both English and Hindi alphabets, the latter mostly within brackets. He rightly made me see that here the use of Hindi alone could cause needless confusion to those readers who do not have any knowledge of this language.

So far as I know, this book is the first of its kind; and I am happy I could do it. It seeks to fix the meaning of such basic concepts as *laya, mātrā, zarab, bol, ṭhekā, tāla, sama* and *layakārī* in the context of both aesthetic discourse and actual contemplation of running rhythm. And where I speak of the Gestalt laws and Kathak dance, I have tried to discuss the crucial questions of rhythmic filling and structure; and to determine the individual contribution of footwork and bodily bearing (*aṅga*) to the wholeness of rhythmic appeal.

But the very singularity of my concern has in part been a handicap. The book is but a lone furrow, and quite without the weight that comes from references to parallel writings. I therefore feel deeply indebted to all those who first made it possible for me to publish this book, and earlier gave me ample chance to work and think for it, by inviting me to participate in national seminars on music and rhythm, or to straight away write on these arts. These friends, all now fond memories which I still gratefully cherish, may be listed thus: Mrs. Uma

Anand and Dr. B.C. Deva (Sangeet Natak Akademi's Assistant Secretaries for publication and music, respectively), and Professor S.S. Barlingay, the well-known editor of the *Indian Philosophical Quarterly*, Poona. I have also felt encouraged, I recall, by the extremely kind reactions which my essay on *laya* elicited from Professor Manfred Junius (sometime with the Institute of Comparative Music, Venice) who not only knew and practised Hindustani music, but remained deeply devoted to it throughout his life.

As is commonly known, a good way to diversify and enrich one's knowledge of rhythm — and to cultivate the ability to follow passages of intricate *layakārī* steadfastly — is close and continual attention to Kathak dance. So I am beholden also to the members of my 25-year-old Kathak team, to its key link in particular, comprising Rani Karna (the noted Kathak danseuse and an Akademi Award winner); and the late Ustad Chhamma Khan, the *tablā* expert of the University of Delhi, a perfect gentleman and an unforgettable friend. I need hardly add that without this association my acquaintance with rhythm would have been poorer than it is today.

Yet, from the viewpoint of the actual *practice* of rhythm — and also, at times, in respect of my understanding of it — my main guide and monitor has been the ablest pupil of the late Ustad Habeebuddin Khan of Meerut, the late Prof. Sudhir Kumar Saxena, who taught *tablā* at the College of Indian Music, Dance and Drama, Baroda University, for a number of years and was himself a drummer of no mean merit. If the book is no mere speculation, it is due as much to his ready and attentive help as to my own deep love of rhythm as an art form. The dedication is therefore heartfelt.

And if the work, as it first appeared in print (1979), seemed passable, it was due to the unstinted help given by M.M. Shungloo, formerly Assistant Editor at Sangeet Natak Akademi, who chose the format and checked the proofs along with Mrs. Uma Anand; and by S.J. Dubey, the then manager of the Delhi University Press, along with A.G. Korde who saw to the printing with patience and seemed ever willing to minimise its errors.

This revised edition, however, makes me feel beholden to a quite different set of friends, and I am as thankful to them as to those who are no longer there to see how the fruit of their kindly assistance has burgeoned. These present friends are: A.N. Sharma (typing); Vinay Jain who has designed the jacket with his usual concern for visual appeal and relevance to the subject of the book; A. Chatterjee who has lent his admirable editorial expertise to all my books brought out so far by Sangeet Natak Akademi, and his usual associate in publication, S.P. Saxena; and Susheel K. Mittal of D.K. Printworld who has taken care of the printing not only of the present edition of the book, but of most of my books brought out by the Akademi.

I regret I cannot put in more detail how their individual assistance has been of help to me; but I can surely cherish, in deep and wordless gratitude, the manifold help they have all along rendered.

**9.2.2012** **S.K. Saxena**

# Contents

# Acknowledgement

I am happy to acknowledge my gratitude to the following who kindly gave me permission to include in this book, with some alterations, my articles which they were the first to publish:

| | |
|---|---|
| *The British Journal of Aesthetics*: | Aesthetic Theory and Hindustani Rhythm |
| *IL Veltro* (Rome): | Croce's Aesthetical Theory and the Rhythm of North Indian Music |
| *Indian Philosophical Quarterly* (Poona): | The Concept of *Laya* in Hindustani Music; and Phenomenology of *Sama* in Hindustani Rhythm |
| *Sangeet Natak* (New Delhi): | Form and Content in Hindustani Rhythm; Aesthetic Character of some Asymmetrical Rhythms: An analytic study; and The Fabric of *Āmad*: A study of Form and Flow in Hindustani Music |
| *Marg* (Bombay): | The Role of Rhythm in Kathak Dance |

# 1

# Aesthetic Theory and Hindustani Rhythm[1]

## Introductory

THIS essay is, in part, a response to the call for internationalism in aesthetics. Two features of Hindustani[2] music, vocal *ālāpa* and *rhythm*, have not yet been given the notice they deserve. The former is singing without words and rhythmic accompaniment. At its best, it seems an intense diffusion, a kind of atmosphere, rather than a form with clear-cut outlines.[3] It is perhaps the most deeply satisfying aspect of Indian music. But attention to rhythm is of help in checking more ideas in our philosophic concern with matters relating to art today. It is this that I here seek to argue.

But is rhythm one of the arts as they are commonly regarded today? Can it lay claim to an independent status?

---

1. The present form of this article differs not only from the talk given on the subject to participants in the Aesthetics section of the World Philosophy Conference (University of Delhi, 2 January 1976), but from the essay published, under the same title, by *The British Journal of Aesthetics* in its Summer 1976 issue, vol. 16, no. 3.

2. *Hindustani* here means "north Indian".

3. I must add that I am here reminded of the following from P.B. Shelley's *Epipsychidion*:

   One intense diffusion
   One serene Omnipresence

My answer is, yes; but I know that many would disagree. Today, in India, rhythm is presented and admired mostly as accompaniment; and a lay listener would perhaps question the view that rhythm is autonomous. But, I may point out, it is also a fact that in our main music conferences even today, a *solo* rhythmic recital is often the main draw of an entire session of music. In our country indeed it has ever been so. Sculpture, in the West, had to shake off subservience to architecture. Painting too had to win its freedom from representation. In the case of our rhythm, on the other hand, it is the heightened emphasis on *accompaniment* that seems to be of relatively recent growth. The primal test of a drummer for us has ever been his capacity for *solo* playing.

The musicologist may protest by pointing to our well known word *sangeet*. It certainly covers both music (vocal, instrumental) and dance, and *does not omit rhythm*. How then is rhythm independent? My reply here is that if the same word is used for many things, they are not thereby prevented from functioning severally. There is indeed no dancing with *ālāpa*; nor any vocal filigree with *tatkār*[4] or pure dance. It is true that, as is indeed quite manifest in our dancing today, the arts called *sangeet* can be interwoven easily. Further, there is in fact one element which is common to them all, that is, *laya* or pace as duly regulated. But, *it* is not the only or dominant integrative way in which dance and music blend. In the case of an expressional dance number, for instance, they may all have to subserve, in the main, the demands of the *theme* rather than the requirements of *laya*.

I can here draw help also from theory. But to facilitate understanding let me first outline our rhythm quite simply. A rhythmic recital comprises a cycle and quite a few patterns. The cycle is a whole of a specific number of beats moving at even speed. The first beat here is at once the focal beat or *Sama*. From it we set out as we follow the rhythm; and to it we

---

4. *Tatkār* is a display of pure footwork in Kathak dance.

return, accurately, completing a round or *āvṛtti*.[5] The patterns that are woven across (or within) the cycle can be infinitely various in respect of content and manner, but they must all in the end close at the *Sama* actually or heighten it ideally.

The cyclic quality of our (basic) rhythm at once favours the suggestion of wholeness. If the unique manner of the cycle has been truly "established";[6] if, further, the accents neither seem to tug at, nor look blurred in the flow; and if, finally, the playing has the requisite measure of auditory charm, the rhythm may even *seem to move to a clear inner impetus.* All this conduces to concentration on the form and inside of the rhythmic whole itself. It is indeed quite easy for a duly played cycle to appear a miniature of what Dewey calls "an experience" — marked out and self-complete.[7]

But the independence of rhythm as an art can be argued in a much fuller way. Susanne Langer suggests that an art is autonomous if it can be said to have its own materials, its "peculiar primary creation", and its own creative principles.[8] So, I may now set out to see how rhythm meets all these requirements, and one or two more; and also, in passing and subsequently, its value for aesthetics.

## Rhythm as an Art

A. *The material of rhythm* is doubtless distinctive. It is mnemonic syllables (or *bols*) that aim at seizing the manner and character of sounds produced by striking the drum(s) in specific ways.[9]

5. How, even *aesthetically*, the *Sama* is both the source and destiny of rhythm will be brought out later.

6. This is the English word for our: *quāyem karnā.*

7. A much better illustration of the point in question would, however, be a *quāyedā*; for, such a pattern has a far richer structure than a mere cycle.

8. S.K. Langer, *Problems of Art*, Routledge and Kegan Paul, London, 1957, pp. 78-79.

9. I do not here speak of *mātrā*s or beats. These are all material

→

They are mere letters or meaningless bunches of letters, like *tā, dhā, tin, dhin* (ता, धा, तिन, धिन); but in every case they seek to be formal analogues of actual sounds. They are not patently unmusical, but they mark but one or two notes of the musical scale. Their function is to make us identify the actual sounds drummed, and their beauty arises from the manner of their grouping and clear execution.

Now, it is possible to hold with some show of reason that because of this material, rhythm is not only distinctive but *important* among the arts. One may here build on Herbert Read's way of arguing for the pre-eminence of *music*:

> . . . almost in music alone, it is possible for the artist to appeal to his audience directly, without the intervention of a medium of communication in common use for other purposes. The architect must express himself in buildings which have (a clear) utilitarian purpose. The poet must use words which are bandied about in the daily give-and-take of conversation.[10]

Now if, as here, the rank of an art is made to depend on the requirement that its medium is *not* used for "other (non-aesthetic) purposes", rhythm, I would say, is superior to music. For, whereas musical notes are in fact sweetly employed, say, by some hawkers in their typical cries, or by some bells to chime the hour pleasantly — purposes which are both clearly utilitarian — the mnemonic syllables (or *bol*s) of rhythm are never employed for any non-aesthetic purpose. Have we ever seen anyone using the following collocation of *bol*s (rhythmic syllables) in everyday conversation: तकिट तकिट धिन तधिगिन धाधा गिन (*takiṭ takiṭ dhin tadhigin dhādhā gin*).

Nor do the syllables of rhythm refer to anything external.

---

→ *organised* as accents of an even flow, and so are the *content,* not the mere material of rhythm. As for the content and form of rhythm, see chapter 6.

10. Herbert Read's essay, "A Definition of Art", included in *Aesthetics and the Arts*, ed. L.A. Jacobus, McGraw Hill Book Co., 1968, p. 4. Bracketed words added.

A good rhythmic recital is quite non-representational. Yet, because of the excellence of its own inner organisation (and clarity), it can be so absorbing that it may induce in knowledgeable listeners a state of self-forgetfulness and attune them in *tādātmya*[11] with the winged variform beauty of rhythm. Of course, if he so decides, the drummer *can* produce syllables that may appear to *resemble* everyday sounds and familiar happenings, such as the movement and noise of a train as it steams out and gathers speed; but whenever this is attempted, those who really know the *art* of rhythm only feel amused. Our rhythm is indeed very true to the ideal of "pure" art.

Here, I may add, it would of course be wrong to contend that rhythm *as played* represents or imitates *bol*s *as recited* or thought; and that rhythm is therefore not free from subservience to the external. For, merely as it occurs in speech, writing or thought, a *bol* is nothing self-complete. It is meant to be played. It receives the supplement it intrinsically needs when it is executed on the drums. And *as played*, the *bol*s are not imitated by, but only incorporated in rhythm, like words in poetry.

B. *The primary creation of rhythm* is, in my view, *the seemingly automotive and essentially articulate symmetry of pure pace*. The keywords here may be explained as follows:

By "symmetry" I mean beauty of form. Everything in the region of rhythm is indeed required to seem well organised and shapely. This is true of both the basic rhythm-cycle and the patterns that are woven within and across it.

As for the epithet *articulate*, I think it is truer of our rhythm than of any other art. Langer emphasizes it in the context of music. "A composition", she says, "is not merely produced by mixture like a new colour made by mixing paints but is articulated, i.e. its internal structure is given to our perception." The parts here, it is added, "maintain some

11. *Tādātmya* is imaginative self-identification with the essence of the other.

degree of separate existence".[12] But I do not think this is quite true of musical form. To speak quite generally, where harmony dominates the music it is difficult to distinguish the notes as having a measure of "separate existence". And in Hindustani music *mīṇḍ*s (glides), if suitably employed, are found to make for, rather than to weaken the form; yet it is impossible to say that the notes in a *mīṇḍ* retain "some degree of *separate* existence". Such existence is here neither present nor desired. In fact, what distinguishes a *mīṇḍ* as a formal device is the quite opposite fact that the notes it comprises seem to *flow into one another*.

Nor is articulation, as Langer interprets it, indispensable to painting. The structure or the organization of details is not here mainfest in the case of every work. Consider, for instance, the masterpieces of Turner, the famous English painter of seascapes and landscapes. Take his well-known work *Snowstorm*. Turner himself feared its details would not be manifest to the onlooker. That is indeed why he had to exhibit the work with a long, descriptive rubric: "Snowstorm: steamboat off a harbour's mouth making signals in shallow water, and going by the lead". And yet the work *is* a masterpiece, "one of the vastest representations", as Ruskin said, "of the sea in motion, and of clouds and light".[13]

In respect of rhythm, on the other hand, articulation is always a key requirement. Here, even in the case of such patterns as *relā* or a *rau* which are meant to be presented at quick pace, we insist on the clarity of syllables, without of course accenting them at the expense of requisite fluency. Generally, the *bol*s are required to be "cut out". This detail of manner is called *bol kāṭnā*; and playing which meets this requirement admirably is called *khuśkhat* (ख़ुशख़त). The syllable *"dir, dir"*, in quick playing, may seem an exception to this

12. S.K. Langer, *Feeling and Form*, Routledge and Kegan Paul Ltd., London, 1963, 3rd impression, p. 31.

13. Giuseppe Gatt, *Turner*, A Dolphin Art Book, Thames and Hudson, 1968, p. 37.

general rule; but even here, we may note, the effect sought is one of *tremulous* fluency, *and the palpitation must not be quite eclipsed in the flow*. It should now be easy to see why the old masters would be, as a rule, averse to playing at hectic speed[14] where the syllables are bedimmed and seem a mere flowing lump.

Its *automotive* character is another main feature of rhythm. The meaning is not that rhythm *somehow* seems self-propelling, but that (in principle) the length or brevity of the very first syllable or beat as played or recited[15] — or its own temporal character — directly determines whether the entire subsequent playing is to be leisurely or brisk. In *paḍant* (or recitation of *bol*s) it is in fact quite easy to see the point that if one utters the first beat slowly — in the manner of a drawl, so to say — the entire subsequent counting has to be just as leisurely; and if the same beat is then spoken sharply and briefly,[16] the following beats too must be quickened correspondingly. I wonder if we can anywhere (in the region of art) find a more obvious instance of immediate determination of the whole form by the character of a part. And this is, I may add, a *clearer* indication of the "autonomous form" of rhythm than Langer's following remark on some records of African music in which the constructive power of the drum is paramount:

> . . . Anyone familiar with many works of that sort would probably feel their structure and mood almost from the opening beat.[17]

---

14. An oft-quoted example of such masters is the late Ustād Natthu Khan of Delhi.

15. In the case of Indian rhythm, most of the sounds that the drummer produces while playing can be recited by him, as syllables or *bol*s, the playing and the speaking being related by similarity of mere manner. Recitation of the rhythmic syllables is for us an important aspect of the drummer's art.

16. I may add that the point I am here trying to make is borne out better in recitation than in playing the first beat (*bol*) unless the drum used is *pakhāwaj* which can easily produce sounds that tend to prolong themselves.

17. S.K. Langer, *Feeling and Form*, p. 125.

The automotive symmetry of rhythm is, however, not uniform. It has three main expressions:

> a pattern flitting across yet ultimately within — and variegating — the basic rhythm (-cycle);
>
> or making for, and (so to speak) efflorescing at the *Sama*; or, much less commonly,
>
> deviating purposively, but for a mere moment, from the focal beat, and yet not losing sight of it.

The first is the common effect of patterns after the basic rhythm (-cycle) has been established. The second and the third may be called, respectively, the rhythms of orientation *and* abandon or willed waywardness *and resilience.*[18] *These* have been often missed by those who have written on rhythm.[19] So I may comment on them at some length:

THE RHYTHM OF ORIENTATION

When a well-designed integration of *bols* is being played by the drummer, it often happens that — from a particular point within its fabric — the pattern (so to say) gathers and activates itself perceptibly and tends towards, and finally blooms forth at the *Sama* in delightful self-completion of its own form. The *Sama* here appears as the destiny of a clearly oriented rhythmic flow, and not merely as a tame, if unfaltering terminus. Such flow is of help like a clear direction line (of look) in a painting; and form is here heightened as a *passage, and not as a mere process* of efflorescence. Perhaps in no other art is the precise point

---

18. The two italicised words had to be added after listening to some *pakhāwaj*-playing by Bhai Baldeep Singh, a young man who is very well versed in hoary Sikh music and rhythm.

19. As by Frye, where he speaks of the various kinds of rhythm. See his *Anatomy of Criticism*, Princeton University Press, 1957 (PB), pp. 251-81.

    Langer too speaks *only* of the setting up and release of tensions, and of continuity and repetition where she discusses rhythm. See her *Feeling and Form*, pp. 125-32.

or region of organization, or the dominant motif or movement, so clearly identifiable as in our rhythm.

It may also be noted, in passing, that — as seems requisite for any art that claims to be independent — in respect of rhythm too we have some criteria that apply to it uniquely. One of these is the drummer's capacity for a "blended" employment of the two drums. The reference here is obviously to *tablā* which comprises two drums; but the point needs clearing. The thing is that each drum has its own share in the fabric of playing. The "left" drum is meant to work up effects of a certain breathing continuity (called *sāṅs*) and of depth and inwardness; and the "right" one contributes crispness, discreteness, sweetness, fluency and clarity. The requirement is that (at least) in playing the basic rhythm-cycle the use of the two drums should appear duly coordinated, so that the playing may seem neither a mere succession of disconnected sounds, due to undue dominance of "the right one", nor a mere booming loudness due to overmuch emphasis on the left, but rather a mellow, flowing round wherein the details occur daintily, without being blurred in, or marring resonances of the left drum. Another requirement which relates to rhythm alone is the drummer's ability to come back to the *Sama* with split second accuracy.[20]

Now, this second criterion, I insist, is a more definitely usable requirement than the criteria which govern evaluation in the field of other arts. Two critics, equally competent and watchful, may find it difficult to decide whether an item of music is or is not properly structured *or* expressive. But two listeners who have but a fair knowledge of rhythm are almost bound to agree as to whether or not the drummer has reached the first beat accurately. For them it is as easy a matter to judge as the fact of a man's arrival sharply on time.

## THE RHYTHM OF ABANDON AND RESILIENCE

Some patterns are so knit and played that they end a little

20. And in a well-designed way.

after or before the *Sama*. The deviation is here willed; and is demanded by the very economy or ebullience of structure. The *Sama* is overstepped or just not touched; but its precise location is heightened in idea by its regulated refusal to comply. A *part* of this artifice may not seem new to those who are familiar with the arts. It is indeed common knowledge that inspired artistic content may well overrun, so to say, the bounds of prefixed extent, and thereby vivify "form" ideally as internal structure. See, for instance, the following on poetry:

> Form does not lie simply in the correct observance of rules. It lies in the struggle of certain living material to achieve itself within a pattern. The very refusal of a poet to sacrifice what he means to a perfectly correct rhyme, for example, can more powerfully suggest the rhyme than correctness itself would.[21]

But, I believe, it is not *so* easy to realize the other half of the matter, that is, the truth that our awareness of "form" may be heightened even by the act of falling daintily *short* of the normal stretch, in response to the immanent needs of design. Yet this is exactly what is done by our patterns that are made to end a little before the *Sama*.[22] In the region of sculpture a parallel of this structural subtlety is perhaps provided by a detail of Rodin's way of working. Once he had succeeded in finding the precise livingness or expression in a figure or bust, he would often stop and leave, say, the hands and feet unfinished — all without detracting from the seeming self-completeness of the work (as contemplated).

## THE RHYTHM OF SIMULTANEITY

But a better known rhythm — and easier to follow — is that of simultaneity. I have here in mind the kind of rhythm that *distinguishes* the drummer's art of providing "accompaniment"

---

21. Stephen Spender, *World within World*, Hamilton, London, pp. 313-14.

22. Such rhythmic patterns are called *anāgat.*

to the main performer, say, the *sitārist*; that is, the rhythm of similarity, or parallel flow, and of co-extension and unitive advent. The reference is to a consummate kind of *saṅgat*.[23] Where the music seeks to dally with rhythm, the drummer may seize forthwith the manner (*andāz*) of the *sitārist*; and without ever slackening his hold over the cycle, may so adapt his own playing to that of the main performer that the two flowing forms may seem a quite free confluence, and finish at the *Sama* with perfect simultaneity. Here, *what* syllables the drummer plays is not the basic thing; and what counts, I repeat, is only his unerring grasp and replication of the *manner* of the music. And, as for the instant of jointly reaching the *Sama*, it here satisfies us not in detachedness, but largely because it consummates a flowing *design*; and the net effect, because of parallel form and rhythmic turns, is one of intertwining.[24]

C. Rhythm also has its own "*principles of constructing* its final creations".[25] Some of these resemble poetic craft, such as the artifice of *quāfiyā radeef* (in the case of a *quāyedā*)[26] which is similar to end-rhymes; and there is also, in the making of rhythm, a free use of the Gestalt laws of perception such as those of figure-ground and common destiny. However, I may here dwell on only one constructional device which is at once basic to, and distinctive of rhythm. This is the act of so filling

23. The other kind, which is easier and more current today, is quite different. Here the drummer reproduces the rhythmic parallel *after* the *sitārist* has finished the pattern and has begun playing the basic *gat* (composition) again. But this, I protest, is closer to *solo* playing than *saṅgat* which literally means "accompaniment", and not mere following or reproduction.

24. The Hindustani word, here, is *lipaṭnā*.

25. S.K. Langer, *Problems of Art*, p. 79.

26. A *quāyedā* is an impressive, elaborate and methodically organized pattern. The terminal syllables of its two sections should be similar in sound, though not identical in content, such as: *tīnākinā, dhīnāginā* (तीनाकिना, धीनागिना).

a stretch of some beats, or the duration *between* two separate beats, with orderly bunches of *bol*s that rhythm gets invested with the *spatial suggestions of teeming, being crowded, or overflowing* with them. A single syllable so inserted may even come to look like a wedge holding the neighbouring ones apart. The richer and the more orderly such filling of *bol*s within a narrow time-length, the greater is the title of the drummer to acclaim. From the viewpoint of this artifice, rhythm may well be regarded as an aesthetic demonstration of the divisibility of time.

But the *form* of its filling (of *bol*s) at once divides rhythm from actual, lived time. This, however, is not the only reason for regarding rhythmic time as "virtual". There are many little elements of happy seeming that characterize rhythm. Whether as the matrix of a solo recital, or as providing "accompaniment", how exactly a *cycle* affects us on the whole, turns (also) on its relation to the patterns which it initiates, supervenes or sustains. Thus, when in a solo recital the drummer lapses back to the cycle steadily, after executing a *tukḍā*[27] of extra fluent pace, the *ṭhekā* may *seem to be* slower than it really is. And if, while providing simple[28] "accompaniment" to, (say) the singer's filigree of *svara*s, the drummer goes on playing the *cycle* steadily, the rhythm may be felt as a mere moveless background, not as being occurrent or flowing, though some actual process is obviously there. Here, the question of *drut*[29] or *vilambit*[30] is not raised at all, and what we admire is only the drummer's seeming fixedness.

Again, any rhythmic pattern can be made to look a little more fleet than it really is by just gradually accentuating its

---

27. A *tukḍā* is a small rhythmic pattern, not exceeding two *āvṛtti*s of the cycle.

28. By *simple* accompaniment I here mean the steady playing of the *ṭhekā* alone, not imitating the manner of the vocalist's patterns.

29. *Drut* means allegro.

30. *Vilambit* is adagio.

closing syllables. But, actual time may be more sweetly surpassed when the playing makes the *Sama* appear as the climax of a shapely rhythmic upsurge. Here, as we follow the flowing form approaching its terminus, we only *think of* the *Sama*; and *as thus apprehended*, it cannot seem extended. The unfoldment that we watch is that of the pattern. And when it ends immaculately at the *Sama*, we just nod at the fusion rather than judge how long the *Sama-bol* lasts. It does in fact occupy a measurable time, but it *seems* instantaneous. Calculative following as a quiet *counting* of beats — to which our awareness of lived time may be, in some anxious moments, similar — is here quite suspended. Assuredly, we do not reckon time exactly when a tension is relieved, or a target just attained.

And if, during the process of making a pattern (appear to) move designedly towards the *Sama*, the drummer also gradually increases the intensity of the constituent *bol*s, the additional suggestion of an *ascent* — not of mere reaching, but of an upflow — will be clearly worked up.

## Rhythm and Aesthetic Theory

We may finally make some explicit comments on the relevance of Hindustani rhythm to modern aesthetic theory — to the following concepts, in particular: *living form* (as used by Susanne Langer in *Mind : An Essay on Human Feeling*), *embodiment, symbol* and *expression*.

a. The concept of *living form*, I believe, gets a new meaning in terms of those patterns which (for some time) abandon the basic rhythm in movements of diverse design, without really going astray. Such "wanton heed" is at once a kind of drummer's self-testing, a check of the firmness of his own grip over *laya*; and rhythm that is seen to rearrange itself in numberless varying ways *within set confines* must be credited with a kind of creative self-possession.

b. In the light of this fact, it hardly seems proper to speak of rhythm as *embodiment*. This particular word, favoured by L.A. Reid, suggests inertness. Rhythm, on the other hand, is an occurrent art. It happens; and we follow it as it runs its course. We see it being made. Further, in playing any pattern the drummer may — with guarded abandon and distinct aesthetic gain — shorten or withhold one syllable, or tarry at or displace another against its set speed and location, without of course failing to mark (or suggest) the *Sama*. And this can make for an effect that is wholly new. Thus, quite apart from the design of the patterns he chooses to play, the drummer may impart an extra bit of quite unexpected sharpness to the *Sama* by playing the penultimate *bol* a little later than its grammatically set moment. This ever-present room for creative variations is not at all provided for when we speak of rhythm as embodiment.[31] Above all, with regard to drumming which is extremely fluent, and may seem to have the rapidity of a torrent, it would be as improper to use the word "embodiment" as to say that a waterfall *embodies* a flow.

c. Can (an exposition of) rhythm be said to be a *symbol*? My answer is here in the negative. Whatever is a symbol permits the question; "what does it symbolize"? But this is just what cannot be asked in respect of rhythm. It simply *looks* lively, ebullient, torrential, steady, sparse or involute. If however we *have* to regard it as being in some sense a symbol, it would be proper to call it a presentational one, in Langer's sense. As we listen to good drumming, it is

---

31. For similar (and other) objections to the view that embodiment is the key aesthetic concept, see my article: "Embodiment and the Quest for Key Aesthetic Concepts" in *Contemporary Indian Philosophy* (ed. Margaret Chatterji), George Allen & Unwin Ltd., London (1974), pp. 321-52.

just not possible to detach what it says (or how it looks) from its syllabic material.

d. Nor is *expressiveness* any truer to rhythm. I have yet to see a drummer or a critic saying that rhythm is expressive of something. The commonest words of critical acclaim here are: fluent, effortless, methodical, sparkling, brilliant; and the key features of rhythm, I repeat, are clarity and organization of syllables.

(Here, I can visualize a plansible objection. If rhythm neither represents nor expresses life-content, how is it significant at all? *My* ready answer is that it charms us by its very "look", like beautiful objects of nature which are not ordinarily said to symbolize, express or embody anything.)

e. But perhaps the clearest way in which Hindustani rhythm is relevant to aesthetic theory is the infinite ground for thinking it provides to the philosopher of art. Analytic writing on the basic concepts of our rhythm has only begun,[32] and the whole rhythmic discourse of the unlettered *ustāds*,[33] often quite unclear but never without insight, is waiting to be analyzed.

32. The first step here, I believe, is my essay on *laya*: see chapter 3.

33. *Ustād* here means a professional Muslim musician or teacher of music or rhythm.

# 2

# Our Rhythm and Croce[1]

It appears to me that some seeming obscurities of Croce's aesthetic theory are lightened if we view it in relation to Hindustani rhythm and the present essay is but an attempt to justify this impression.

But why do I choose rhythm rather than the better known arts of, say, music, poetry and painting? Is rhythm an independent art at all? The answer to the first of these questions will emerge only towards the end of the chapter, that is, when we have seen how *rhythm* is specially illustrative of Croce's ideas. As to the independent status of this art, I turn forthwith to justify it.

### Rhythm as an Art

a. There is, to begin with, the clear evidence of fact. Even today, at our bigger music "festivals", *solo* expositions of rhythm are freely presented as important items in different sessions; and if the drummer is a really competent one — say, like the late Ustād Habeebuddin Khān of Meerut[2] — such rhythmic recitals can

1. This essay is a slightly modified form of my article: "Aesthetic Theory of Croce and the Rhythm of North Indian music" first published in the Italian journal *IL Veltro* (3-4-Maggio-Agosto, 1976) and of the paper presented, under a similar heading, to the Dante Society of Delhi at the University of Delhi on 15 February 1975.

2. Regarded by many as a model of technique, fluency and appeal →

captivate both lay and knowledgeable listeners. So, rhythm may well be said to be an independent art in the view of those who present music in a big way.

b. One can also appeal (we have seen)[3] to aesthetic *theory* to prove that — in so far as it has its own unique material, manner and criteria of evaluation — rhythm is a distinct and important art.

c. Further, our rhythm (or *tāla*) quite meets the modern requirement that art should seem significant because of its own inner organisation, rather than through a convincing representation of external reality or expression of some basic human emotion. And it is important to see how this specific adequacy of rhythm is traceable to its various features:

> There is, first, the fact that our *tāla* admits of ever newer inner shapings. The basic form of rhythm is *a specific* number of beats as combining to make a *regular* succession, like moments marked *evenly* in time. But in Hindustani rhythm, within the chosen extent of flow — and remaining *on the whole* true to its tempo — many little *decelerations and spurts can be brought in restrainedly.*[4] Nor is there any limit to the number and location of accents, in addition to the set ones of a cycle, within the speed and measure of the flow in question, it being largely dependent on the creative skill of the drummer as to which particular moment of the flow is to be emphasised.

---

→ among the drummers of north India. *Tablā* is the two-piece drum, popular today in the field of north Indian music.

3. In chapter 1. For brief comments on the general relevance of Hindustani rhythm to modern aesthetic theory, also see my article: "Aesthetics of Hindustani Music", in *Sangeet Natak* (Journal of our Central Academy for Music, Dance and Drama), New Delhi, no. 28, April-June, pp. 14-15.

4. That is, according to a design; or intentionally *and* with an eye to *beauty.*

> The syllables (or *bols*)[5] too that make the filling of the flow *between* the beats are alike various in respect of both number and character.
>
> Secondly, and this is noteworthy, in so far as the *syllables* here are all without ordinary meaning or quite non-representational — and (positively) sounds of changing step, character and embedment — attention is not only invited to rhythm, but is entirely prevented from wandering to thoughts of things and happenings in reality. Aestheticians sometimes speak of art as a *presentational* symbol;[6] and in so doing they seek to provide for the truth that, though a work of art does say something, its "meaning" is quite fused with what we find presented in it. Now, of the truth of *this* idea our rhythm, I believe, is perhaps the best available instance. The "meaning" (or significance) is here indivisi*ble* — and not only undivid*ed* — from what directly meets the ear; and the mind only follows interestedly the varying sound and movement of rhythm.

Now, I may outline some key aesthetic ideas of Croce before turning to see how our rhythm is of help in understanding them. What first claims our attention is here is his singular view of intuition and expression.

## Croce: Intuition, Expression

By "intuition" Croce means the spiritual (or inner) *activity* of having a *vivid* image *or* perception. I *see* this paper clearly; it is intuition. I vividly *imagine* myself as writing in another room; that too is intuition.[7] This would suggest, as Croce indeed

5. A *bol* is mnemonic syllable, a letter or a tuft of letters, all alike meaningless. It is a way of identifying the various sounds that the drums produce when they are struck (or pressed) variously at different places. These *bol*s are therefore the material of our rhythm.
6. The reference here is to the view of Mrs. Langer.
7. B. Croce, *Aesthetic: As Science of Expression and General Linguistic*, Vision Press, London, 1962 rpt., p. 3.

believes, that "the distinction between reality and non-reality is . . . secondary to the true nature of intuition".[8] But what I here want to emphasise is his view that intuition is an *activity*, and that the spirit intuits "only in mak*ing*, form*ing*, express*ing*".[9]

Elsewhere, however, Croce also says that:

> To intuit is to express; and nothing else (nothing more, but nothing less) than to express.[10]

Here, there is a seeming discrepancy. In the second utterance Croce says, quite categorically, that intuition is nothing but expression. But in the earlier one (see the closing sentence of the regular para above) he seems clearly to hold that intuition is not merely expression, but also making, or forming; or that expression is just a part, however necessary, of intuition. *This* is more clearly held in the following:

> . . . Be it pictorial, or verbal, or musical, or in whatever form it [may] appear, to no intuition can *expression* in one of its forms be wanting; it is, in fact, *an inseparable part of intuition*.[11]

Now, how are we to reconcile the two sides? Perhaps the only way to do this is to regard "expression" itself as *including* forming, making, etc. In the light of this suggestion, the first utterance — that the spirit intuits "only in making, forming, expressing" — may be regarded as *a gradual ascent to the full meaning of intuition*, so that expression (as understood by Croce) may be said to be truly a making too. This is borne out by his own following words:

> Intuition . . . is distinguished as *form* from what is felt and suffered, from the flux . . . of sensation, or from psychic matter; and *this* form, *this taking possession, is expression*.[12]

8. Croce, *Aesthetic*, p. 3.
9. Ibid., p. 8.
10. Ibid., p. 11.
11. Ibid., 8. Italics added.
12. Ibid., p. 11.

So "expression" is really a form *at work*: or it is at once a form*ing*. For the sake of understanding we may indeed distinguish *intuition* from disorganised sensations by saying that it is a form; but as manifest in experience — or as it is found — intuition is this form as actively organising ("taking possession" of) the psychic material. This *activity* is expression. It includes, or is itself a "forming". "Expression", which Croce regards as being inseparable from intuition, is not any expression, but *formed* expression. Intuition, correspondingly, is not the mere having of suggestions or sensations, but their active organising.

Further, and this partly follows from the remarks just made, though the fact of intuition is (in Croce's view) never separate from expression, a distinction between the two may well be made *from the viewpoint of their individual relation to knowledge and experience in general*. Thus, whereas intuition — as that "knowledge of . . . individual things" which is provided by imagination — is opposed to the knowledge of *relations* between things provided by the intellect,[13] "expression" is (by Croce) distinguished from impressions on the one hand, and from expression in the sense of the external activity of making art, on the other. The latter dual distinction *is* present, if not quite manifest, in his following basic thesis:

> Art is the expression of impressions, not expression of expression.[14]

The way "expression" is here related to "impressions" enables us to make another distinction between intuition and expression. Quite generally, expression may be regarded as the (necessary) objectification of intuition:

> That which does not objectify itself in expression is not intuition.[15]

13. Croce, *Aesthetic*, p. 1.

14. Ibid., p. 13.

15. Ibid., p. 8.

Here, however, Croce would like us to remember that what he calls "expression" is no external activity but only the holding up of some content, as it were, before the mind. And where he speaks of art and the aesthetic, "intuition" is used to emphasise the *individuality*, and "expression", the *manifestness* of an experience. This is borne out by the following:

> What *intuition* reveals in a work of art is . . . character, *individual physiognomy*.[16]
>
> When we have . . . conceived *definitely and vividly* a figure or a statue . . . *expression* is born and complete. . . .[17]

But, I repeat, the difference is only one of emphasis. It is not to be regarded as warranting a separation of intuition from expression. Croce indeed is careful to add that expression *too* has the unity (or continuity) of a process:

> A corollary of the conception of expression as activity is the indivisibility of the work of art. Every expression is a single expression.[18]

Finally, the fact that Croce keeps it *so close to intuition* may be taken to suggest that "expression" is an inner activity. This is indeed (we have seen) a view which he openly professes.[19]

And from the other side, the coupling of "intuition" with "expression" means that, though it cannot be seen from the outside, *intuition* is, so to speak, always the setting up of something before the mind.

## Our Rhythm and Croce

But if, as Croce indeed maintains, intuition is formed expression, where exactly do we find that intuition, that having of a vivid *image* which is at once and *clearly* a "forming"

16. Croce, *Aesthetic*, p. 20. Italics added.
17. Ibid., p. 50. Italics added.
18. Ibid., p. 20.
19. Ibid., pp. 50-1.

or "making"? The answer, I fear, is not quite provided by some of Croce's own favoured instances:

> . . . The perceptions of the room in which I am writing, of the ink-bottle and paper that are before me, of the pen I am using . . . ; — these are all intuitions.[20]

a. We have rather to go to the arts where the very first step is obviously a kind of making. But here, I believe, rhythm is markedly relevant, because the moment one begins rhythm, a speed is *actively* set (we assume) for all subsequent work. Here, indeed, the very first intuition (or clear awareness) of a beat *as a mātrā*[21] is at once a forming or making of *laya*.[22] But this must be clarified:

   To put it roughly, the manner of rhythm is similar to counting steadily at a chosen speed. *Our* rhythm, we have seen, is cyclic. But, and this is precisely what is here of significance, the temporal character of the very first beat — that is, the time which one takes, more or less, in speaking (*or* playing) it — directly determines the pace at which the *entire* cycle is to be played.[23] Thus, if one begins counting sharply, the inviolable norm of steadiness demands that the same alacrity be kept throughout. If, on the other hand, the opening is slow and deliberate, what follows immediately, nay, the full cycle too must move and seem leisurely, in response to the same basic requirement.

   In other words, the moment I begin the right kind of

---

20. Croce, *Aesthetic*, p. 3.
21. The word *mātrā* literally means "measure".
22. Quite generally, *laya* may be taken to mean the *flow* of musical time which the beats are seen to measure. For a detailed examination of the meaning of *laya* see chapter 3.
23. What follows is partly a repetition of my similar argument in the first chapter. But it is here demanded by the context.

rhythmic counting, I choose the pace to be followed all along. The clear awareness or utterance of a beat, *as the beginning of rhythm*, is thus at once regulative of the process to follow. The "intuition" here is clearly a *forming*.

b. We may dwell a little longer on the fact that a necessary character of the whole rhythm — that is, its moving at a set pace — is determined by the length or brevity of the very first beat. I may say at once that this particular feature gives us some definite theoretic help. In so far as determination of the character of a whole by that of its parts is a clear meaning of the concept of organic unity, what we have just said about rhythm also lends point to Croce's following utterance:

> (The activity of artistic expression) is a fusion of impressions in an organic whole.[24]

I may add here that the "individual physiognomy"[25] of which Croce speaks, is (as a rule) quite manifest in our rhythm. What it here means, however, is not merely the cyclic self-completeness referred to earlier, but the ordered character of the inner accents of rhythm.

c. In Hindustani rhythm, indeed, the formed character of an articulate whole is the main ground of appeal.[26] And, in so far as this character is obviously an inseparable part of rhythm as "symbol", the word cannot be taken as signifying something to which "meaning" is *merely conjoined*:

> The symbol has sometimes been given us as the essence

24. Croce, *Aesthetic*, p. 20.

25. Ibid., p. 5. The Hindustani word here, in the region of rhythm, is *shakl* which literally means a face with its individual features.

26. I say, "main", not "the only" ground, because the heard sweetness of playing also counts.

> of art. . . . But if the symbol be conceived as separable — if the symbol be on one side, and on the other, the thing symbolised, we fall . . . into the intellectualist error.[27]

d. Finally, our rhythm is, in my view, of greater help than any other art in seeing how (in some cases) the following words of Croce could appear quite sensible:

> The aesthetic fact is altogether completed in the expressive elaboration of impressions. When we have achieved the word within us, conceived definitely the motive, expression is born and complete. If after this we should open our mouths — *will to* open them to speak . . . this is all an addition . . . a *practical* fact, or fact of *will*. . . . The work of art (the aesthetic work) is always *internal*.[28]

Croce's meaning here is that artistic expression, or the real making of a work of art, is a purely internal happening; that the moment I have been able to form a tune and to hear it sung in the mind, the music *as a work of art* is quite complete; and that if I then sing it out to others I certainly *share* it with them, but do not add anything to the music itself. The work of art is completed *within* the mind.

In support of this rather unusual view, Croce appeals to the evidence of some very eminent artists. Thus, we are told, the great Michelangelo once declared:

> One paints, not with the hands, but with the brain.[29]

Again, we may add, there is the case of Leonardo who once stood just gazing at *The Last Supper* for days together — without touching it with the brush — and then made the following remark on this attitude of intense, but quiet contemplativeness:

---

27. Croce, *Aesthetic*, p. 34.

28. Ibid., pp. 50-51.

29. Ibid., p. 10.

> The minds of men of lofty genius are most active in invention when they are doing the least external work.[30]

Now, it is difficult to accept the view that the making of a work of art is, in general, a *purely* internal affair: and most of the artists and aestheticians today would here disagree with Croce. Thus, Reid cites with approval Barbara Hepworth's explicit mention of how, in her own abstract drawing, the process of creation is vitally determined by the material character of lines and curves.[31] Our own *ālāpa* singing too is a challenge to Croce. Here, what happens may be put as follows. The notes which open the music are naturally heard by the singer, and they may seem to be tender or firm. Now, this specific character of notes as heard may *itself* seem to call for a particular phrase or turn of voice. So the making of music is here not merely subjective. We cannot deny that thinking *is* here done. Distinguishing two adjacent notes or linking two distant ones by means of a shapely pattern is as clear a demand on the mind[32] as the act of relating two concepts. But the thinking is here done essentially on the basis of what is sung *and heard*. The making of Hindustani music, which is often embellished with *improvisations in response to open reactions of the audience,* is clearly, though of course not entirely an overt process.

Our *rhythm*, however, may be said to support Croce's view to a very large extent, if not entirely. My point here is that rhythm can be composed *and enjoyed* very largely within the mind; for in both these aspects the essence of rhythm is a steady movement *of the mind* across a chosen extent of beats. In the act of composing rhythm the mind just goes on pecking the flow, held and followed quite ideally; and the absence of

---

30. Croce, *Aesthetic*, p. 10.

31. L.A. Reid, *Meaning in the Arts*, George Allen and Unwin, London, 1969, p. 108.

32. Cf. John Dewey, *Art as Experience*, Capricorn Books, New York, 1958 (7th impression), p. 46.

real hearing does not vitally affect the form and inner accents of what is composed, exactly as one can do mental counting with ease. In respect of enjoying rhythm too, though the heard quality of playing may well affect the fullness of delight, what makes the response really intelligent is, in essence, one's ability to follow *with the mind* the measure and meander of rhythm. If we add to all this the non-representational quality of its syllables, rhythm would at once seem to be much more capable of being independent of *outer* activity, meanings and values than any other art.

# 3

# The Concept of Laya in Hindustani Music

THE present essay is but the beginning of an attempt to understand the basic concepts of Hindustani or north Indian rhythm in the light of relevant discourse which has not so far been made an object of explicit attention.[1] Of these I here choose just one: *laya*. The frame of reference, however, has got to be fairly wide; for, considered as (musical) duration that is aesthetically regulated,[2] *laya* is in fact the only common feature of our *ālāpa*[3] and rhythmically organised singing, instrumental music and dance.[4] There is one other consideration which calls for some fullness of approach. The common Indian word for music is *sangeet* and it stands for both music and dance.

Now it seems to me that in the whole range of Hindustani

---

1. It surely was such a beginning when it first appeared in *Indian Philosophical Quarterly*, Poona, vol. I, no. 2, January 1974, for which I feel indebted to the late Prof. S.S. Barlingay, the editor.
2. Rather than measured by counting the beats it may comprise.
3. *Ālāpa* is music minus language and rhythmic accompaniment. For Indians, the ability to sing effectively without these two aids is the hallmark of a great musician. Singing without language, but *with some drumming*, is a subsidiary meaning of *ālāpa*. In its basic form, *ālāpa precedes* music accompanied by rhythm.
4. The classical dance-form that can be put under Hindustani or north Indian music is only Kathak.

*sangeet*, *laya* is clearly superior to rhythm. By rhythm I understand musical duration *as measured by beats*. *Laya* is not necessarily subject to such measurement. Its full meaning, however, is by no means obvious; and I may set out to determine it by considering not what the ancient works have to say on the subject generally, but how the word is actually used today in specific contexts, and how the fact it stands for really informs the different aspects of our music variously.

### Laya in Ālāpa

The fact that *laya* permeates good *ālāpa* is widely known. How it does so has, however, to be determined with care. The singing of a note for exactly the right length of time, so that whereas it may well appear full-blown, it does not look exaggerated to the point of monotony; due regulation also of the time taken in covering different notes with a view to producing varied and likeable effects; and, above all, a carefully graded increase of the speed of singing — these are, in my view, the chief meanings and manifestations of *laya* in the context of *ālāpa*. What distinguishes all these features of *ālāpa* is their common freedom from the employment of a specific number of beats as constituting a rhythm-cycle. The singer here proceeds entirely on the strength of his own capacity for judging the propriety of music; and, for the listener, the only sources of appeal in *ālāpa* are: euphonic sweetness, structural propriety, feeling or some ideal quality, such as a look of inner attunement; and the diversity of manner, besides of course the skill of rendering the *rāga*[5] in

5. Classical Indian music — which, of course, includes south Indian or Karnatak Music too — always renders a *rāga*. A *rāga* is a melody-*type*. It is not a song. Many songs can be sung in the same *rāga*. Every *rāga* is organised around its own key notes, and has therefore a sensible individuality which a trained listener can perceive quite clearly. A dual *rāga-tāla* form characterizes all classical *songs*. But *ālāpa* is free from *tāla* or cyclic rhythm, though it has got to be done in, and according to the grammar of, the *rāga* chosen.

question correctly and adequately. The (relatively) external aid of rhythmic *accompaniment* is here not available to the vocalist. So, if his performance is to be effective at all, he must concentrate throughout on the tunefulness and variform effects of his singing alone; which in turn calls for a very close subjective involvement with the music. This at once reminds us of an important, traditional but general sense of the word *laya*, as distinguished from its meaning in casual *aesthetic* parlance — that is, *laya* as the mind's self-identification with the object of attention or pursuit. Understood in this general sense, *laya* can of course be easily present in *ālāpa* as well. But in so far as close attention is a condition of success in *every* field of activity — whereas our concern here is *only* with musical duration and rhythm — I propose to ignore this general meaning of *laya* in our subsequent discussion.

Now, how musical duration (or *laya*) actually enters into sonant *ālāpa*[6] and conduces to its effects may be brought out as follows:

Suppose the vocalist sings the tonic *for a mere instant* and then *immediately* provides a steady, *elongated* rendering of the adjacent note, *komal r̥̥ṣabh*. The effect worked up would be one of *mere emergence* if the transition from the tonic to the other note is accomplished *quickly*, though without a break; and it may be one of *emergence from within something* in case the passage is smooth and relatively *leisurely*. In the latter case the singing may appear to have about it a touch of inwardness as well. The point to be noted here is that the *time* taken in passing from one *svara*[7] to another, or in rendering any single note, contributes vitally to the net look of a *svara*. To me it appears that the element of time, thus incorporated, stimulates a kind

6. *Ālāpa* is the opening movement of our classical instrumental music too. But the ideal of *ālāpa* is, in the case of north Indian music, provided by the *singer* of *ālāpa-dhruvapada* music. *Dhruvapada* is the song, always set to a specific rhythm, which follows *ālāpa*.

7. *Svara* is the Indian word for the musical note.

of linear imagining, and that the two together, aided by his feeling imagination, enable the musician to invest a *svara* or a phrase with an emotive or ideal hue. It is indeed a fact that many different factors conduce to the overall effect of *ālāpa*, which has to cover all the *svara*s of the *rāga* being sung; and that they do this with a jointness that is very close.

But the point has to be clarified. I may do this as follows by reverting to the instance cited above. If the *r̥ṣabh* in question is *steady* and broad — and is, like the tonic, located in the middle register — the effect would be one of emergent effulgence; but if the note in question is rendered very finely (or thinly) — yet very steadily and tunefully — and if it is located by the side of the tonic in the higher register,[8] the effect may be one of looking at something far-off, *or* of detachment, provided the *r̥ṣabh* here appears smoothly, yet *quickly*, after a fine and *fleet* touch at the *sā*.[9] Or again, if proceeding steadily from *ni* in the lower register, the voice touches the D flat (in the middle register) for just a *moment*, and then lapses back quickly to the preceding note, the effect worked up may be one of a mere linear droop *or* of sheer langour. In the case of an orthodox Indian singer — that is, because of some traditional moral images or attitudes — such employment of musical duration can profoundly influence his (or her) own immediate mental state.

Imagine, for instance, a devotee hallowing the dawn with *svaras* of a morning *rāga*. Steadying himself with the basic *sā* (tonic) he sings to saturate himself (say, informally, at home) with images and attitudes that are appropriate to the hour — the rising sun, yearning in prayer for a chastening of the self, pouring *arghya* or "holy water" at the sacred idol, and liberation from enslavement to things and riches of the world. A *brief* but sure touch at the tonic followed *immediately* by *komal*

8. The three voice registers — treble, middle and bass — are in Hindustani called: *tār, madhya* and *mandra*.

9. The Indian letter for the tonic.

*re prolonged* firmly and sweetly, at once blends the mind — by suggesting effulgence — with the fact of the rising sun. The same note (D flat) touched while descending from *gā* (E) provides an euphonic analogue of the downward slant that the act of pouring *arghya* describes. As attunement grows through the aid of *svaras*, the feeling of detachment may also deepen, and the singer may reinforce it by keeping to *sā* (tonic) merely ideally and by letting the voice *linger* repeatedly at the *re* (D flat), now *faintly* — yet sweetly — the note becoming a symbol of ethereality.[10] Surely, the purpose of *ālāpa* is not merely to indicate the constituent notes of the *rāga*; and it is clearly improper to hold, as has sometimes been done, that the appeal of *ālāpa* is merely perceptual.

All this, however, is a very inadequate account of the aesthetic character of *ālāpa*. I have said nothing about the various formal *tonal* devices that distinguish this most interesting genre of our classical singing from the bulk of our present-day music in general. But in relation to our concern with *laya*, what I have pointed out is for the present enough; and I may now turn to consider *laya* as it appears in rhythm or *tāla*.

## Laya in Rhythm

The transition may seem abrupt, but it is not really so; for a clear link is provided by a requirement to which *laya* in *ālāpa*,

10. Cf. Tagore's remark: ". . . Indian music concerns itself more with human experience as interpreted by religion, than with experience in an everyday sense. . . . Our music . . . takes us to the lonely region of renunciation. . . ."

    Traditionally, and in principle, Indian music aims at God-realisation. How this ideal is at least thinkable, and how the basic concepts of Hindustani music are quite intelligible in the context of this idea — all this can be argued. See, for instance: "Essentials of Hindustani Music", by S.K. Saxena, in *Diogenes*, Spring 64, no. 45. I must add, however, that the remark cited above is certainly not true of the bulk of Hindustani music today.

and *laya* in rhythmically organised music are both alike subject — the requirement that sudden, unwarranted, or aesthetically unsatisfying changes in tempo are to be avoided all along. If this be taken along with the consideration that the requirement just mentioned can be met — and its fulfilment *seen — also with the aid of beats,* we at once gain access to some important meanings of *laya* in the context of rhythmically ordered singing. These may be brought out by considering some (Hindustani[11]) phrases from actual discourse[12] relating to such music as is "accompanied" by a rhythm-cycle:

(a) *Laya laṭak rahī hai yā ubhar rahī hai*

These are protests which may have to be made sometimes by the main performer, say, a vocalist, to his drummer-accompanist. They signify an unwarranted slackening or acceleration of the set *speed* of playing, and either defect may have to be removed to enable the *sthāyī*-singing to run properly, that is, at the right pace which the singer himself may not be able to re-establish all at once.

(b) *Laya quāyem hai*

When extended as a compliment to the drummer, this remark signifies his ability to keep the basic *speed* of the rhythm chosen unchanged, not only when the cycle is played independently, but also *after* — or within or against — the execution of some intricate rhythmic patterns.

(c) *Laya girā lo, baṛhā lo*

These are suggestions which may sometimes be given to the

11. Hindustani is the language of a majority of north Indians. It is a blend of two languages: Hindi and Urdu.
12. The analysis that follows does not all along directly illumine the meaning of *laya;* but where it does not do so, it should enable us to understand some other important words in our rhythmic discourse.

drummer, to lower or raise the *pace* of playing slightly. The requisite change, however, has to be made quite gently. In speaking of *vilambit* or *drut laya,* on the other hand, we do not have any specific pace or occasion in mind.

(d) *Chauṅsaṭh kī laya*

This is a phrase which is sometimes used (by Kathak dancers) for a very *slow* rendering of *tritāla,* a rhythm-cycle of 16 beats. It means that the playing here is desired to be four times slower than the "normal" speed of the cycle. However, in so far as there is, in the case of rhythm, no generally accepted measure of "normal" pace, the phrase in question does not stand for anything quite specific. It is in fact used for any speed which one may regard as being very slow in relation to his own conception of average tempo.

*(e) Tāla meiṅ hai, laya meiṅ nahīṅ*

This remark is sometimes made by way of criticising a musician who somehow manages to gain access to the *Sama* (or the first beat of the rhythm-cycle), but is *not* able to maintain *even speed* or the equality of intervals *between* the various beats. Incidentally, the simplest — but by no means the ideal — meaning of being-in-*tāla* (or correct in respect of rhythm) is the ability to mark just the *Sama* accurately.

(f) *Tabaliyā aisā toṛhā chalā ki lehre wāle se laya nikal gayī*

What is meant hereby is the failure on the part of (say) the *sāraṅgī* player who provides the *lehrā* (that is, the measured rhythmic line) to hold on to the speed of (may be) the basic flow; and perhaps also to remember — as a consequence of the basic lapse — the location of the main accents, the *khālī* and the *bharī,*[13] of the cycle being played.

---

13. *Bharī* means a beat that is played. *Khālī* is the offbeat.

(g) *Laya kā andāz*[14] *yā laya ki tamīz*

These commonly used phrases mean:

> first, one's ability to determine (or develop) accurately the speed of the flow of (subsequent) music from the manner, leisurely or brisk, of its very beginning;[15]
>
> secondly, to retain — as long as required — one's hold on the speed fixed as basic;
>
> thirdly, *to improvise rhythmic patterns* of varying speed, extent and emphases not only *without any overall loosening of the hold just referred to, but primarily with the help provided by mental attunement*;
>
> and fourthly, to remember the fundamental speed so unremittingly that any temporary change of pace — introduced intentionally for the sake of working up new and beauteous effects, say, of seemingly wanton abandon and concomitant resilience — may be quickly assimilated into the run of the basic flow, through a skilful adjustment of the speed of what comes in the wake of the creative variation.

All or any of these meanings may be conveyed when we compliment a vocalist or instrumentalist[16] as being truly *layadār*, — that is, competent in respect of his hold over the rhythmic aspect of the ongoing music.

(h) *Laya se khelnā yā khilwāṛh karnā*

These words are used to describe the ability to *sport* with *laya* freely, but without faltering; that is, to introduce such (proper) variations or patterns in or against the flow of *laya* as seem effortless, improvised and brief, rather than long, intricate, and premeditated.

---

14. This phrase, as against the alternative one, may also be taken to mean the distinctive manner of (the flow of) *laya itself*.
15. This ability is very essential for the drummer-accompanist. Otherwise, the very opening stages of his playing are likely to be marred by hasty self-corrections.
16. The reference here is to an instrumentalist who is the main performer, as distinguished from a mere accompanist.

(i) *Layakārī karnā*

This stands for the execution of rhythmic variations and patterns of *all* kinds, whether spontaneous, brief and dainty, or prefixed, large and impressive.

(j) *Tān meiṅ laya kātnā*

Here, what is meant is the way in which musical patterns can be varied beautifully in respect of their rhythmic emphases. This phrase is indeed occasionally used, as appreciation, in respect of a *taan* which is made to "cut" the fabric of *laya* at such subtle[17] moments as are *not* normally marked in the rhythm-cycle as played.

(k) *Laya kī kāt tarāsh*

Whereas the word *kāt*, even in the context of rhythm, simply means "cut", "cross" or "divide", the Urdu word *tarāsh* stands for the idea of carving out shapely slices or figures from the matrix with loving care. Both words, *kāt* and *tarāsh*, are freely used in actual musical discourse, but the word *tarāsh* is here preferable, because it directly suggests the idea of careful and dainty as against random segmentation.

(l) *Laya kā bul*

In common Hindustani parlance, the word *bul* stands for a twist (not a knot) in a string or rope. In the region of rhythm it is used to describe such a brief and sudden, yet identifiable turn in the (even) musical flow of *laya* as does not look obtrusive, but only provides an added touch of alacrity, so to say, to the run of *laya* in a gently subtle way. The word *badal*, on the other hand, signifies any kind of change in flow.[18] Thus, *dugan* and *chauguna*, which stand (respectively) for the double and fourfold quickening of *laya*, or the rhythmic variants called *āṛh* and *kuvāṛh*, are only changes or *badal*s in

17. Subtle by virtue of the angle at which it pecks the flow of *laya*.

18. Another common meaning of *badal* is exchange or transposition.

general. They are not *buls*, for they affect a much wider stretch of flow than a *bul* with its brevity ever does. Sometimes, indeed, a *bul* is so brief and dainty that only a highly trained and very vigilant *rasika* can notice and relish it.

(m) *Laya kā chakkar yā halquā*

Here, *kā* and *yā*, stand for "of" and "or" respectively; and the key words are: *chakkar* and *halquā*. Considered in itself, the word *chakkar* means a circle or round. In ordinary parlance, however, it can also mean an engagement which permits no easy headway, a diffcult situation which one can neither get out of nor handle satisfactorily. More generally, however, the word *chakkar* stands mainly for the ideas of *unity and continuity, repetitiveness, containment, and self-completeness*. It does *not* convey, in our daily conversation, the sense of an internally measured flow. Now, turning to the playing and impact of rhythm in general, we may say that the (italicised) features just referred to characterise, and the phrase in question is used with regard to, the following multiform aesthetic situations:

First, when the *tritāla*[19] cycle is so played — say, at a lively pace, and long and effectively enough to secure our total involvement with the flow — that the conscious counting of beats soon recedes into the background, and the mind is merely swayed, in subdued delight, by an unbroken flow that seems not only self-complete, but self-complet*ing*. Here, the beats of course abide, and it is surely by quietly heeding them that the playing remains grammatically correct. But the felt variety of the beats (or *bols*)[20] as played; their regulated intensity serving — as required — to articulate the flow; and, above all, the sweet steadiness of manner — these details of drumming here totally offset the need to count. The mind

19. *Tritāla*, a rhythm of 16 beats, is the most popular cycle in the region of Hindustani classical music.

20. A *bol* is a mnemonic syllable by means of which we identify a specific sound produced by the drummer by striking a particular part of the drum in a specific way.

just relaxes in utter self-abandonment to the flow, keeping to measure effortlessly. The *mātrā*s (or beats) here do not *hold* our attention. They seem directly to make for the movement which animates them; and what here occupies the mind is merely the feel of a flow that sways us automatically. As for the emphasis called *Sama* (or the first beat), it does not here look inert and manifest like the centre of a circle, but is only felt as sweetly, yet perceptibly *implicit* in the centripetal and centrifugal flow.

*Secondly, during the playing of a quāyedā*: Here, the effect called *laya kā chakkar* may be produced — and the phrase aptly used — when, after opening the pattern reposefully, the drummer turns to bedeck its various sub-sections with a close, but orderly filling of *bol*s. Here, it is the compact successiveness of the syllables, their fitting embedment in divisions, as also the slight spurt with which they are occasionally made to get at a basic emphasis of the cycle, that make for the suggestion of unbroken continuity. True, in the case of some specially intricate *quāyedā*s what interests us specially is the *bul* that they throw up with delightful unexpectedness, and which, as a variant, is not only distinct but dainty. Yet, perceptible though it always is, such a syllable never seems to disrupt or disturb the flow.

Thirdly, after a spell has been cast on the listeners by some steady and tuneful repetitions of the *sthāyī-antarā*[21] of a properly organised *tarānā*,[22] provided its content is not sparse.

Here, too, the two key factors for the production of the effect in question are closeness of musical syllables and clarity of approach to the *Sama*. But the effect is readier if the

---

21. *Sthāyī* is the first line of the song. *Antarā* follows it, employing higher notes of the musical scale.

22. *Tarānā* is a *vocal* composition distinguished by its effective employment of mnemonic syllables.

composition describes a fairly extensive *āroha*[23] and *avaroha*.[24] A *vilambit khyāl*[25] does not normally provide for the essentials just mentioned; and this is precisely why its *independent* singing is not ordinarily able to conjure up any *chakkar of laya,* though it may well appeal to us because of some other excellences.

To conclude: the phrase, *laya kā chakkar,* stands for a flow that seems unified and organised, self-complet*ing* and not merely independent or isolated; and, above all, looks measured *without our having to measure it.* If a cycle is merely played (and followed) once or twice *and slowly,* it would of course be a distinct something; but it would not appear to evoke a *chakkar of laya* because the playing is not as sustained and compact as is requisite.

The phrase may now be considered in its alternative form: *lay kā halquā.* Literally, the word *halquā* means the area or orbit of influence. Taken along with *laya,* it conveys the significant idea that it looks steadfast, clear and roomy on the inside, and that the round of rhythmic flow permits ideal indwelling and may even seem to encompass us. This is quite different from what the phrase, *ṭheke kā halquā* means; which is (as already pointed out) simply the number of beats a cycle actually comprises.

(n) *Laya kā dhakkā yā ghooṅsā*

Where the flow of *laya* gains access to the *Sama* not only *in a manifestly well-designed and increasingly intense way,* but correctly and sharply, the knowledgeable listener may express his approval by acclaiming the impact as a winsome *laya kā dhakkā yā ghooṅsā.* The experience thus referred to is no mere cognitive approval of structural accuracy, *but is felt as a shock of delight.* In the case of vocal music, the suggestion in question is the effect

23. Musical ascent.

24. Musical descent.

25. *Khyāl* is the more popular form of North Indian classical vocal music. A song in this form is also called *khyāl.*

of a well-designed *āmad*[26] or that part of the *sthāyī* (first line of the song) which seems an organised and self-evolving access to the *Sama* or the first beat.

(o) *Laya kī jātiyāṅ*

A *jāti* is a specific way in which *laya* may be made to flow. It owes its distinctness to the precise way in which it organises its emphases or beats. The direct reference here is only to a manner of movement, and so to *laya*. But, in so far as a *jāti* is inconceivable apart from a specific number of beats (with their emphases), and also because we may freely speak of the *jāti* of a rhythmic pattern *that finally conforms to a cycle*, it would be truer to say that the phrase in question marks *a distinct passage of the mind* from mere *laya* (as found in *ālāpa*) to the strictly measured run of *tāla* with its *mātrā*s and syllables.

(p) *Laya-pradhān yā tāla-pradhān*

Such a way of speaking is relevant to both music and dance; and in both contexts it refers to two alternatives: the dominance of rhythmic flow and continuity *or* of beats, their order, and the way they are emphasized.[27] Thus, while doing a *ṭhāṭ*[28] a Kathak dancer may either dance very daintily, presenting mainly the undivided continuity of *laya* through a gentle wavy employment of arms and upper part of the body; or relatively quickly, with greater emphasis on footwork

26. *Āmad*, incidentally, is a very clear instance of the operation of the Gestalt laws of coercive design and common destiny in Hindustani music. For a fuller account of *āmad* see chapter 8 or: "The Fabric of Āmad: A Study of Form and Flow in Hindustani Music", by S.K. Saxena, in *Sangeet Natak*, op. cit., no. 16, April-June 1970.

27. The *Sama* too is a beat, though the focal one; and where its centrality is heightened by showing how the flow moves towards it designedly, it is clearly rhythm or *tāla* which dominates.

28. *Thāṭ* is the traditional opening item of a Kathak dance recital.

which generally chimes with the *mātrā*s, and distinct arrivals at the *Sama*, without of course neglecting the basic posture and the requisite overall grace of the number.

Now, the conclusion of our discussion so far may be that *laya* in rhythm is open to the following multiform characterization:

> Speed of musical flow which, be it quick or slow, is all along even,[29] evenness being manifest here in the equality of inter-*mātrā intervals* (see above, a to f); the basic flow that *permits — and controls* as their continual, if implicit point of reference — the various rhythmic patterns and divisions (g to k); *unity and continuity* of flow (l and m); *orbit and extent of* this run (m); the *impact of its (seeming) self-completion* (n); and, finally, its distinct *manner of movement* (o).

In brief, *laya in rhythm* means a flow which is (when established) even, and appears one and continuous so long as the music lasts[30] has distinct ways of running its course, and its own orbit or extent; permits and regulates, as their ground and underrunning anchor, a variety of effects and arrangements; and which — by virtue of its running around, and attaining to, the central beat — can look well oriented and complete, without being cut short, as it wheels (without faltering) its flowing rhythmic rounds.

Now, only one of these features of *laya* characterizes *ālāpa* as well: the quality, we may say, of being the willed locus of musical changes and effects. Steadiness of flow or speed is admittedly an important meaning of *laya,* but it cannot *as such* be regarded as a *basic and pervasive* feature of *both ālāpa* and rhythmic singing; for,

29. *Laya* may be quick or slow, but once it *has assumed* a certain speed it must proceed steadily so long as the musician does not himself wish to change it and with due reason.

30. Because the drummer goes on playing and marking the flow uniterruptedly; and also because, by way of preserving the unity of the rhythm-cycle, the flow is imagined to persist even where it is not marked audibly on the drums.

> first, as long as it is actually there, evenness of speed is itself, specially in the case of *ālāpa,* the result of the artist's own active willing; and
>
> secondly, though never randomly,[31] the *ālāpiyā*[32] is free to sing two adjacent *svaras* or tufts of notes *at inequal speed,* simply for the sake of working up some specific effect or making the distinctive nature of the *rāga* being sung a little more manifest.

So, if a definition of *laya* be demanded, we could perhaps offer the following:

> *Laya* is musical duration which is duly controlled, but not necessarily with the (objective) aid of beats in respect of its speed; and which permits such a creative variety of pace and emphasis in its melodic content[33] that it seems utterly removed from what we commonly mean by time. In *ālāpa* (we must add) the regulation of *laya* is much more subjective — that is, dependent on the musician at work — than in the case of beat-measured singing.

By way of clarifying and justifying this definition, I think it necessary to make the following additional remarks:

First, duration is aesthetically as relevant to the articulation of a single note as to the rendering of an expansive musical phrase or pattern. Thus, the *tār sā* (upper tonic) may be either touched with the brevity of an instant, and so skilfully and daintily that it may continue to throb in

31. That is, without caring for likeable effects, as distinguished from propriety in respect of mere evenness of speed.
32. A musician who specializes in singing *ālāpa*.
33. Here, I purposely avoid such words as "expression" and "embodiment". Rhythm perhaps does not *express* anything, though it may well seem to be taut or relaxed, ebullient or (even) coy. Nor does "embodiment" seem adequate to the *flowing* form of most rhythmic work. Perhaps the safest way to speak of rhythm is to say that it *appears* organised and variform, provided "appears" is not taken to imply a contrast with what is "real".

the listener's mind even when it has ceased as a sound; or rendered so long and soulfully that it may seem to soak us in sweetness; or abruptly cut short (as if) in the mid, in which case it will appear *half-fed,*[34] so to say, and clearly unsatisfactory. Again, by singing it for a longer time than is given to its adjacent notes, a *svara* can easily be made to appear an emphasis, a bearer of some effect — say, of emergence — or a revealer of the distinctive hue of the *rāga*.[35]

Secondly, I choose to interpret *laya* as "controlled", not necessarily steady or unchanging musical duration. For, whereas it is not in fact all along steady, the tempo of actual music — even where it changes — is set and controlled by the musician himself.

Thirdly, our definition says that — because it itself is regulated by the artist — *laya* can only be said to permit, not itself to produce or control the many variations that are often seen to diversify it. It is of course true that in the case of rhythmically organised music, the flow of *laya* — as marked by the drummer — vitally controls a good deal of creative work, by virtue of the demands that the *Sama* be duly (if eventually) arrived at; and that the evenness of *inter-mātrā* intervals be, in general, maintained.[36] But *ālāpa* is subject to no such demands; and in so far as for our definition we need features that are common, I choose the word "permits".

Fourthly, allied to the above is the distinction (duly made

34. In the situation here referred to, the late Ustād Chand Khan would actually use the words put in italics, but of course in their Hindustani form.

35. Understood as the regulated duration of the stay of voice at a particular note, *laya* seems essential for the technical and emotive propriety of *rāga*-rendering. Thus, if the voice lingers for more than an instant at the (note) *r̥ṣabh* in a recital of *rāga puriyā*, a dual offence is at once committed against the technical accuracy *and* the frequently (if slightly) pathetic, drooping imagery of the *rāga*.

36. Or at least not awkwardly flouted.

in our definition) which relates to the subjective and objective determination of *laya* in *ālāpa* and rhythm respectively. When *ālāpa* is being done there is no drum to mark the rhythm, and the flow has to be regulated entirely by the performer himself. The determination here is subjective.[37] On the other hand, in music which is "accompanied" by rhythm, the drummer, as we know, quietly indicates some requirements of rhythmic accuracy which the singer has to reckon with; and the flow of *laya* in such music, is rarely — in slow *khyāl* singing perhaps never — so thoroughly assimilated by the vocalist as to make it entirely unnecessary for him to look at the drumming with a view to locating a point for assistance in gaining access to the *Sama*.

Yet, even here (we may note) the regulation of *laya* is not *entirely* objective. In *vilambit* singing, in particular, where the interval between any two successive beats is naturally big, the vocalist must draw on his own ability to keep the flow steady; for he cannot go on looking at the drummer all along. What here enables him to keep the *laya* steady is not the laboured and conscious process of counting the beats, but that non-calculative kind of estimation which Kant has called *aesthetic*.

It is indeed the musician himself who turns *laya* into the material of beauty. *Laya* only permits, I repeat, but does not itself produce any changes or emphases. As it runs through a cycle, it is indeed differentiated; and its key emphases — the *Sama* and the offbeat in particular — are as a rule unmistakable. But it is only when they have been played by the drummer for quite some time — and with due regard to both temporal steadiness and *aural appeal* which, in the case of *tablā*[38] playing, calls for a very skilful and blended use of

37. But it is not merely so. For, the technical demands of the *rāga*, as an *objective* melody-type, have to be met throughout; and these include the requirement that the important notes of the *rāga* in question be treated *for the right length of time*.

38. The more popular drum in the field of classical and light classical Hindustani music and Kathak dance. Comprises two pieces.

the "left" and the "right" drums — that a spell is worked up by the round of *laya* which may *now* seem disembodied, and on its own wings afloat (so to say), inducing in the drummer (or the singer) such intense self-attunement with the flow that lovely, little patterns of sweet and sure step may simply seem to well up from *laya*'s own fabric. The seeming spontaneity of creation is here but a consequence of the artist's own prior meticulous work.

I may next explain why I prefer to define *laya* as musical duration rather than as musical flow. My reasons here are briefly as follows:

(a) Duration means continuance in time, or time indefinitely. The word *laya* too is used mainly for an essential *temporal* feature of music. On the other hand, when we speak of a musical flow we may mean merely the various notes traversed, or the melodic way they are sung (or played) without directly giving any thought to the tempo of music.[39]

(b) Again, when we speak of a *flow* we refer, in general, to some movement from one point to another, horizontally — so to say. On the other hand, *laya* can be present (we have seen) also in the steady and properly timed rendering of a single note — say, the *tār sā* — from which (if the vocalist so desires) dainty little flourishes may simply seem to drip. What we have here is no flow, as commonly understood, but only the passage of musical time or duration. A *svara* at which the voice lingers may seem to *last in time*;[40] and the right word for *its laya* would be "duration", not "flow".

---

39. I hasten to add that such a restricted interpretation of "musical flow" is only possible and legitimate, not necessary. Speaking generally, "musical flow" includes the flow of rhythm too; for, music is a blend of melody *and rhythm*.

40. Longer than it actually does, so that musical duration remains different from actual time.

Finally, I turn now to see how, as our definition insists, *musical* duration differs from actual or everyday time:

What is *given* to us in actual duration is some physical happening or a state of the mind, or both. The duration *created* by music is, on the other hand, inlaid only with *svaras* and rhythmic turns. Again, whereas (if considered from the outside) a musical recital is clearly an event — and so itself occupies a definite stretch of actual time — *within* its magical domain the various features of time as experienced in real life, say, as awaiting a friend's arrival, or as regretting a mistake which could have been avoided, are all dispensed with; and neither rhythm nor melody presents any actual content or happening of the world we daily deal with. Simultaneity, here, is *not primarily* a matter of parallel physical processes or detached, concurrent happenings; as a semblance, it is here grounded instead in an inwardly affirmed shapeliness of rhythmic or melodic design and attainment. The delightful acuity of a perfectly simultaneous access to the *Sama* by the (principal) musician and his drummer would of course be missing if their moment of marking the beat in question is not *actually* the same. But if the musician realizes the *Sama* correctly, yet abruptly — by just looking at its occurrence in the drumming, it would be just as little artistic as nodding in harmony with the ticks of a clock. On the other hand, if the same rhythmic propriety is achieved primarily by the intrinsic run of the basic structure of one's chosen *sthāyī* or *gat*,[41] or by the subsidiary shapeliness of a pattern — prefixed or improvised — the concurrence would be truly in tune with the demands of the art of music. Where the main performer and his accompanist both lose their hold over the basic flow and form of the cycle, and — after weaving a few random patterns — yet land jointly at a point by force of mutual understanding or just by chance, the point is either not the *Sama* at all; or if it *is* the *Sama*, it fails to appear what it

41. The basic, rhythmically organised tune in the case of instrumental music.

aesthetically should, that is, the natural end-point *demanded immanently by the very design of a flow.*

Even successiveness in music is not just a matter of "before" and "after". It is rather a passage of beauty *inter*wrought — as in the case of complementary musical phrases or notes that make for *saṁvāda*[42] — or of upflow and ultimate flowering, as in the case of an *āmad* rightly designed. Duration in music is never mere time. Its instants often twinkle;[43] its fluidities tend to tranquilise us and in *āroha* (or ascent) may even appear to yearn, in case the tonal volume is duly regulated.[44]

It is indeed important to see how musical duration is *not* actual time. The two are of course not wholly unrelated, because the run of music does take some actual time. But, in so far as rhythm is often mistakenly regarded as *merely* a matter of measured time, it seems necessary to heighten its differences from actual time. The following, in addition to what we have already said above, should make the matter clearer:

A slowly played rhythm-cycle does take more (actual) time than a *drut* (or quick) execution of the same. But to say just this is to consider the matter merely from the outside, and very inadequately. Whether as the matrix of a solo recital, or as providing "accompaniment", how exactly a cycle affects us, on the whole, turns (also) on its relation to the pattern which it initiates, supervenes or sustains. For instance, when in a solo recital the drummer lapses back to the cycle steadily,

---

42. Musical consonance.

43. I have here in mind the *dyut* rendering of the *tār sā* (upper tonic) by the late Padma Bhushan Ustād A. Rahimuddin Khan Dagar. The note would be touched with the brevity of an instant; and so suddenly yet sweetly, that it seemed to sparkle like a star.

44. This certainly was the effect of quite a few *āroha* (ascending) patterns in an exposition of *rāga puriyā* by the late Shri Behre Buwa, one of our more soulful singers of yesteryears.

after executing a *tukḍā*[45] of extra fluent pace, the *ṭhekā*[46] may *seem to be slower* than it really is; and, as incidental to "accompaniment", it may *appear to be a mere moveless background*,[47] in which case the question of *drut* or *vilambit* does not dominate the mind, and applause is extended mainly to the drummer's steadfastness. In case *laya* is "thrown very high up", as they say, and if the drummer too promptly follows suit, we may certainly be struck by the sheer speed of the *ṭhekā*; but even here what is admired by trained listeners is not quick speed alone, but its maintenance *consistently with the inner clarity and structure of the cycle*. The proper execution of *bols*, evenness of *laya*, and preservation of rhythmic structure and shapeliness — it is these, and never *mere* speed or loudness, that delight the knowledgeable listener.

Again, though in wedging a limited temporal stretch (or number of beats) with a close filling of *bol*s the drummer certainly avails of the *actual* divisibility of time, the enrichment is always expected to be done *in accordance with some design*, so that it is never a case of merely calculative subdivision of time. Moreover, in such cases, the intenser the filling of *bol*s, the more "crowded" will the pattern appear, investing rhythm at once with a distinctive semblance of spatiality. In actual life too, it is true, a period of time may look packed with events and overt activity. But such actual content of life does not make any decorative design. This also explains, incidentally, the difference between meaningless sounds that occur around us freely in our daily experience and the mnemonic syllables that our rhythm builds on,[48] always as a simple flourish or pattern, or as the multiform structure of an intricate *quāyedā*.

45. A brief rhythmic pattern.

46. The basic rhythm-cycle as played, as distinguished from the patterns conforming to the idiom of the cycle.

47. Which it is really not. The *seeming* slowness and movelessness are both "virtual" elements.

48. These syllables — such as: *tā, dhā, dir, dir* — are methodically employed *only* in rhythm. The theoretical importance of this fact has already been brought out in the first chapter.

# 4

# Tāla, Bol, Ṭhekā

In spite of its basic importance as that which permeates our entire *sangeet*, *laya* is not the most *obvious* feature of the temporal aspect of our music. What strikes us generally is musical duration *as cyclic* or *tāla* which is our favourite word for rhythm in music. It stands for musical duration (or *laya*) as articulated, measured and organised in terms of rhythmic cycles — each having its own extent and character — by building on a specific number of beats or *mātrā*s and *bol*s (or mnemonic syllables) in determinate ways.

Now, as such a way of speaking implies, *tāla* may be interpreted in two distinct, though allied senses: as standing for the *general idea* of flow that is measured with the help of beats or for an *individual rhythm-cycle*. These indeed are the two basic ways in which we generally think and speak of *tāla*. Those who know music not only distinguish *tāla* in rhythmically organised singing from mere *laya in ālāpa*, but freely speak of individual rhythm-cycles as *tritāla* or *chautāla*. Again, when we emphasize the supreme value of a proper *bandish* for good *khyāl* singing or *sitār* playing, we have in mind the ideal of proper organisation in terms of cyclic rhythm (and *rāga*) generally; and when we ask for (say) a *bedam chakkardār* pattern in *ektāla*, the reference is obviously to a *particular* rhythm-cycle. The full meaning of *tāla* can, however, be brought out only by attending as follows to the individual ideas implicit in the definition proposed in this very first para of this chapter.

1. What is vivified and organised by (or as) rhythm is *musical duration* or *laya*. *Laya* we have chosen to regard as controlled duration which admits of ever new creation in terms of effect and imagery. So, it may well be said — in fact, it is commonly admitted — that the surer the drummer's (or musician's) hold on the flow of *laya*[1] in and through the *tāla* chosen, the greater will be his ability to create immaculate patterns effortlessly within the limits, and in conformity with the distinctive idiom, of the specific cycle being played.

   It would be wrong to suppose that such patterns can only be correct, intricate and fluent. Not only the set onward lapse of even inner emphases which rhythm directly presents, but the subtle and wilfully created suggestions of a tense expectancy or a dainty hesitancy in approaching what is nonetheless desired,[2] are all evocable by a good drummer. Yet what makes for such delightful semblances is (in part) the fact that *tāla* is throughout enlivened with *laya*. Therefore, to deal with rhythm as a mere succession of various *mātrā*s is at once to ignore what unifies and steadies them from the inside; and to blight, in consequence, their conduciveness to patterns which, with all their seeming abandon, are prevented by one's hold over *laya* from really going astray.

2. Mere *laya*, however, is by no means enough. It doubtless makes for evenness of passage; but the only identifiable changes it can produce, wholly by itself, are those of pace. What turns it into the material of countless shapely patterns and winsome tiny turns

1. Of *laya* considered as the equality of inter-*mātrā* intervals.
2. The first suggestion that I here speak of relates to a well-designed *tiyā* that appears to be heading for the *Sama*, specially where the three segments are of rising intensity; and the second one is the usual effect of a well-designed *anāgat* pattern.

and twists is its employment of beats and emphases. It is the *mātrā*s and *bol*s that make *laya* articulate, and enable us to organize it into cycles of different extent and character.

As is widely known, our rhythm runs in cycles. It begins from and returns to the first beat, completing a round; and then sets out again to describe another. Every cycle builds on a fixed number of beats. This, however, is by no means a complete account of its individual nature. The following factors too have to be taken into account: the character of the *bol*s or mnemonic syllables it employs for identifying the *mātrā*s; the way the beats are marked or merely suggested on the drums; and the specific speed it may seem to demand for its own characteristic effect. To illustrate, though they both employ ten beats, *sool tāla* is generally distinguished from *jhaptāla* not only by its different *bol*s and emphases, but by its intrinsic need for a relatively quicker pace. *Dhamār*, on the other hand, calls for a slower pace of playing; and its full character is not brought out if we refer only to its *bol*s, emphases and number of *mātrā*s. All this, however, must be dealt with at some length.

3. A *mātrā* marks a basic and equal subdivision of *laya*. We say "basic" and "equal" with a view to keeping the *mātrā*-marked intervals distinct from the other, bigger sub-sections (or *vibhāg*s) of a cycle which may comprise individually an inequal number of beats, and so be of different temporal extent. That the intervals in question are basic is further borne out by the consideration that in the fixed structure of a cycle as played ordinarily — as against its free and creative handling by an expert — the space *between* any two adjacent *mātrā*s is not marked, though in the hands of a seasoned drummer, it may be filled instinctively with some gentle flourishes which serve to suggest the

ceaseless flow of *laya* through the cycle's inner markings.

As for the function of a *mātrā,* it is easy to see how it is basic. Rhythm is nothing if it does not flow steadily; and it is difficult to keep a flow steady — and to follow it unwaveringly — without subdividing it, which is exactly what the *mātrā*s enable us to do. They mark equal intervals, and their places are fixed.

By bearing this in mind we can see a difference easily. A beat (as *mātrā*) is not quite identical with a mere emphasis. A *mātrā* is of course an emphasis too; it shows the mind pecking *laya,* so to say, which it at once diversifies. But it must occur at the right place or instant, for its function is also to measure, and not merely to mark. On the other hand, a *ẓarab* (or emphasis) — except as implicit in a *mātrā* — is not thus set. It is an emphasis which, in pursuance of some creative design, the artist can lay *anywhere* in the flow of rhythm, even at places unmarked by the *mātrās,* just with a view to working up effects of novelty or "wanton heed and giddy cunning".[3]

We must also remember what a *mātrā* does not do. It only vivifies and measures, but does nothing to disrupt the *laya*-flow. The point here is not that actual time itself keeps flowing even in the interval between two marked (or spoken) beats, but that the mind — not only of the drummer, but of the listening *rasika* — must throughout maintain and hold on to the ideally apprehended and even flow of *laya;* for otherwise the very basis that keeps the *mātrā*s evenly apart will disappear, annulling their claim to be marks of equal subdivision. This is an important point; and I may have to clarify it a little later, in the context of what is to be said about *bol*s.

3. The reference, here, is to Milton's well-known poem, *L'Allegro,* line 141.

4. Just as we need *mātrās* to vivify *laya* and thereby to hold on to it, so we need *bols* to identify the *mātrās* themselves. But, what exactly is a *bol*? Now here, again, our answer should provide not only a criterion for distinguishing *bols* from sounds which are *not bols*, but also a little insight into the relevant language used casually, but never inanely by our *ustāds*. Both these needs, I believe, are met by the following definition:

   A *bol* is a *letter* or a mnemonic tuft of letters. It enables the listener to identify — and the drummer, also to build creatively on — the sounds *actively* produced out of the drums *with an eye to producing some effect of beauty*. This beauty, grounded in *bols*, may be either the intrinsic charm of perceptual clarity, softness, intensity or of some other striking auditory characteristic; or the merely relational beauty of sequence, contrast and similarity.

   The italicised words and phrases in the above may now be attended to individually. Our *ustāds* often use the word *aksharas* (letters) while speaking of rhythm; and they would like us to believe that a sound which does not correspond to (at least one) *akshara* is not a *bol*. But this has to be brought out, and I may do it right away.

   It is possible to produce out of the right *tablā* a sound describable as a dot of resonance, by first *striking* the inky portion and then *touching* it gently with a finger *tip*. This sound will of course be clearly audible; but, in so far as it does not resemble any letter, it cannot be said to be a *bol*. The fact indeed is that only those *aksharas* have been selected as *bols*, and then woven into patterns of various kinds, which can be said to resemble the sounds produced by striking the drums at various places in different ways.

   We *identify a mātrā* — as marked on the drum, or even as recited — by speaking of it either as a letter, such as "k"; or as a combination of letters such as "kat", both "k" and "kat" alike being *bol*s. But no tuft of letters, howsoever big, is allowed to become a meaningful word; and the non-linguistic character of our rhythm remains intact all along. The general principle at work here simply is that the *bol* should resemble (more or less) the sound produced by the drummer in respect of openness, crispness, weighty or elongated sound, fluency, tremulousness and such other *purely formal* features of sound. Numerals as spoken do not admit of such a variety of formal auditory characteristics. Besides, if they are recited in the right order, numerals keep the mind focused on the act of conscious counting which, in the case of effective drumming or proper listening, becomes quite subsidiary. Words, on the other hand, are not generally used to provide sheer auditory effects except at times by some consummate poets. Further, as ordinarily used, they do not make for the suggestion of a flow that lapses back to the point of its origin. Except in the case of *tarānā*s, a *sthāyī* uses meaningful words; and this probably is why, even when it extends from *Sama* to *Sama*, it does not appear to be self-completing in the manner of a rhythm-cycle as generally played. Why we do not use words (such as पहली, दूसरी) to identify the *mātrā*s should now be clear. Of course, for indicating the mere extent of a particular cycle — as distinguished from its actual, heard character — we may have to speak only of the number of *mātrā*s it employs; and, avoiding the *bol*s, recite them as numerals as we do in simple counting. But in actual drumming the *mātrā*s, all conjoined with some *bol*s, do not appear as merely numbered; and we simply miss the charm of rhythm if we ignore the *bol*s which, unlike their numerals, not only mark the *mātrā*s or help our counting them, but cover them and the gaps between them with variform sonant touches.

It may be of help to dwell a little longer on the relation of a *mātrā* to a *bol* before we turn to discuss the aesthetic character and varying use of *bol*s. Considered as the mere unit of a cycle, a *mātrā* is essentially temporal: it only comes before or after other *mātrā*s. On the other hand, a *bol* has a sonant character as well. Again, the *mātrā*s of a cycle cannot be changed, neither in respect of their set location in the flow, nor in that of their number in a particular cycle. But the *bol*s *can* be shuffled at will, though of course not capriciously. In fact, even those *bol*s that name the *mātrā*s can be spoken out or played (by the drummer) at moments which deviate from the basic beats, but of course *according to a set design*, testifying to the artist's ability to deal with rhythm in a spirit of creative abandon. Again, unlike the *mātrā*s, the *bol*s can be played (or recited) in a way that may appear to wilfully overflow or daintily fall short of the set round of rhythm. As we know, this is exactly what is done by the drummer in executing patterns of *ateet* and *anāgat* variety.

Yet, though it is certainly the *bol*s which enable the (performing) artist to identify the *mātrā*s, and so to deal with rhythm in numberless creative ways, we must not underestimate the value of *laya* and beats. In patterns of every kind the basic evenness of movement, the offbeat and the focal beat and (above all), the seeming wholeness of the round (or *chakkar*) of *laya* as against its inner markings — these have all to be kept to continually. The vocalist has to be specially wary in this respect; for if, as is too often the case, he has learnt to gain access to the *Sama* from a particular *bol* as marked on the drum, instead of developing a ceaseless sensitiveness to the basic *laya*-flow of the rhythm-cycle being used, even an accidental bedimming of the clue may at once lead him woefully astray.

Finally, every *bol* has to *be* such, and *played* in such a way that it may somehow contribute to the beauty of the phrase or pattern which includes it. Such insistence is by no means unnecessary, for any rhythmic cycle or pattern can be played in a way which may be grammatically correct, yet aesthetically insipid. An accomplished drummer, on the other hand, plays the *bol*s in such a way that they seem neat, shapely and effortless in themselves; articulate the *laya* without any rough-edged emphases; and make directly for integration in the chosen pattern.

All these excellences are emphasised by our experts in their everyday rhythmic parlance. *Bol kāṭnā* means playing the *bol*s neatly, so that they are easily identified and seem well trimmed or shapely. In the early stages of playing, we are told, the *bol*s of a pattern have "the thickness of a rope". Later, it is added, they get mellowed into "silken strings" under the finesse of mature, fluent playing. The truth here suggested simply is that a properly played *bol* asserts itself only to the extent of vivifying the flow of *laya*, so to say, instead of appearing a mere imposition on it. This is indeed the evidence of competent drumming.

Phrases like *bol banānā* and *bol bharnā* refer particularly to the relational propriety of *bol*s, as distinguished from their individual excellences. *Bol banānā* stands for the practical device of changing the speed or location of a *bol* in such a way, and with such continual mindfulness of the basic flow, that the variation itself may call for some quick adjustment of the *bol*s that follow, which has to be done forthwith, satisfying the drummer himself as a breath of subtly held abandon and impressing the listener as a mark of the player's consummate hold over *laya*. *Bol bharnā*, on the other hand, refers simply to the act of *filling* the space between *mātrā*s with a close, but orderly bunch of *bol*s.

Negatively, mere sounds which are neither likeable in themselves nor conducive to the beauty of others are not *bol*s at all by orthodox standards. An illustration is here provided by the graded, but not musical effects of loudness which are sometimes produced, as a piece of sheer exhibitionism, by playing at the left *tablā* in the "reverse" way.[4]

*How* exactly the *effect* of a *bol* is determined not only by its own perceptual character, but also by its integration with other *bol*s is not my present concern. In fact, no one can accomplish this task adequately; and I have to content myself with the general remark that to seize the net character of a syllable in actual drumming we have to reckon with the following main considerations: (a) the way the *bol*, as a sound, enters into silence — assertively and full-blown or gently as a whisper; (b) the character and speed of the *bol*s which provide it with a context; (c) its own temporal extent; (d) the speed at which it is played; (e) and how exactly — that is, from which part of the skin and by what specific employment of fingers or palm — it is actually produced. All in all, a *bol* as played admits of very different effects, the more easily identifiable of them being: roundness, daintiness or mellowness, sharpness or incisiveness, *sāṅs* or a certain breathing kind of depth and continuity, fluency and tremulousness. The chief effects of rhythmic *patterns*, on the other hand, are: continuity, unity in diversity, self-differentation or unwinding (or *bul kholnā*), regulated wantonness, sheer ebullience or a winsome semblance of self-restraint.

The context of a *bol* or its embedment in a pattern is indeed of great importance; and it would be very wrong to believe that the appeal of rhythm consists merely in our ability to identify the diverse, individual

---

4. That is, from the *kinār* to the inky round.

character of the various *bols*. The truly aesthetic concern with rhythm is an exercise of one's ability to perceive the *bols* in relation to the rhythm-cycle which is their unchanging support. How exactly they follow or occasionally deviate from it; the design of the way they hasten back to the basic flow; whether they fill it up wedgewise, or in a gathered or relaxed manner — all this must all be kept in view while opening to or explaining the magic of rhythm.

5. This leads me to an analysis of the nature and significance of a rhythm-cycle. References to its various kinds or forms will here be but incidental, my main purpose being simply to discuss the idea of a cycle in general. To facilitate understanding, we may proceed piecemeal:

    a. To begin with, as has already been pointed out, the identity of a rhythm-cycle does not depend only on the number of *mātrās* it employs. *Teorā* and *rūpak* both employ 7 *mātrās* each; *ektāl* and *chautāla*, 12; and *āṛhā chautāla, jhoomrā, dhamār* and *deepchandi* are all cycles of 14 *mātrās* each. Yet everyone of them is distinct from its temporal colleagues in respect of the following individual features: the number and position of accents; nature and number of *bols*; location of the offbeat, and of the *Sama*, which sometimes occurs on the left one; and, in quite a few cases, the precise speed needed for fullness of effect.

    b. If, as is only proper, a cycle be regarded as an ordered whole not only of a fixed number of *mātrās*, but of some specific accents and *bols*, it may be said to heighten the individual character of a *bol* by putting it in a setting of other *bols*. Thus, to illustrate, in the case of the *7-mātrā* cycle called *mughlai*, the incisive brevity of the *bol "kat"* (कत) — which is here the syllable for the *Sama* — is thrown into bolder relief by its contrast with the long and relaxed *dhāge tirkit* (धागे तिरकिट) and *tātirkit* (तातिरकिट) which precede and follow it. A simpler illustration of the same truth is provided by the contrast of the brief and open *nā* (ना) with the closed and gently elongated *dhin* (धिन) in the *tritāla* cycle. Again, we have the mutual opposition of the *khālī* and *bharī* points of the cycle. The latter are actually played; the former may be merely suggested.

c. However, a little more light may be thrown on the organised character and internal cohesiveness of a rhythm-cycle by making the following observations on the nature and aesthetic centrality of the *Sama*.

First, as has already been hinted, the *Sama* not only initiates, but consummates the cycle. Moreover, after executing his chosen patterns — melodic or rhythmic — the musician is required to return to the *Sama* with split second accuracy. The ability to do so — and in a beautifully designed way — is in fact an important criterion by which we judge the quality of the music or rhythmic play going on.

Secondly, the centrality of the *Sama* may be heightened by the sharp and definite way in which it is actually played, as in the case of *dhamār*. In fact, the *Sama* of every cycle has, in principle, to be shown as a quite distinct accent. According to our ancient works on rhythm, the ideal sound for *Sama* is a *dhakār* one — a sound which is definite and clearly audible. This perhaps is why those who play the *tritāla* cycle as *nā dhin dhin nā* (ना धिन धिन ना) instead of as *dhā dhin, dhin, dhā* (धा धिन धिन धा) tend to make the *Sama* appear a little unconvincing.

Here, however, a doubt can beset us. The syllable *dhā*, as it is played on the drum, is indeed a loud sound, and is therefore clearly heard. But it is *not a sharp* sound; and so, if considered in itself — or as apart from the well-designed way in which it may be arrived at — it may not seem very pleasing to the ear because of its relative breadth. On the other hand, if a *Sama,* which comes at "the left one", is played not only loudly but sharply and crisply, the effect may be positively delightful. Here the likeableness of effect is due to the fact that the *Sama-syllable* coincides with the brief being of the *mātrā,* which it relates to. Now, this is exactly as it should be, even theoretically. The function of a beat is to mark and measure the flow of *laya* or musical duration. The shorter the time it itself takes in being played or recited as a *bol,* the less will be the unmarked duration in its own occupancy. Its deviation from its ideal of marking will in that case be minimal. But the little time that must always be taken in articulating the *Sama-bol* is not only some (unavoidable) deviation from the ideal of a maximally fine subdivision of *laya,* but is also useful to us in fixing the speed of subsequent rhythm.[5]

In spite of all these details, however, my treatment of rhythm-cycle has so far been a little abstract. So the following points in respect of its actual playing may now be added:

First, though we have so far used the two words interchangeably, a distinction must be drawn between "rhythm-cycle" and *ṭhekā.* The latter stands for the fuller idea of a rhythm-cycle regarded as *an unchanging support* of the drummer's own decorative work — or as a moveless background by looking at which the vocalist or *sitārist* avoids going astray. This is why the ability to play the *ṭhekā* steadily for long spells must be considered as a major excellence of the drummer's art. Unfortunately, this is often forgotten today when both the drummer and the audience prize only the playing of some very quick patterns.

Incidentally, the way we here interpret the word *ṭhekā* is, on the one hand, warranted by its use in popular parlance — where it generally conveys the sense of a guarantee of dependability — and is, on the other hand, a clear pointer to the truth that, with all its inner accents and organisation, the

5. As already brought out in the first essay.

cycle still remains subservient to *laya* or steadiness of passage or pace.

Secondly, even the most careful choice and integration of *bols* will not make the cycle look internally unified unless "the left" and "the right" ones are played in the truly complementary manner — blended as one, as the *ustāds* say. The left one is believed to contribute only two *akṣaras*, *dh* (ध) and *k* (क). It is attuned with a low note; and, if we go merely by the syllables it is expected to use, its chief contribution to the total playing may be said to be the effect of depth. But — and this a matter which relates to actual practice — if it is wielded in the right way, the "left one" can contribute *sāṅs*, or an effect of depth *and breathing continuity* within which the discrete *bol*s (produced by the right drum) all appear a little enveloped and so held as one. Assuming that it fulfils also the basic requirement as to the proper articulation of individual *bol*s, such a way of playing can at once invest the *ṭhekā* with a charm of its own.[6] The beauty here is all along intrinsic, utterly free of a representational look.

Conversely, where the interval between adjacent *bol*s or beats is so long that the sound of the left one cannot be made to envelop them, the *ṭhekā* naturally loses its requisite look of cohesive singleness. This at once gives us a warning as to the impropriety of trying to play it excessively slowly. In a very sluggish *tritāla* exposition — say, at what is sometimes called *chauṅsaṭh kī laya* by Kathak dancers — not only does the *ṭhekā* lose its unity, making it impossible for the listener to hold on to the constituent *bol*s of the cycle in one unified act of attention; even the *lahrā* on the *sāraṅgī* is deprived of its flow, and this because the bow has to tarry so long on individual

6. If played in this ideal way, the *tritāla ṭhekā*, even at *madhya laya*, can charm us with its sweet, unbroken swing, the left one contributing what is technically called *lau* or a steady glow (लौ) in addition to the effect of a deep and breathing continuity, called *sāns* or *ās*.

*svaras* or phrases that they seem frozen and disjointed, cancelling the requisite suggestion of a seamless musical *flow*.

Finally, an attempt may be made to describe our experience when we attend to a *madhya laya tritāla ṭhekā* as it is sweetly and steadily played for a while. To begin with, there is (on our part) some effort of conscious attention. After a few rounds of the cycle — their precise number depending on our measure of familiarity with the technique of it, as also on the quality of playing itself — the element of deliberate counting disappears. The beauteous, winsome quality of the playing elicits self-forgetfulness, and makes for *tādātmya*. Instead of attending to it with a sense of strain, we now feel swayed by, or as flowing along with the *ṭhekā*. Whereas counting is a conscious, calculative process, and mere repetition can soon grow boring, the process of freely following a manageable count, sweetly and evenly marked, is always a likeable process; and it is this which constitutes the basic appeal of rhythm. Once this magic becomes operative, the discursive activity of thinking recedes. The playing of the various *bol*s of course continues; and we certainly remain aware of them. But, and this is here the crux of the matter, we do not now distinguish them too actively. Our experience here is the felt awareness of some accents in or of a flow — of the rhythmic emphases in such a way that they do not even seem to ruffle, much less to disrupt the unity of the flow. Yet, however non-relational it may be, the experience is *also* — in a positive, if subconscious way — the awareness of a *measured* flow. For, when there is any unwarranted increase or decrease of speed, we are disturbed by the change at once. Here too, we may note, *laya* seems more important than the mere diversity of beats and *bol*s.

# 5

# Phenomenology of Sama in Hindustani Rhythm[1]

FOR those who know Hindustani rhythm it is easy to identify the *Sama* when (and where) it comes. Many can even anticipate it. But hardly any one ponders at length as to what *Sama* does in its setting of rhythm and melody. It is this gap which I here seek to narrow, in respect of rhythm taken generally. My findings, however, will be quite limited. But this is unavoidable; for, how exactly we *sense* the *Sama* depends on numberless details. What precise pattern it completes is one of these. How it itself is played is another. No study can exhaust these differences of manner and context. The drummer at work can always bring in some new ones; and what is here actually experienced — or the phenomenal — cannot be quite captured by the grasp of theory.[2]

But one *can* light up the area of enquiry, and do some

---

1. This essay is a slightly altered form of my article, bearing the same title, published in *Indian Philosophical Quarterly*, Poona, vol. IV, no. 3, April 1977. But its original basis is the paper: "*Sama* in Hindustani Rhythm: A Psycho-Aesthetic Study" presented to the Conference on *Psychology and Music* organized by Sangeet Natak Akademi (New Delhi) at Poona, on 12 January 1975. All the *tablā* "illustrations" for this paper were provided by my brother, the late Prof. Sudhir Kumar Saxena from the Music College of Baroda University.

2. My own present study is limited, I repeat, in one other way. It directly relates only to the rhythm of north Indian Music.

basic thinking. This is exactly what I here propose to do. Now, let me first see what the subject chosen means. This will enable us to determine how it requires us to proceed:

To begin with, *Sama* may be understood as simply the first or focal beat of the rhythm-cycle.[3] But because under "rhythm" we include both the basic cycle (as *ṭhekā*) *and* rhythmic patterns, and also because the ability to play them properly is as much a test of a drummer's competence as his success in holding on to the chosen *laya* steadfastly,[4] we have to give some thought to rhythmic *patterns* too. Now, it is true that every kind of pattern does not highlight the *Sama*. A *quāyedā*, for instance, is noted more for its inner shapeliness; and, in some cases, for its inclusion of a subtly varied tuft of syllables. Yet, at the same time, the *Sama* cannot be denied its regulative value. If the *Sama*, as completing a round of *laya*, is lost sight of, the *bul*[5] or creative twist will only be heard, but *not look delightfully wayward*. In *judging* that a rhythmic phrase or even a single accent is "displaced", we have always to view it in relation to *a set flow*: and *this* we are enabled to do necessarily, if partly by remembering the *Sama*.

The *Sama*, I maintain, is always a key determinant of rhythmic arrangements; and it often becomes striking because of its regional context, that is, by virtue of what immediately precedes it. But whatever be the reason of its hold on our notice, we never quite forget it, unless the very fabric of rhythm which it distinguishes is utterly ignored. We may only bear it in mind quietly, or make for it purposely, as in following a well-shaped *āmad*.[6] Or we may have to struggle to

3. Such a characterization of *Sama* is of course very incomplete. But it is convenient as a starting-point. And, later in the essay, it will receive due supplement.

4. Which is at once to remember the *Sama* too. *Ṭhekā* is the rhythm-cycle regarded as the unchanging support of further rhythmic work.

5. *Bul*, in Hindustani, means a brief twist.

6. On the relation of *Sama* to *āmad* in vocal music, see chapter 8.

keep to it, as in following an intricate *quāyedā*. But, whatever be the way of our being related to it, we have to keep the *Sama* continually in mind, as an act of conscious orientation or as quiet, but continual fidelity to what is at once a recurring source and climax.

I may now turn to the word "phenomenology". It stands for a point of view which is quite different from the merely grammatical one. But let me explain. After which *mātrā* does the *Sama* appear, and at which drum? What precisely is the *bol* which marks it? By what calculative method has a pattern been composed — simply through a division of its total beats into three equal segments, or also by requiring them to be played at graded speeds? Questions such as these relate to the grammar and technical details of rhythm. They are *not as such* the subject of this essay. I propose rather to deal with a quite different question. How, in relation to the *Sama*, does our rhythm *seem* (or *appear*) *organised*? It may here at once be added that I only wish to distinguish, not to separate "*seem* organised" from "*is* (actually) organized"; and that this restraint is forced on me not by mere theory, but by a matter of fact. During actual composition one must of course organize the beats (or *svaras*) in a particular way. But, at the same time, one has also to look, quite often, at the part so far organized, just to check how it *seems* and makes for due onward passage.[7]

I may now but the different ideas that I propose to discuss in respect of *Sama*, all organized as follows:

> *Sama* is the first or focal *mātrā* (or beat) of the rhythm-cycle as treated musically, clearly spoken *or* merely contemplated in idea. In principle, it is to be kept in mind continually as the

---

7. I may cite here the view of Coleridge that, as engaged in composing, the mind suffers "alternate pulses of active *and passive* motion".

   Owen Barfield, *What Coleridge Thought*, O.U.P., London, 1972, 78. *My* emphasis.

major accent of a generally even flow of *laya*;[8] and is, in fact, often made designedly to work up effects of occurrent order and clear orientation.

Here, however, we must forthwith mark a difference. As played on the drum or as merely recited, the *Sama* is at once a *bol*, or a mnemonic (yet spoken or speakable) syllable. But this is not necessary when we mark the *Sama* only in the mind. Here, one is *not bound to* (quietly) *Speak* the *Sama*-syllable: the marking (which goes with a *Sama*) may occur as just a very light and merely ideal pecking of *laya*-flow by tacit attention.

Let me now explain our proposed definition of *Sama* by focussing on its key words, and by making some needful distinctions. This will at once bring out the main angles from which one has to look at the *Sama*.

## Sama as the Source of Rhythmic Design

As the *first mātrā*, the *Sama* is a *stimulus*. It impels and enables the mind to get attuned to what is to follow. Indeed, it is the first beat not merely numerically, but as the pace-setter. As a matter of principle, the time taken in articulating the *Sama-bol* itself at once fixes the speed of the flow that follows. Putting the two ideas together, we may speak of *Sama* as the source of rhythmic *design*, in case we take this word to mean, as we should, also the evenness of *laya* or rhythmic movement. As a cycle, the rhythm not only begins from, but *is determined by* the *Sama*.

## As Focal Beat

Yet, the *Sama* is not merely the first, but *the focal beat* of a cycle. From it we set out, and to it we return.[9] This is quite common

8. *Laya* is the controlled, yet not necessarily *beat*-measured, flow of musical duration.

9. In many cases, certainly not in all. A *sthāyī* or rhythmic pattern may take off from any *mātrā*. But when we indicate the character of a rhythm-cycle we begin from the *Sama*. As for "returning", one may end the patterning a little before *khālī* from where the *āmad* may build-up its access to the *Sama*. Nor is it proper to →

knowledge. But we are prone to forget this, and often say merely that the *Sama* is the first beat, ignoring the necessary complement: "of the cycle". In truth, *Sama* is the name of a key accent *of a regulated flow or rhythmic stretch*. The beat which marks it is not the full meaning of *Sama*. The flow which it initiates and completes (as a round) is implicit in what we mean by the word. Therefore, when later in the essay we turn to study the *Sama*-beat in relation to its context, it will only be doing what the beat (as properly understood) itself demands.

It is, I may add, *Sama* as the focal point of a cycle which imparts to rhythm, and to music which repeats a cycle visibly,[10] a suggestion of self-completeness. This is quite missing in *ālāpa* where we only have *laya, no tāla. Ālāpa* works up an atmosphere which may well seem unbounded. But it never appears self-complete in the manner of a round.

### A Beat or a Mātrā?

Yet the *Sama* is a beat or *mātrā* too. As such, it enables us to measure the flow, to steady or vivify the *laya* whenever it is needed[11] — as after the execution of intricate patterns — and to keep it generally in check.

Such talk, however, is a little glib; and we must make it clear what it means to say that the *Sama* is a beat *or mātrā*. A *beat* is a recurrent stroke, or its sound or moment. Repetitiveness, so clear in rhythm, is implicit in the very meaning of the word *beat*. A *mātrā*, on the other hand, is a measured quantity. This word is closer to measure than to recurrence. But it does

---

→ assume, as we shall later argue, that every pattern *appears to return to the Sama*.

10. This happens most clearly when a simple *drut sthāyī* or *gat* is presented more than once.

11. For instance, when the main performer is weaving a specially intricate pattern, the *tablā* accompanist may try to be of help by playing the *Sama* and the approach to it specially clearly.

not signify absolute separateness. In fact, to speak of a measure is at once to imply the complement — "of something". The *mātrā* here measures *an extent of the chosen flow of laya*. To sum up, as a *beat* the *Sama* means that it is to be repeated (or played) as the end of the cycle — a point that we have already emphasized; and considered as a *mātrā,* the *Sama* is the measure of a flow.

The second idea deserves a little more attention. The essential function of a *Sama,* I insist, is *not merely* to mark or divide, but to measure. I do not deny that it serves as a mark *too*. Failure to *notice* it would weaken our awareness of both the character and speed of the cycle. Also, it generally serves to distinguish one rhythmic pattern from another. What is more, it must freely be allowed *to appear doing this*. In order to enable a rhythmic pattern to have its full impact on the listener, and to *appear self*-completed, it is generally advisable not to begin the second pattern immediately on the finish of the first one, when the *Sama* appears as the end-point. Here, the little bit of quiet which follows it allows the *Sama* to flower as desired; and this serves to sever, not of course the flow of *laya,* but certainly the form of a pattern from that of the following one. This is sometimes ignored in Kathak dancing, with the result that the presentation comes to appear a bit too flowing, and deficient in inner segmentation.[12]

Yet, I insist, the *full and basic* function of the *Sama as a mātrā* is to measure, not merely to mark. This can be argued as follows:

a. In an ongoing recital the marking or dividing just referred to is no *radical* splitting. The proper awareness of rhythm is, so to say, *bifocal*. Immediately, of course, we notice and follow the patterns presented directly. But this mere confluence will itself be quite unrhythmical if we loosen our hold on the underrunning *laya*. So the *Sama* which divides patterns as segments *of rhythm* does so only as long as it serves

12. For a clearer presentation of this point see chapter 9.

to measure and steady, as a guide-beat, the flow which it itself (partly) articulates.[13] What is divided, is not really the basic *laya*, but only the patterns; and the *Sama*'s activity of marking or dividing still remains subject to its *function* of measuring.

And this, I believe, is important aesthetically. For a trained contemplator a good work of art can appear to articulate all that it comprises. Its parts are not merely mixed, like paints rubbed indistinguishably into oneness.[14] Nor are they only put together like pebbles in a heap. They can of course be distinguished. Yet they also nourish and are rooted in some common significance. Now, in the region of rhythm what keeps the *mātrā*s at their proper places and so truly distinct from, yet also rightly related[15] to one another is their common grounding in *laya*; but, if only implicitly, *laya* itself rests (if not entirely) on our awareness of *Sama*. So I conclude: the essential articulateness of rhythm as art is *in part* due to *Sama*. (I say "in part", advisedly. For, besides *Sama*, there are many other factors which ensure articulation in rhythm. What is articulate is also clear. Clarity, in turn, presupposes the right technique of executing *bol*s; their proper temporal arrangement in relation to one another, for *any* two *bol*s cannot be played tightly; and the requisite look of clarity also forbids hectic playing.[16]

13. This, however, is only half the truth. For, *laya* too determines the proper location of *Sama*.

14. Cf. S.K. Langer, *Feeling and Form*, p. 31.

15. The relation here — though also one of perceptual difference, if the *mātrā*s be regarded as related to *bol*s — is basically an interval of time.

16. This rule, I am sorry to say, is just not heeded by most of our drummers today. They care much more for fluency and loudness than for clarity and fineness, and mostly generate mere excitement which is often quite undiscriminating.

b. Again, suppose we require the *Sama* only to mark, not really to *occupy* the *laya*-flow. In that case, in order to meet the requirement, the *Sama* as played will have to be maximally fine. But then it will be a very brief and light stroke. This, in turn, will require the following *bol*s too to be played quite quickly,[17] making all leisurely rhythm improper in principle. No one can approve of such an attitude to *vilambit* playing. So we have to accept the alternative — I mean the suggestion that the purpose of *Sama* is to measure the *laya-flow.* This view provides quite fairly for both reposeful and lively rhythm. Whether the subsequent *bol*s are to be played slowly or briskly depends on the temporal length of the *Sama-bol* itself.[18]

Even apart from the points just used as argument, it is easy to see why "measuring" has to be regarded as the *full and basic* function of *Sama*. Measuring includes marking and dividing in a way, though not as utter sundering. To measure is at once to insert distinctions into what is measured; and the latter — that is, what is measured — at once becomes one unit as against the rest.

This, however, is a bit too general, though surely not untrue. What is important here is to mark the *special* nature of the measuring involved. To measure rhythmically is clearly not to portion what is visibly given as mere inert extension, as in plotting a stretch of land, but to hold on to *laya* which is, in the main, grasped *by the mind*. What is more, in fixing and keeping to this flow — or even in merely following it[19] — one has to remain steady, sometimes even to try to do so, may be with some actual felt strain. The inter-*mātrā* interval

17. This is here the demand of internal consistency of design.

18. The overall *laya*, however, where rhythm is "accompaniment", has to be fixed with an eye to the rhythmic demands of the composition chosen by the main performer.

19. As in merely listening correctly to a rhythmic recital.

must be kept[20] all along even, but the effort here involved is also some implicit *self-steadying*. If in his attention to rhythm the listener wavers in this inner balance even for a second, the *mātrās* may wobble, unhinging the very basis of rhythm's flowing fabric. The steadiness here demanded, we have seen, is helped greatly (though not entirely) by *Sama*. Hence I insist that measuring *of the kind just indicated is the Sama-bol's basic function.*

Yet, it would be wrong to suppose that the function of *Sama* is never essentially to mark. I say so with an eye to the use of *Sama* as *destiny* — a concept which is yet to be discussed, and which is clearly opposed to the idea of *Sama* as the source of rhythmic design. Where it *begins* rhythmic work, the *Sama* may well appear to be definite; and, as played, deliberative. But I wonder if here it can ever appear sharp, and not merely loud. We aim, in such cases, at fixing a speed; and in virtue of the time that its own sound occupies, the *Sama* is therefore admittedly a measure, suggesting (I repeat) by its own extent the *laya* to be followed. But where it occurs as the climax of a shapely rhythmic upsurge, its function is, as a rule, quite plainly to mark.

## Sama as "Bol"

In its other main forms, however — that is, as the source and as target of rhythmic arrangement — the *Sama* as played has an audible quality which not only receives, but deserves attention. In case its *chāṁṭ* is used properly, and if the playing is *drut*, a well-tuned "right one" can quite soon work up a kind of serial sweetness that helps concentration, our holding on to *laya*; and so also the proper notice of rhythm's other details.

The *Sama as uttered* too deserves a separate mention. I say so not because of the general importance of *paḍant*[21] in our

20. We cannot truly say: it *is* even. It is continually *kept* thus, may be quite without conscious effort.

21. *Paḍant* is the proper recitation of mnemonic syllables or *bols* of rhythm.

rhythm and dance, but in view of a specific consideration. The fact that the *Sama can directly fix* the subsequent speed to be followed — and this by its own temporal length — can, in my view, be better illustrated by speaking than by playing the *Sama* on the *tablā*.[22] And in so far as such regulation is probably the most easily identifiable instance of an important excellence of works of art — I mean the determination of the essential spirit of a complex whole *by the manifest character of its parts* — the importance of *Sama* as recited should seem quite obvious.

## Sama as Contemplated

With regard to the merely ideal awareness of *Sama* something has been said already. But whereas there I spoke of the *Sama* as *thought of*,[23] now I prefer the word "contemplated". The latter is, I think, truer to how *Sama in fact appears* — that is, as an accent (in a flow) which, in spite of its obvious distinctness, never appears isolated.[24] What is *thought of* may well be explored merely on its inside, ignoring its (outer) context. But even the simplest awareness of *Sama*, as the centre of a cycle, demands even counting, and so a continual ideal hold on the even flow of *laya* preceding the *Sama*.

It may be objected, quite properly, that what is *here* regarded as (outer) *context* can be accepted as such only if the *Sama* be thought of as just one beat, however important; and that if, as I earlier insisted, by *Sama* we mean the focal beat *of a rhythm-cycle*, what I now speak of as consideration of the context should really be deemed as mere internal attention. To this I would rejoin:

first, that if the *Sama* is thus understood as the *recurring centre*

22. The *pakhāwaj* is not so handicapped, in virtue of the deeper (or longer) resonance of its strokes.

23. The reference, here, is to the concluding part of point 3.

24. Except to those who do not really know rhythm and enjoy only the loud, and often unpleasant *sound* of the *Sama*.

> of a cycle, we still mean to emphasize[25] the centre, whereupon the remaining cycle at once becomes the context of what is emphasized; and secondly, that if this way of understanding — and its tendency to abstract, if very slightly — be rejected, and an appeal be made to the *Sama*-beat as appear*ing* enwreathed in, and integral to a cycle, "contemplation" still remains the right word, for the experience here cited is quite undivided, though awareness of a *distinct* outside is of course here absent.[26] To conclude, if we *understand* the *Sama* as the centre *of a cycle,* we have also to *think* that the context is in fact not left out; and if we *experience* it as occurring in a cycle, the *Sama* directly appears as both making for, and as made by the cycle. Therefore, the right word for our experience of *Sama* is in either case "contemplation".

How the *Sama* as contemplated may serve, in the main, to mark the *laya*-flow has already been seen. But the linkage of this one idea with our actual rhythmic practice is so rich and variform that I feel impelled to say something more about it:

a. First, it fixes an ideal for actual playing. The *Sama* which marks the *laya*-flow merely in idea is maximally fine. As already brought out, it does not seem to *occupy* time.[27] Therefore, drummers whose *minds* are steeped in the habit of keeping *laya* steady, and who no longer depend on the ear for noticing *Sama*, often affirm it but ideally, by refusing to *play it* very clearly where the design of the prior patterning yet makes us expect it. What is more, in conformity with their merely ideal — and often a little reverential — attitude to the *Sama*, they prefer to adopt a quiet, steady and mellow style of playing generally.

   I may here invite attention to two opposite ways of opening a recital. Today, when a *vilambit gat* begins,

25. Though not to isolate.
26. By "contemplation" I understand the undivided awareness of the details of a whole.
27. Which is not the same thing as just being *in* time.

the accompanist normally takes off with an elaborate pattern that ends *climactically and quite loudly* at the *Sama*. The aim here is at winning the applause of the listeners. But some rare drummer who delights in the contemplation of *laya* (as against audible rhythm) may behave quite differently. He may quietly unwind a pattern that is subtly arranged — but is gentle in accents — so softly, yet surely, that the *Sama* can be sensed nearly quite without sound, and is here vivified essentially in idea, the corresponding nod (of his own, as also of the main musician) being wholly involuntary in such cases. The purpose here is not to elicit general approval, though it often comes automatically from the knowledgeable; but just to imbue the mind with the essential character of a particular rhythm. *The* Sama *which exhibits itself, even to the poorly trained, is (as a rule) quite different*[28] *in appearance from the one which induces and enables a genuine* rasika *to dwell in the region of a particular rhythm.*

b. Secondly, in our rhythmic practice, an essentially ideal emphasis on the *Sama* also occurs in terms of *ateet-anāgat* patterns. These figurations are marked not by withholding the *Sama-stroke* entirely, but by making it fall willfully a little[29] after or before the fixed location of the *Sama-beat*. In so far as the *Sama as played* is here in both cases "displaced" from its *set* place in the cycle, these patterns are classed as *visham*. All this is fairly well known. But some additional remarks here seem necessary. Merely to stop ostentatiously a little before, or just to nod a little after the *Sama* — which practice is popularly called *jagah dikhānā*[30] — is only to show that one knows the location of the *Sama* and can therefore deviate purposely from its beat. It does not

28. In both loudness and appeal.

29. Yet quite identifiably.

30. Or, rather crudely, *muṅh-mārnā*.

become an aesthetic act unless it is done according to a running design. The fact that the performing musician emphasizes a *mātrā* before or after the *Sama* is of course easily *noticeable,* but a *pattern* which appears to slightly overflow, or ends just a little before, the focal beat primarily because of the regulation of its own run is *noteworthy.*

Rhythm, of course, is not the only art where form appears as essentially a matter of inner structure and not of mere observance of outer, prefixed rules, say, with regard to the location of *khālī* at a particular beat. But the artistic subtlety of designedly falling just a little short of the set normal length is nowhere *so* clearly manifest as in the sweet self-withholding, so to say, of our *anāgat rhythmic* arrangements.

c. Thirdly, and this is yet another way of affirming the *Sama* merely in idea, a pattern packed with *bol*s in three clear *āvṛttis,*[31] may be so played that at its first two places the *Sama* is deftly withheld. Here, if the moments of quiet are just of the right extent, and if the (contextual) *bol*s that they punctuate are close yet clear, *the quiet pauses will appear integral to hearing!* What happens here is — and it is a clear operation of the Gestalt law of good design or common destiny — that the configuration of the pattern is so coercive and its content of syllabic filling so intense that we are easily enabled to fill up, imginatively, the little gaps ourselves.

Mark that I speak here not of the silence that *precedes and follows* the pattern, as aestheticians speak of sculptures and architectural works organizing the "emptiness *around*"[32] them, but of pauses (or vacancies) interwrought. In the *art* of sculpture, of course,

---

31. An *āvṛtti* is a segment in the form of a round.

32. Cf. S.K. Langer, *Feeling and Form,* p. 88.

parallels can be easily found. I do not know how far the Gestalt laws enable us to understand the organization of *heterogeneous* elements. But art certainly helps. Just as rhythm turns moments of quiet into seeming accents of repose in an audible flow, a Henry Moore bronze may reveal an oblong aperture which lends life to the *figure* not only by letting in some light, but by inviting the eye to explore its interior, so that the space therein may appear to be show*ing* us the inside of the figure.[33]

## Sama and Laya

In spite of all its importance, however, the *Sama*-beat or *bol* is by no means independent. It is but the major accent in *an even flow of laya*. Let me clarify this in terms of the following individual remarks:

a. Awareness of the true character of the *Sama-bol* means neither that we know it (merely in theory) as the first of the beats that a cycle comprises, nor that we simply notice it when it comes — say, on being struck by its mere loudness — but that *we follow how it occurs as the centre of an even cyclic flow*. The ability to anticipate, locate, or deviate voluntarily from the *Sama*-beat depends essentially on one's ability to keep to the ongoing *laya* unfalteringly. This is the basic requisite for a proper relish of the subtlety, variety, and accuracy of our rhythmic patterns.

b. Yet, the *Sama*-beat itself may help us in checking whether *laya* has been truly even. It is the chief point where we can steady ourselves. Yet, it is *not the only* accent where we *raise or decrease the laya*. That can be

33. I refer here to the eleven inches bronze done by Moore in 1939. It is a bronze cast of lead original in the Victoria and Albert Museum, London; and was on display at the Exhibition of the artist's photographs and bronzes organised by our Lalit Kala Akademi and British Council, New Delhi (6-15 December 1973).

done by the drummer *anywhere*, through judicious quickening or elongation of any detail of playing.[34] But whenever this is done, the temporal distance of the *Sama* from the detail in question is also duly adjusted. Where, on the other hand, a change of *laya* happens to be involuntary, the ideal hold on the *Sama* too slackens forthwith; and the whole playing begins to totter.

**Sama as Destiny**

I may turn, in the end, to what is perhaps the most widely admired feature of *Sama*, that is, its *advent* as the end of a shapely rhythmic flow. I choose, to begin with, the word "advent" because it can be used not only where the *Sama* arrives as the climax of *what seems to be* a rhythmic *ascent* but also where it is just gently indicated as the close of a flow that *appears refluent*. The former is, in my view, easier to "illustrate" than the latter. But let me here make some remarks of theoretical value:

a. In the case of a melody what is most easily noticeable is its up and down movement. This is so because the music here follows, by and large, the ascent and descent of a scale. In rhythm there are no graded tones as making a scale. Yet if, during the process of playing a shapely pattern which seems to move clearly towards the *Sama*, the drummer *also* gradually increases the intensity of the *bol*s, the additional suggestion of an *ascent* — not of mere reaching, but of an upflow or a kind of *āroha* — will be noticeably produced. Two factors are here built on: graded intensiveness and clear orientation of the last few *bol*s as they run towards the *Sama*. Here, therefore, the *Sama* is of help

34. In practice, this requires the instantaneous cooperation of an understanding *lahrā*-player.

    *Lahrā* is the set tune which is played steadily and repeatedly along with drummers or dancers to keep the basic rhythmic measure quite clear to them.

in bringing the *character* of rhythm just a little close to the felt and organized character of a melody. To speak of melody *and* rhythm, or to say that a vocal *bandish* and a *tāla* can have the same *Sama* is, on the other hand, relating them only from the outside, so to say. Being (or flowing) together is surely not the same as appearing similarly organized.[35]

I may here add that in such cases — that is, where a pattern delights us by appearing to aim at, and by marking the *Sama* as its target — the principle at work is the Gestalt law of good contour. But the law itself — as explained in books on psychology — says nothing about the increasing intensification of the *bol*s which is really the drummer's own independent doing.[36] Here, however, my precise meaning has to be clearly put. I suggest only that the laws of perception are *not quite adequate* to art. They do not *exhaust* the creative possibilities of rhythm. But I do not say that the laws in question are *not at all relevant* to rhythm. Relevant they truly are, and I hasten to illustrate this positive point. Just think of the principle of contrast, and then attend to the following cycle of seven *beats*:

| 1 | | 2 | 3 | 4 | 5 | 6 | 7 |
|---|---|---|---|---|---|---|---|
| *Tin* | (ऽ)[37] | *tā* | *tirkit* | *dhin* | (ऽ) | *dhāge* | *tirkit* |
| 1 | | 2 | 3 | 4 | 5 | 6 | 7 |
| *तिन* | ऽ | *ता* | *तिरकिट* | *धिन* | ऽ | *धागे* | *तिरकिट* |

The *Sama-bol* here is *tin*. Its *seems* one,[38] a little elongated,

---

35. The point will become clearer if we here think of the right kind of rhythmic "accompaniment" or *saṅgat*.

36. Yet, in so far as it heightens the suggestion of orientation, such intensification will be quite in accord with the Gestalt law of common destiny. I failed to say *this* while presenting the Paper.

37. It must be marked that (ऽ) is here not a syllable, but only signifies the lapse of rhythmic time.

38. Though it in fact has *two akṣara*s or letters.

fairly steady and closed (or बन्द). The preceding tuft of *bols* is *tirkit*. This cluster of letters appears internally diverse, marked by a touch of successiveness, relaxed and a little lively. Now, the *contrast* — of the diverse with the undivided, of the lively with the firm — is here essential for producing the distinctive effect of the *Sama-bol tin*. This contrast — and with it, the singular effect of *Sama* — will both disappear if we introduced a touch of successiveness *into the Sama-bol itself*, say, by turning the steady *tin* into a quicker two-in-one: *tin-tin*.[39]

It would however be wrong to suppose that the actual, heard character of *Sama* depends on its relation to the immediately preceding *bols alone*. In the case of a bigger rhythm, it may in fact be found to depend on the inner organization of the entire cycle. This is clearly so where the *Sama-bol* is not exactly *repeated* anywhere else in the cycle; in which case it appears as a distinctive figure against the whole structure of the *ṭhekā* — quite in accordance with the Gestalt law of figure and ground.

But, whether the cycle is big or small, the actual heard character of the *Sama* is different from the *Sama* as merely *thought of* as being the centre of the cycle. The phenomenological is one thing; the merely ideal, quite another. Further, we have to remember that the Gestalt laws are no arbitrary imposition of intellect on everyday experience. They stand for ways in which experience itself appears organised. One does not have to be an intellectual to use the Gestalt laws. This partly explains the fact that many beautiful rhythmic compositions have been created by such masters of *tablā* and *mridaṅga* as had no formal education at all.

b. Care should also be taken to distinguish where *and how the Sama* comes to appear as the climax of an *ascent* from its occurrence as the natural end of a passage which looks like a rhythmic *reflex*. In its second form specially, *Sama* calls for some extra thinking. It is

39. Without, of course, exceeding the permitted length of a *mātrā*.

common to speak of it as the beat from which the rhythmic flow begins, and to which it also returns, accurately and winsomely. But let us just ponder over the idea of *return*. What exactly is that which should (in principle) appear to come back to the *Sama*, the counting of (say) the drummer or the rhythmic flow itself? We may recall, at this point, that a similar question can be put with regard to a vocal *bandish* that claims to be good. Does the composition *itself* appear to move towards the *Sama*? Is it so designed on the inside? Or is it only the singer who is able to come back to the focal beat, just because *he* knows where it is? Arriving at the *Sama* should seem to be an impulse of the *bandish* itself. Similarly, because of the flowing and seemingly undivided way it is played,[40] the rhythm *itself* should appear to lapse back to the first beat. Rhythmic patterns can indeed appear either merely to reach the *Sama* correctly, yet tamely; or to end climactically at the focal beat. My own experience is — and it is of course quite limited — that the (rather uncommon) suggestion in question (of appearing to lapse back) is clearly worked up:

> if a symmetrical rhythm-cycle, say *tritāla*, is chosen for playing — I say "symmetrical" because then alone can a rhythm easily *seem circular, as against appearing only quickly repeated;*
>
> if the *ṭhekā* is played neither very slowly — in which case it may be difficult for us to perceive the rhythm as a seamless run and impossible to sense it as circular; nor very quickly, for then the recoil, the turn*ing*-back, will not be visible — but at *madhya laya;*
>
> if, further, the cycle is so played that the work of the two drums appears blended as one, *the left drum* enveloping — and so unifying — the articulate *bol*s of the right one, with

40. Say, as a skilfully blended use of the two drums and a mellow style of playing, and (of course,) also as aided by the proper attention of a knowledgeable listener.

> its own breathing depth, called *sāns*; whereupon the listener's attention will remain gripped by the playing, and the experience seem self-complete in the manner of a circle;
>
> and, finally, if the re-touching of *Sama* is prefaced with a flourish — *of gently diminishing loudness*, such regulation being implicit in the requirement that the beat in quetion has to look as the point of *return*. A flourish, I may add, is a little shorter *and lighter* than a regular pattern. It does not appear to crowd or burden the listener's attention. Nor does it ever satisfy us deeply. But here, in the case of the rhythmic run in question, it helps by making for a *facile* return to the *Sama*.

This is the only convincing instance that I am able to provide, of rhythm's *really appearing to go back to the Sama*. A *chakkardār paran* is of course *said* to be circular. But it does not *seem circular*, if that be taken to mean a perfectly manifest *return* to the focal beat.

I may add that I insist on drawing a distinction between the *listener's returning to* the *Sama* and the *rhythm as itself appearing* to repair to its source. The former is a matter of only knowing and finding where the first beat is or where it occurs. The latter, on the other hand, is at once some creative ordering and *seeming* — a suggestion psycho-aesthetic. By "seeming" however, I here mean not only "being presented to attention", but only apparent or, in aesthetical language, "virtual"; for how can one really return to a moment which has ceased to be? And this one fact should be enough to expose the error of roundly speaking of rhythm as division and arrangement of time, without specifying that though, like every other event, rhythm as a whole does occur *in* time, the time that *it deals in* is its own virtual realm, the image of time that it itself conjures up with its created elements of simultaneousness, repose, succession and seriality.[41]

---

41. For explanatory remarks on these "virtual" elements of Hindustani Rhythm, see the first two chapters.

c. Patterns which arrive at the *Sama* merely correctly — that is, neither as the point of directed return nor as a climax — are aesthetically insipid. In two possible playings of the same pattern, it is easy to see the point of contrast between the *Sama* that comes as a mere terminus — weak and cheerless — and the *Sama* that emerges as the *climax or destiny of a shapely, powerful and onward* passage. In *both* cases, it is true, the playing can be correct grammatically. But whereas in the first case the playing will be only correct, not effective because of lack of graded emphasis, and the *Sama* will just occur rightly without being winsome, in the second case, because the pattern is played with *due inner accentuation*, and (I may add) a duly graded deepening of the *bol*s as they approach the *Sama*, this focal beat will appear as it aesthetically should, that is, as the climax of a regulated flow. It would help if I here drew a collateral distinction. *To say* that *Sama* is central because it both initiates and completes a rhythmic round is one thing. *To see it is so appear* is quite another. One way to truly make it look central is to play such patterns (I repeat) as appear clearly to move *towards* it, and end at it by virtue of the very manner of their inner design. The *Sama* here appears as the target[42] of their flow and therefore central, providing, I may add, a very clear operation of the Gestalt idea of "common destiny". But this "appearing" actually comes to pass only when we are able to *follow* the flow; which in turn requires that the rhythm-cycle be neither very narrow nor very quick. This is why the manifest suggestion of a shapely and directed access to the *Sama* cannot be ordinarily produced within the narrow confines of the rapid rounds of, say, *sool tāla* as it is commonly played.[43]

42. Not merely outer, but inwardly affirmed.

43. Which is, as a rule, played quite quickly.

The simplest illustrations of the point in question are provided by the patterns known as *tiyās*. A *tiyā* has three distinguishable, yet similar segments. These may either be equal in respect of length, or may carry a common content of syllables at a methodically rising speed. In either case, the *Sama* appears as the climax where the pattern seems completed, and towards which it all along moves in a way which is clearly designed. The point where the movement originates may occur anywhere within the fabric of the cycle; but most commonly this point of activation[44] is either the *khālī* or the *Sama* itself. There is hardly any limit to the number of such patterns. But what they all do in common is to show the *Sama* as destiny and as climax of the rhythmic flow, specially if the last few strokes that herald its advent show a deepening intensity.

But the *Sama* can assume a still different form. It may come neither with the force of a climax, *nor* as the (so to say) exhausted finish of some anaemic playing, but as the gently satisfying self-completion of a rich, elaborate and well-organised pattern that unfolds itself steadily and is internally distinguished by such a subtle variation — called a *bul* or *badal* — that attention is here held by the *whole* inner fabric of the movement, and is *not dominated* by the advent of the *Sama*. In such a case the *Sama* satisfies like the natural conclusion of a logical movement of thought. It does not dazzle us with the force of a climax; and the delight is, on the whole, spread out evenly, with the *bul* providing a welcome variant.

The *Sama*, I conclude, is not merely the straight *target* of a rhythmic run but is often seen to share its aesthetic value and role with other accents of the cycle, without ever giving up its basic significance as a *checkpoint* for the evenness of *laya*.

---

44. Sometimes this point may well be a quite unsuspected recess of the cycle, providing a delightful rhythmic version of what Mrs. Langer means by "subtle activation" in our felt life. See her *Feeling and Form*, p. 27.

# 6

# Form and Content[1]

THE purpose of this essay is to discuss the aesthetic problem of form and content in the context of north Indian rhythm. Of the various questions in terms of which this problem is generally dealt with in aesthetics, the following two may be said to be cardinal:

*a*. What are the individual (aesthetic) meanings of "form" and "content"?

*b*. How exactly are the two inter-related?

Other questions — such as those that relate to the primary *and secondary* meanings of "form", the difference of (aesthetic) content from mere material; or to the relative superiority of the one over the other — are but subsidiary; for they can all be reduced to one of the two we have specified as *a*. and *b*.

An *aesthetical* study of Indian rhythm is a need of the day. In contemporary India not much analytic work has been done on rhythm in a serious and sustained way; and this article is bound to seem unclear at places simply because even the basic meanings of the concepts of Hindustani rhythm, not to speak of their relevance to contemporary aesthetic theory, have not so far been made an object of explicit enquiry.

Before, however, I turn to look at Hindustani rhythm in detail, it seems essential to disucss the two questions generally:

---

1. First published in *Sangeet Natak*, 18, October-December 1970, under the title "Form and Content in Hindustani Rhythm".

## The Meaning of "Form"

Turning first to *form*, our concern has to be with the *basic aesthetic* meaning of the word. Such meaning is that which is, on the one hand, helpful in keeping art distinct from what is not art — say, craft and the numberless objects that we deal with in daily life — and is, on the other hand, applicable not only to all the arts, but to all the various *sub-types of structure* in the region of any one art, such as *dohā* and *chaupāyī* in Hindi poetry or *quāyedā* and *relā* in Hindustani rhythm. Keeping these guiding considerations in mind, I may now try to get at the needed meaning as follows:

1. Form is not the mere outline of a work of art. So to regard it would at once be to delimit its applicability to *some* works of art. We may well speak of the *outline* of some paintings which mainly present figures and clear shapes. But a poem, on the other hand, can be said to have an outline only in the sense that it is possible to make a list of the main points of its content; which sense, it is plain, relates "outline" to the poem very differently from the way it may be said to belong to some simple paintings and to works of architecture generally.

2. Nor can "form" in aesthetics be taken to mean mere shape. The word "shape", it is true, has some dictionary meanings which are freely regarded by aestheticians as being distinctively relevant to all art objects. Thus, it does not simply mean "disposition in space", but "form", or "apparition" — a word which Susanne Langer regards as a fair alternative to "appearance" in speaking of dance[2] — and "pattern", which *we* propose to employ in speaking of almost everything in our rhythm excluding *laya, ṭhekā* and the individual accents of rhythm. But, as we use it ordinarily, the word "shape" stands for something

2. S.K. Langer, "The Dynamic Image: Some Philosophical Reflections on Dance" included in *Aesthetics and the Arts*, op. cit., 78.

abstractable, that is, something which remains intelligible even if the specific *content* which happens to have the shape in question is ignored. Thus, to borrow (with some change of words) an illustration from Langer, our meaning is readily understood when we ask the shopkeeper to show us another lampshade *of the same shape, but in a different colour and size.* In respect of works of art, on the other hand, such talk is plainly impossible. It just does not make sense to say: "Write out another poem of the same shape (or form) but in a different metre, or with a different (though synonymous) set of words," because the shape or "form" of *a* poem is the shape (or form) of *its* present specific content. Vary its rhythm or its filling of words, and you change its *form* at once. In other words, the details of content, here, are not merely within the poem, but are inseparable from its *form*.

3. This leads us to say that the form of a work of art means only the *intimate unity* of *its* contents. Where we speak of art in the abstract, *form* stands for the idea of organization of content *in general*; but where our concern is with a particular work of art, "form" has to be understood as the unique organisation of the *specific* content of the work in question. In either case, in the meaning of artistic "form" a reference to content, as general or specific, is always implicit; and there is no real incongruity between the view of Alexander who regards form (generally) as "the system or relations in which the parts of the material are unified"[3] — rather than "as mere arrangement in space and time" — and Mrs. Langer's insistence that, as opposed to the shape of (say) a lampshade, the form of *a* work of art is not abstractable:

> We may abstract a shape from an object that has this shape, by disregarding colour, weight and texture, even size; but

3. Alexander, *Beauty and Other Forms of Value*, p. 46.

> to the total effect that is *an artistic* form, the colour matters, the thickness of the line's matters.[4]

4. In thus interpreting it we at once facilitate the realization as to how *form* is linked with some important aesthetic concepts such as "regional quality", "significant form", and "aesthetic gratification". In a work of art organization does not generally proceed as a perfectly even distribution of emphasis over its content. It is freely required to have an aesthetic centre — such as *Sama* in rhythm, or the linkage of the *vādi* with other close *svaras* in our classical music, or a dominant figure in painting. This at once makes for some striking regional quality; and helped by the general cohesiveness of internal organization, it makes the work a "significant form" — significant in the non-contentious sense of being interesting in itself. This, I believe, is really a safe way to interpret "significant form". To translate "significant" as "expressive" would be at once to make for the questionable view that *all* art is expressive — of some feeling or emotion. On the other hand, it seems unquestionably true to say that "if the literature of twentieth-century aesthetics and art critcism has favoured any single definition of art, it is that each work of art is an end in itself".[5]

   As for the closeness of "form" — interpreted as above — to "aesthetic gratification", it should now be easy to see; for,

   > gratification is aesthetic when it is obtained primarily from attention to the formal unity and or the regional qualities of a complex whole. . . .[6]

---

4. S.K. Langer, *Problems of Art*, op. cit., 25-26. My italics.
5. W.H. Bossart, "Form and Meaning in the Visual Arts", included in *Aesthetics and the Arts*, op. cit., 8.
6. M.C. Beardsley, "The Aesthetic Point of View", published in *Metaphilosophy*, vol. I, no. 1. January 1970, 46.

5. In understanding "form" as that which makes a work of art significant *in itself*, we are helped also in keeping art distinct from craft and our daily activities which all draw value from the fact of their being conducive to ends that are generally external, in the main.

**The Meaning of "Content"**

To turn now to the meaning of (artistic) content, one general truth seems to issue directly from what we have said about form: content is that which is, or appears to be there (in the work of art) considered not in itself, but *as it is there* — that is, as uniquely organized in, or by that individual work. The *āroha-avaroha* in terms of which we indicate to a beginner the grammatical character of a *rāga* is the mere material of music — as distinguished from its subject-matter, say, the text of a song. It becomes the content of (good) music only when, by being incorporated within the structure of a *sthāyī* or *gat*, it either appears as the very orientation of a musical flow towards the *Sama*; or as the up and down movement of *taans*, in which case it may strike us as the very breath of the freedom with which the latent richness of a melody-type unfolds itself, provided (as is necessary) the specific character of the *rāga* being rendered is kept all along manifest in the (grammatically true) rendering of the *sthāyī* or the *gat*.

**Form-content Relation**

If a question be put, as has often been done in the history of aesthetics,[7] with regard to the comparative value of form and content — or about the precise relation between them — we may set out to answer as follows:

a. The very fact that the question has been posed and discussed implies the possibility of a distinction

7. Thus, whereas Longinus, Hartmann and Hegel emphasize theme or idea, Plato and Kant prefer the formal excellences of measure and harmony to subject-matter or content.

between form and content.[8] We have ourselves distinguished the two, if not very explicitly. Content is *what* appears organized, and form means *that and how* it is organized *in* a work of art. The distinction can be vivified by comparing "content" with its existence outside the work, that is, as mere material. To illustrate, the sweet and swinging emphases of a *tritāla ṭhekā* as played by an expert drummer are obviously quite different from a summary verbal mention of its sixteen *mātrā*s and grammatically fixed accents and sections (or *vibhāg*s) or as simply *recited* in the way of a mere succession of beats and *bol*s. And the clearer our awareness of this difference, the greater may be our admiration for the drummer's way of actual playing; which would naturally heighten our sense of the distinction between what is being played (content) and how it is being played (or form). In the case of an occurrent art, the realization of the difference in question is further facilitated by the fact that the way content is here *being organized* — as distinguished from its merely *appearing organized*, say, in a completed painting — can be actually observed and followed.[9]

b. Considered as the artist's way of handling (or playing the *bol*s), and as being a clear index of his own creative authority over material which is merely given, form may indeed be ranked higher than content;[10] for, it is

8. This has to be said because some philosophers of art have categorically denied the propriety of this distinction. Weitz is one of these. He insists that content and form each comprise all that is there in the work of art, and that the distinction leads to "misdirected or specious aesthetic disputes". To me, however, the distinction in question is not only possible, but necessary.

9. Say, when the drummer is doing what is called *laya banānā*, or when he employs a shapely, self-evolving access to the *Sama*.

10. Cf.: ". . . In proportion as poetry becomes more intense the content is *entirely remade by form* and has no separate value at →

(in a way) the very generator of "content" as aesthetically regarded.

c. But where a question is put about the comparative superiority of form or content *in a specific work of art*, care must be taken to interpret "form" not as the artist's way of handling or style in itself (and as *generally recognised*), *but as manifest in the work in question.*

d. While discussing the problem of form-content relation, two points of view should indeed be always borne in mind. *Within the work of art*, form and content are required to be held so intimately as one that they may appear almost indistinguishable; for the distinctive idiom of art is non-discursive, and its aim is to create a complex whole which is internally very intense, and so interesting in itself. *For purposes of understanding*, however, form must always be distinguished from content. Otherwise, in addition to other difficulities, it would be impossible for us to admire, say, a drummer for his magical ability to produce, by means of his adroit handling, a multiform wealth of beauty afloat out of the meaningless material of some beats interjected into ideally apprehended rhythmic flow (or *laya*).

e. But then, in *thinking* of form *and* content (as matter or material), do we necessarily, and on the whole, run counter to the indivisible unity of a good work of art? No, we do not; for, in the very act of trying to distinguish the nature of the one we have to refer to the other. To think of form *and* content in the way *we have done*, is thus only to realize *understandingly* the extreme closeness of form and content in an authentic work of art.

---

→ all." (My italics). Roger Fry on poetry, quoted by Sparshott in his *The Structure of Aesthetics*, Routledge and Kegan Paul, 1963, pp. 348-49.

Why music is often ranked higher than the other arts should now be clear. Here, probably more than anywhere else, we find it very difficult to distinguish content from form. It is, in our view, easy to understand how "in [the case of] music we have no *permanent* means of deciding which of the many aspects we shall call the subject and which the treatment".[11] The difficulty may be seen even in our concern with a single note. As one of those *svara*s that merely make up a musical phrase, it is a detail of content; but as that at which an ascending melodic movement culminates, or as the *vādī svara* to which the other notes repair (off and on) in aesthetic subservience, so to say, the note in question also seems to organize *or form* what, as thus related to it, would appear mere content.

My task, however, is to deal with the concepts of form and content mainly in the context of Hindustani rhythm; and to this I turn presently.

### Form in Hindustani Rhythm

*"Form" in Hindustani rhythm may be said to stand for the idea that a definite number of beats, aided by specific "bols", some emphases and the "Sama" — whether marked or merely suggested — is seen (being) organized either directly into a cycle, or in general, or at least in eventual, conformity with the specific character and extent of a cycle.*

The individual ideas implicit in this definition may now be explained, so as to clarify what form really is in the region of Hindustani rhythm:

1. Leaving out mere *laya*,[12] the durational aspect of our music may be said to appear in two main forms: cycles and patterns. The word "form", as aesthetically understood, is equally applicable to both. It is to provide for this shared relevance that, in our

11. D.F. Tovey's article, "Handel as Composer", in *Encyclopaedia Britannica*, 11th edn., vol. XII (1910), 913. My italics.
12. Specially *laya* as found *in ālāpa*.

definition, we speak of *two kinds of organization* of beats and *bols*: (a) "either directly into a cycle" or (b) "in general or at least in eventual conformity with the specific character and extent of a cycle".

2. Yet, care should be taken to see the difference between the form of a cycle and that of a *premeditated* rhythmic pattern. Both are of course, in principle, internally organized; and are therefore "form" in the basic aesthetic sense of the word. But whereas (the form of) a properly played cycle itself looks self-completing — in so far as the *Sama* is a salient accent of its own structure — the form of a pattern appears completed only when it actually attains to or at least suggests, the focal beat *of the cycle*. If it is taken wholly by itself, and not as related to the (*Sama* of the) cycle, it would seem to be a mere collocation of *bols*, quite without any destiny, so to say, and not a rhythmically completed pattern. The form of a pattern may therefore be said to be subsidiary. It becomes fully manifest only when it gains access to the *Sama of the ṭhekā*. What is more, as a matter of principle, its entire manner of movement has to conform to the distinctive idiom of the cycle.

3. Where the patterns are *improvized*, as in the case of extempore *saṅgat* which the drummer may be called upon to provide to (say) the *sitārist*, their form is (in principle) judged — till before they reach the *Sama* — mainly by marking not only their correspondence, in respect of manner of movement and temporal extent, with the playing of the main performer, which itself is required to be properly structured, but also how they run parallel to, or deviate wilfully from, and yet hasten back to the full, basic flow of the *ṭhekā*.[13] The awareness of total form, in such cases, depends as much on the listener's exercise of trained attention

13. This is necessary. So, our definition speaks of the need for at least "eventual conformity with the specific . . . extent of a cycle".

as on the objective propriety of the playing itself. And, though the filling of some *bol*s has always got to be there, the drummer is *here* guided more by his attentive observation of the rhythmic manner and extent of what the main performer does — and, what is more, throughout, if but subconsciously, by his hold over the basic form of the *tāla* — than by rigid adherence to any set *bol*s. In other words, *predetermined bol*s, beats and emphases are *not always essential* for the form of a satisfying rhythmic pattern.

4. Where a pattern organizes itself in such a way that it both evinces its own inner design and yet deviates (momentarily) from the normal flow of the cycle, the right aesthetic response on the part of the listener is both rich and difficult. It is the awareness of a form (here, of the *ṭhekā*) as sustaining, and as itself being highlighted (as an anchor) by another distinct form (or the pattern), each perceived in its own distinctive character, and yet as related mutually, so that the total experience, though internally diverse and aesthetically very satisfying, is by no means blurred, but is rather a happy witnessing of how two distinct forms can be interlaced winsomely.

   Here, however, what is experienced, *as a flow,* is only the pattern. The form of the cycle, on the other hand, is sensed only as pleasing steadfast background. Thus, it is clear that *in our music the form of rhythm is not always experienced as "occurrent" or flowing, though some actual process is always there.*[14]

5. Yet, the suggestion of oriented flow is a very important feature (of the form) of our rhythm; and it can enliven a pattern even as a palpable passage of efflorescence

14. On the other hand, as pointed out by Susanne Langer, a shape that is static may well suggest a dynamic form. S.K. Langer, *Problems of Art*, p. 19.

(or खिलना). Thus, when a well-designed integration of *bols* is being played by the drummer — while the *sāraṅgī* simply goes on marking the speed and extent of the chosen cycle — it can happen that, from a particular point within its fabric, the pattern may appear to gather and activate itself perceptibly, and tend towards — and finally bloom forth at — the *Sama* in a manner which makes it seem distinct not only from the *ṭhekā*, but from its own previous parts. The reference, here, is to what I have elsewhere spoken of and explained as *āmad*. In my view, it can play as important a part in contributing to the form of rhythm as a line of look often does in making for coherence of different figures in a painting.

6. The artistic device just referred to can, however, characterize the form only of a rhythmic pattern, not of a rhythmic cycle. The run of *laya*, as it shapes a cycle, is required to be (on the whole) even and steady. A pattern is subject to no such necessity. In actual practice the form of a cycle, as it itself is, is just not used as a ground for that close and intense filling of *bol*s which makes the essence of charm in the case of quite a few rhythmic *patterns*.

7. There are some other features or effects too which can characterize the form only of a pattern, never that of a cycle as such. The two most obvious of these are *ebullient* self-assertiveness, as in the case of patterns called *ateet*; and a semblance of self-restraint as illustrated by patterns of the *anāgat* variety. The latter can be winsome in the way of a coy hesitancy, if the playing is not only soft, but properly patterned.

The reason for the (cycle-pattern) difference I am trying to make out may be brought out thus. It is of course true that neither a cycle nor a pattern can have a form without employing a specific number of *mātrās*, *bol*s and some emphases. But, whereas the *Sama* and the other emphases conjoined with the *bol*s of a *pattern* may be shifted — of course, in a planned way, and with an eye to heightening the overall beauty of its form — the same cannot be done in the case of a cycle without damaging its essential nature. If the *bol*s of the *ṭhekā* are displaced from their corresponding *mātrā*s, its character as an unchangeable support — which is one essential meaning of the (Hindi) word *ṭhekā* — would at once disappear and leave in its wake only a variant of the cycle. In the case of playing a *tukḍā*, on the other hand, it is commonly regarded as a mark of skill if, in a spirit of guarded abandon, the drummer shortens or withholds one (prefixed) *bol* or elongates or displaces another — as against their set speed, length and location[15] — without of course failing to return to the *Sama* immaculately, either in terms of an audible stroke on the drum or simply as a mere well-timed quiet nod.

Whether it is actually played or merely suggested, the completion of a *ṭhekā* must always be made to appear *at* the set *mātrā*. In the case of some *patterns*, on the other hand, the last audible *bol* may occur a little *before* or *after* the fixed location of the *Sama*. The reference here (I repeat) is to patterns of *anāgat* and *ateet* type. In such cases, the *Sama* is suggested and quietly affirmed through the very intentional and properly designed quality of the way in which the playing avoids it.

This, incidentally, prompts me to explain why in the definition which opens this entire section devoted to form in the context of rhythm, I have spoken of it as *bol*s, emphases, etc. that are sometimes seen as *being* organized. If a cycle or a simple and evenly flowing pattern is played out in the set way, the playing just appears organiz*ed*. But, where the drummer *is* shuffl*ing* the *bol*s intentionally, beautifully, and without losing sight of the *Sama*, we get the extra suggestion that the pattern is *being actively* organized.

Our treatment of "form" may now be allowed to end. I have, of course, not said anything about the numberless details of the way in which rhythmic organization actually takes

15. This is called *laya banānā*.

place;[16] but, interesting though it certainly is, the matter left out is hardly demanded by our present purpose which is simply to determine the general meaning of "form" and "content" in the context of our rhythm.

**Content in Hindustani Rhythm**

Here, too, we may begin by proposing a definition:

> *Whatever appears (or is visualized) as organized in a rhythm-cycle or a rhythmic pattern — either manifestly or as ideational reference — at the particular speed at which it is played, may be regarded as the content of rhythm.*

To facilitate understanding, this definition may be explained at some length and piecemeal as follows:

a. Considered in themselves, the beats, *bol*s and the various emphases are only the raw material of rhythm. It is only when they appear organized as a cycle or pattern that they can be said to form the aesthetic content of rhythm.

   I here think it necessary to add that by virtue of its inclusion of *bol*s — which are all alike non-representational — as the bulk of its content, rhythm is quite different from, and may even be said to be superior to some other arts from some specific point of view.[17]

b. In the case of a cycle, in the many inter-*mātrā* intervals *where* it is not marked by beats and *bol, laya* — as the seamless evenness of flow — is throughout supplied by the listener's (or at least the drummer's own) ideal

16. Generally, this is done in accordance with the Gestalt Laws of perception, the most important of them, in our rhythm, being the laws of "figure and ground"; contiguity, similarity and contrast; and "common destiny".

17. Say, if being non-representational is regarded as an important feature of good art.

attunement. The beats only enable us to mark and diversify, and to hold on to, the flow of *laya*. The cycle, itself appears as an undivided unity, essentially because *laya* is found *or visualized* as permeating it. *So, laya (or sheer duration or pace) must also be regarded as a vital part of the content of rhythm.* Here, however, it does not occur as it does in vocal *ālāpa*, but is organized as a cycle of evenly marked accents. It should now be clear that our response even to the basic appearances of rhythm is by no means merely sensuous, just because its flow *between* the beats is all along visualized, and surely not heard.

c. The content of a rhythmic *pattern*, as it occurs in a regular recital, must be said to include, besides its own *bols*, a vital additional factor, that is, *an implicit (yet ceaseless) reference to the basic rhythm-cycle* on which it is based, and to which it has eventually to conform, however devious it may appear during the course of its own run. Unless the flow (of *laya*) running through the *ṭhekā* is continually remembered by the drummer, the pattern is always liable to waver. Likewise, if the listener does not remain all along mindful of the flow in question, he cannot hope to see the precise way — often quite tortuous — in which the pattern moves.[18] So, the non-sensuous element in (our experience of) the content of rhythm consists not only in the ideal attitude of remaining steady in marking or following the *mātrās*, but in a comparative activity of the mind which judges not only the general and (or) *ultimate conformity of the pattern* with the cycle, but its own (earlier) creative audacity in deviating, may be quite briefly, from the run and pace of the ṭhekā.

d. Nor can we leave out from the meaning of its

18. And, of course, his perception of the *form* of pattern too will suffer at once; for, where form is occurrent *the manner of movement* must also be attended to.

"content" *the precise speed* at which the cycle or pattern is being played; for speed is obviously an inalienable element of drumming. What is more, it is not merely included along with, but determines the other details of the content of rhythm. Thus, at the quicker stages of playing, one or two difficults *bol*s — such as are meant, in the main, for slower drumming — may have either to be played differently from the way they ordinarily are, or even replaced with other syllables. Such changes are demanded by the need to keep the playing internally distinct, and (from the outside) seemingly full and complete, even in its more fluent movements. Taken by itself, however, speed is a mere element of rhythm; it becomes the aesthetic content of the latter only when it actively contributes to, and is itself incorporated within, the specific inner character of the cycle or pattern. A drummer who sacrifices clarity of *bol*s for the sake of sheer speed obviously fails to organize a vital quality element of the content of rhythm.

But, it may be wondered, is its speed really indispensable as "content" for a "form" of rhythm? Does speed really *determine* the *specific* character of rhythmic forms? Now, one may feel tempted to answer these questions negatively, in view of the commonly held belief that the *same* pattern can be recited or played at *different* speeds, the implication obviously being that the "form" or design of the pattern will remain the same even if its speed is changed. It is, however, easy to see (as follows) how such suggestions are fallacious.

The matter may be considered either abstractly or with an eye to fact. *Abstractly* speaking, the form of rhythm *means* the form of a *flow*, even as the "form" of painting stands for the idea of there being something visual.[19]

19. To say this, however, is obviously not to exhaust the meaning of "form" in painting.

So, it would be as improper to leave out the idea of speed from the meaning of rhythmic form as to ignore the suggestion of spatiality in describing what the "form" of a painting is. And if we decide to reckon with rhythm *as played*, speed would seem vital in two clear ways. Where the object of attention is a steady *madhya laya ṭhekā* which *has been* played for quite some time, our awareness of speed may well be subconscious; but it is nonetheless there. How otherwise could we explain the fact that here the slightest deviation from steadiness of flow disturbs us at once? If, on the other hand, we see the *ṭhekā* (or pattern) as actively *changing its own speed into a quicker one*, its form too will appear as growing more compact and fluent. So, speed is in either case integral to "form". The pattern or *ṭhekā* that is said to remain the same in spite of the change in its pace is but the abstract idea of a design, not "form" considered as the actual, dynamic integration of its elements.

e. In the simple playing of a *ṭhekā* the drummer occasionally employs some flourishes too — which are not a part of the normal, pre-fixed structure of the cycle — simply for the sake of making the playing appear beautiful, by relieving the monotony of its set, usual manner. Thus, where a slow, expansive cycle like *dhamār* is being played, a *tablā*-player may deftly elongate the effect of every *bol* by suffixing its impact with a gentle rub of the skin of "the right one" (दायाँ) and this partly with a view to keeping his own counting steady, and partly by way of audibly indicating to the vocalist the flow of *laya* even *between* the *mātrā*s. (This, however, is not the only way of filling the inter-*mātrā* gaps). Such flourishes are not regular patterns. Yet, in so far as they contribute to the continuity and richness of actual drumming, they must be regarded as a part of the content of rhythm.

## Form and Content in Hindustani Rhythm

As suggested all along by our examination of their individual nature, form and content are closely interrelated in respect of both fact and aesthetic significance. In other words, they are neither found nor can be understood or relished in isolation from each other. The following additional remarks should make the matter clearer:

a. The form of the unitary and organised character of rhythm depends vitally upon the evenness of flow or *laya* which it articulates. In respect of its actual speed, *laya* in turn depends upon, and is regulated by the temporal quality of the way in which the very first *bol* or tuft of *bol*s is played or rather recited. To illustrate, if the syllable — which marks the *Sama* of *dhamār* — is spoken very briefly (or quickly) as a dainty dot, say, as *k* (क्) the following *bol*s too will have to be spoken at a correspondingly quick pace. Alternatively, if the *Sama* is uttered as an elongated and leisurely *kā* (का), the speed of the following *bol*s too will have to be slowed down accordingly. And in so far as the first *bol* is obviously a detail of content, the interdependence of form and content is thus brought out clearly.

b. In the context of rhythm, we may note, *form* means not only that the *bol*s of the cycle are as held as a single series, but that they are all kept articulate. This, in turn, prohibits acceleration of speed beyond a certain limit; and speed, as already brought out, is an important element of the content of rhythm. The same truth can be seen also by reflecting that the proper *organization* of patterns like *relā*s and *rau*s demands *quick* playing. Generally speaking, just for the sake of winsome form, the content of a rhythm-cycle is to be played neither so slowly that it may become impossible to apprehend its *laya* as a seamless flow — instead of a mere succession of detached, static units — nor so quickly that the clarity of *bol*s may suffer. If *they* grow indistinct, the manifest content of rhythm is only messed up, not duly organized.

c. Our actual experience of the form of rhythm depends on our ability to imagine the flow of *laya* throughout its extent, marked or unmarked. Now, when — with the intent of revealing the aesthetic potential of the unmarked parts of the *ṭhekā*, or as a teasing test of our ability to follow the course of rhythm — the drummer expects us to make some extra effort to visualize the flow towards the *Sama*, the point where he wants us to begin (the effort in question) has to be marked on the drum quite emphatically. In other words, the requirement as to the proper observation of *laya*, which is so essential for responding rightly to the form of rhythm, may determine how exactly the individual *bol*s are made to sound.

d. If, as is only proper, rhythmic form be regarded as an *integration* of *distinct* accents, its role in determining the content of *bol*s should indeed be easy to realise. It is the criterion of proper (aesthetic) *form* which demands that only such syllables be put alongside of one another as can actually be played fluently without undue strain on the hands; that *bol*s be mellow without being indistinct, and clear without being obtrusive; or that they be neither so broad or sharp (except occasionally) as to disturb the unity of flow, nor so weak as to become indistinct themselves. The *Sama*, of course, is generally expected to be a little more distinct than the other *bol*s; but if it is too sharp and sudden it may make it difficult for us, momentarily, to regain access to the basic flow. Further, the requirement of rhythmic form also demands that the *bol*s should not only be correctly timed, but sound sweet to the ear. This will enable the playing to elicit ready attention to their location, thereby making it easier for the listener to follow the flow of *laya* without which neither a cycle nor a pattern can appear organized. What is more, a drummer whose playing is neat and sweet himself appears absorbed in the flow of *laya,* which adds to the overall appeal of his artistry. I may here be allowed to repeat that, though it is certainly occurrent, the form of rhythm is not all along audible; and that a measure of ideal involvement is necessarily implicit in our simplest awareness of the form of rhythm.

Above all, in the region of our rhythm the distinction between form and content can be quite as hard to draw as, by an accepted ideal of art, it is (we have seen) required to be. Thus, such *bol*s as *dir, dir,* if played fluently, directly make for a look of singleness; and so it would be *as* proper to call them a part of *form* as a detail of *content*. Again, the *sāṅs* — or the effect of a deep, breathing continuity — which can be evoked by a proper employment of "the left one" — is not a mere content, but a connecting link, and so a making of form. Finally, the *Sama* does not only occur as a beat, but completes a round directly; and to call it content alone would be merely to ignore what the *Sama* always *does.*

A final doubt may be noted and resolved to ensure some adequacy of treatment. In discussing its aesthetic form and content, I have all along quietly assumed that Hindustani rhythm is an independent art, as unquestionably as being simply an art of accompaniment. But is the assumption justified? I am convinced it is; and in the very first essay I have taken care *to explain why* I think so.

# 7

# Aesthetic Character of Some Asymmetrical Rhythms[1]

THE aim of this chapter is to bring out the aesthetic character of four "seven-beat" cycles of Hindustani rhythm.

By "aesthetic character" I understand what (or how) a thing appears to be when considered from the aesthetic point of view. What this point of view means is of course not easy to determine. The meaning varies as we turn from one art to another. Thus, whereas in the aesthetic evaluation of a novel or play the question of lifelikeness is not generally left out,[2] a similar notice of rhythm calls for no such question. Rhythm, as we generally employ it in India, is essentially non-representational. Its materials are mnemonic syllables in *laya*, not words with their individual meanings. It does not describe or depict anything. Yet, in spite of many clear differences between the various arts, it seems safe to make the following generalization:

> To regard an "object" from the aesthetic point of view is to be intelligently — not necessarily analytically — aware of how it "looks" because of its content *and* unique inner organization, both of which conjoin to produce its specific aesthetic character.

But I must explain what I have just said. The word "object" here stands for whatever is attended to or thought about. It

1. First published in *Sangeet Natak,* op. cit., no. 34, October-December 1974.
2. F.J. Coleman, *Contemporary Studies in Aesthetics,* McGraw Hill Book Co., 1968 (PB), Introduction, p. 11.

may be a (complete) work of art, or an individual item in — or a mere part of — a music, dance or rhythmic recital, say, the opening *ṭhāṭ* of Kathak dance; or, in the case of a solo *tablā* recital, the *ṭhekā* which is not commonly regarded as a distinct item of presentational playing[3] like *peshkār* and the various *tukḍā*s.

"Looks" (in the generalization proposed) means what (or how) the object *directly appears* to perception, not merely visual, but auditory; or, in the case of literary arts, to overall comprehension and relish. Thus, we may speak not only of the look of a painting or sculpture, but of the nimble, yet steadfast "look" of a *drut tritāla ṭhekā*. The "look" of a *poem*, on the other hand, would mean its unity (satisfying or otherwise) as it becomes finally accessible to the interplay of analytic and *imaginative* attention. In following the flow of a rhythm-cycle, on the other hand, what is demanded is a clear awareness of its *khālī* and *bharī*, and of its neatness and general evenness (of flow between the beats), but of course *without* actively understanding *why* a particular *bol* appears delightful at a particular pace and place. Yet, clear and cogent thinking is not so removed from vivid perceiving as it may be thought to be. This should become clear to the reader when he has gone through this essay.

Finally, in suggesting that the aesthetic viewpoint means noticing not the mere look, but the inner organization of the work, I wish to keep away from such dubitable uses of the word "aesthetic" as: "the *aesthetic* delights of tasting a wine discriminately". We can certainly distinguish one taste from other close ones, and also its own inner changes. But nobody speaks of perceiving how a taste is *organized*. I may add that the awareness of how an object of art is organized may come quite easily. Thus, anyone who knows the basic elements of rhythm can "see" (that is, appreciate) the manifestly well-shaped patterns, such as *tiyā*s, heading for the *Sama*, and so

3. This is not to deny that, if only occasionally, some *tablā* maestros do seek to win listeners' applause by a sustained *drut* playing of the *ṭhekā alone*, mostly of *tritāla*.

as highlighting its prominence. Finally, by "aesthetic *character*" I here understand the organized and perceivable appearance of the rhythm-cycle *as a whole*, not any such merely aspectual quality of it as the auditory character of the *Sama-bol* or the particularity of this *bol*'s being indicated, say, on "the left one", as in the case of *roopak tāla*.

Nor should we here ignore what the cycle appears to be *in the context of total playing*. For, ordinarily, the *ṭhekā* provides only a steady basis or background to whatever the drummer does; and just as the aesthetic significance of the first *scene* of a play is inseparable from what it does in the economy of the whole work which it opens, a cycle too (in solo drumming) is not grasped in its full nature as an art element unless it is viewed also as the matrix *of the recital* in which it figures. This aspect of the matter, however, I am constrained to leave out, just for the sake of brevity.

Let me now turn to determine the aesthetic character of a seven-beat cycle[4] the *bol*s of which are as follows:

| | 1 | 2 | 3 | 4 | 5 | 6 | 7 |
|---|---|---|---|---|---|---|---|
| 1. | *Tin* | *nā* | *tirkit* | *dhin* | *dhin* | *dhā* | *dhā* |

| 1 | 2 | 3 | 4 | 5 | 6 | 7 |
|---|---|---|---|---|---|---|
| तिन | ना | तिरकिट | धिन | धिन | धा | धा |

What makes this cycle appear organized is the joint operation of quite a few factors. The point may be brought out as follows:

a. First, as in the case of any other *tāla* of Hindustani music, the *Sama* here serves as the focal beat. From it

4. I owe the knowledge of all the cycles cited in this essay to the late Ustād Chhamma Khan, a drummer in the Music Faculty of Delhi University. For their notation, however, I am indebted to Prof. Sudhir Kumar Saxena, Baroda University, who too is now only a cherished memory.

we begin, and to it we turn again, completing a circle, so to say; which makes the rhythm seem clearly cyclic, and in *that* sense organized.

b. Then, there are the Gestalt principles to be kept in mind — principles, say, of contrast, contiguity, and similarity. Contrast is the most effective safeguard against monotony.[5] It generates interest and prevents fatigue of attention. Contiguity and similarity make it easy for us to hold different details as one. They make for unity. Here, in the case of the cycle in question, the opening *tin* — which is the *Sama bol* — is a closed sound (mark the way we utter *tin* or तिन) and it is followed forthwith by the open *nā* (ना). Further, *dhin dhin* (धिन धिन) and *dhā dhā* (धा धा) are pairs of similars, though in relation *to each other* they show the same closed-open contrast that characterizes the opening *tin nā* (तिन ना).

c. The two *dhins*, if *played properly*, provide — by virtue of their gently elongated quality — some perceptible continuity to the cycle, and so make it appear organized.

d. But the most noteworthy detail is here the *tirkit* (तिरकिट). It occurs at double the speed of any other *bol*. This makes it appear as a distinct figure against the setting of other *bol*s. It is different from other *bol*s not only in respect of its auditory character, but (as already said) in that of its *laya*. This makes it a typical "figure" *of rhythm*.

*This* particular excellence, I at once add, is not to be found in *rūpak tāla* which too, as we know, is a *7-mātrā* cycle:

| | 1 | 2 | 3 | 4 | 5 | 6 | 7 |
|---|---|---|---|---|---|---|---|
| 2. | *tin* | *tin* | *nā* | *dhin* | *nā* | *dhin* | *nā* |
| | 1 | 2 | 3 | 4 | 5 | 6 | 7 |
| | तिन | तिन | ना | धिन | ना | धिन | ना |

5. S.C. Pepper's article, "Aesthetic Design", in *Introductory Readings in Aesthetics*, ed. John Hospers, The Free Press, 1969, p. 69.

The principles of similarity, contiguity and contrast are of course at work here too, but no single syllable in this cycle can be regarded as a "figure" *against* the occurrent context of other *bols*.

In the case of *pashto* which runs as follows:

| | | | | | | | |
|---|---|---|---|---|---|---|---|
| | 1 | 2 | 3 | 4 | 5 | 6 | 7 |
| 3. | *tin* | ऽ | *tak/* | *dhin* | ऽ/ | *dhā* | *dhā* |
| | 1 | 2 | 3 | 4 | 5 | 6 | 7 |
| | तिन | ऽ | तक / | धिन | ऽ / | धा ऽ | धा |

the *Sama-bol tin* (तिन) indeed occurs only once, as in the case of the first cycle considered by us. But the other *bols* here do not provide that touch of alacrity which the *bol tirkit* does in the opening cycle. This is why, if it is played at *madhya laya*, *pashto* looks internally sparse, and has therefore to be played *at quick speed*. Further, the extent of this *ṭhekā* is not so intense that it may heighten, by contrast, the leisurely *tin* (तिन) as a figure against ground.

*Mughlai*, another 7-*mātrā* cycle, has a greater filling of syllables than *pashto*. Thus, see the following:

| | | | | | | |
|---|---|---|---|---|---|---|
| | *kat* | *tā* | *tirkit* | *dhiऽn* | *dhāge* | *tirkit* |
| 4. | 1 | 2 | 3 | 4-5 | 6 | 7 |
| | कत | ता | तिरकिट | धिऽऽन | धागे | तिरकिट |

Be it noted that the *Sama-bol kat* (कत) here occurs only once. What is more, the *dhiऽn* is here to be played (or recited) in such a clearly elonglated manner that, by virtue of its very breathing quality, it may provide a clear measure of continuity to the total playing. But, at the same time, this cycle has two features which, I believe, make it (on the whole) a little inferior to the first cycle from the viewpoint of the ideal aesthetic character of rhythm as a *ṭhekā*:

First, the *tā* occurs at the second beat with such delightful alacrity that it becomes a rival to the *Sama, kat* (कत), in respect of attention-catching value, thereby bedimming the requisite centrality of the focal beat.

Secondly, the two *tirkit*s here (at the third and seventh *mātrā*s), along with the feature just referred to, invest the cycle (as played) with a touch of impetuosity. The feature may look good to lay listeners, but it detracts from the look of stableness demanded by a *ṭhekā*[6] as an anchor of all rhythmic artistry.

I conclude, therefore, that if (as, I believe, it is only proper to suggest) the aesthetic character of a *ṭhekā* be taken to consist in a balancing of open with tight *bol*s, and of a measure of vivacity with an overall look of poise, the first cycle may be said to interest us more readily than the other asymmetrical rhythms I have referred to.

Here, however, an important point may well be made. In the *kind* of interestingness which I have just spoken of, no nameable "feeling" (as emotion) is there; and if our view of *aesthetic meaning* is to cover even such cases of aesthetic experience, I think we have to regard it not as "objectification of feeling", but (with Reid)[7] as "embodiment of value". *Embodiment* will here go with *perceptual* clarity, which is most essential for rhythm; and value may be taken simply as "interest-in-the-object",[8] which would *include,* without being confined to, the object as *felt*-about.

Three more remarks are needed before this essay ends:

First, the source of the charm of the "form" of a rhythm cycle is not mere *articulateness*, but its skilfully *accentuated* moments. Articulateness is the feature of being *composed* of recognisably *distinct* sounds. It means, as Langer says, that the structure of an art object is given to clear perception, in opposition to the unity of mere mixing, as is typified by a

---

6. Even in common parlance, we may note, this word implies stability.

7. See Reid's *Meaning in the Arts*, pp. 193-94.

8. With Perry. See his *A General Theory of Value.*

mixture containing many medicines without at all revealing what they individually are. But, and this is noteworthy, in the case of good rhythmic work the clarity of constituent syllables is often mainly the result of the drummer's *own* active regulation of their intensity — so that some *bol*s appear deeper than the others — partly through such ways of "pressing" the drums as are called *daab gāṅs* (दाब गांस).

Second, because of this very norm, the excessively quick playing of a *ṭhekā* is aesthetically improper, because then its accents tend to get blurred.

And finally, no appeal to the laws of perception can cover the many appearances of a cycle *as played*, and no amount of analysis, psychological or otherwise, can wholly *seize* the creative vitality of an artist. For instance, quite apart from the design of the patterns that he may choose to play, a skilled drummer may impart an extra bit of quite *unexpected* sharpness to the *Sama* by playing the penultimate *bol* just a little *later* than its grammatically set moment. Thus, if the first cycle discussed in this essay is recited in a simple way, no tension will appear *in* the rhythm; and no suggestion of any release of tension a*t* the *Sama*. But, think of a possible change. At present, the last but one *dhā* here (in the first cycle) is *at* the sixth beat. If, however, we speak it a little *after* the 6th beat, by elongating the second *dhin*, the two *dhā*s will tend to come closer together, after which the *Sama* at *tin* will look clearly sharper.[9]

Such variations, I may add, are not only possible but necessary. They save the drummer himself, who has to play the *ṭhekā* for long and repeatedly — and also the listeners from a decline of interest.

---

9. *This* detail, as also all the rhythm-cycles mentioned in this essay — except no. 3, *pashto* — were recorded by the Sangeet Natak Akademi (New Delhi) when I presented my Paper on "Sama" to their Poona Seminar, on 12 January 75. But the detail in question was there illustrated in terms of recitation, not played out on the drum.

# 8

# Sama and Musical Structure[1]

THIS chapter is an adaptation of the paper on *āmad* which I presented at a Seminar organized by the Sangeet Natak Akademi in 1970. I seek here to show how *Sama* serves as a determinant of *musical structure.*[2]

Speaking quite generally, *āmad* (in music) is the act of gaining access to the *Sama*. But one cannot meaningfully speak of *āmad* merely, because it never occurs alone. It is always found inlaid in a *bandish* which it at once shapes and enlivens. *Bandish* is our word for what is spoken of as *form* in aesthetics generally. Here, in Hindustani music, *form* is secured through a *flow* that is not only articulate, but internally organized. In our classical vocal music *sthāyī* is said to *be* a *bandish* or to *have* a form[3] if, when it is sung, it seems intense and organized; and, what is more, also as embodying[4] a *rāga* and a specific

1. First published as "The Fabric of Āmad: A Study of Form and Flow in Hindustani Music", in *Sangeet Natak*, Journal of Sangeet Natak Akademi. When it was actually presented at the Seminar, the paper was duly accompanied by illustrative singing. For a list of compositions used as illustration, see p. 44 of that article.

2. In the light of this wider context my earlier characterization of *Sama* as merely the source and destiny of rhythm seems inadequate.

3. And the knowledgeable are at once struck by it, if it is good.

4. Why I say "embodying", and not merely "conforming to", will be clarified in the next para. However, it may be added here (in passing) that in a recent work, *embodiment*, rather than *expression*, →

*tāla*. As sung, it is always a doubly determinate vocal flow traversing some chosen *svaras* winsomely. Its form is clearly occurrent, and is manifest in specific ways. One of these, called *kanbharnā* by our traditional *ustāds*, operates as integration of a little remotely placed notes or tonal phrases by means of glides, and in such a way that the entire flow would appear (more or less) as a directed approach to the *Sama, or as āmad*. So, in addition to *āmad* — and as related to it — I have to speak of the form and flow of our music generally, and of such allied concepts as *bandish, sthāyī, tāla, ṭhekā* or rhythm-cycle, *ẓarab*[5] and *Sama*.

Now, *bandish* is for us a very important concept. Its exact relation to *rāga* and *tāla* is to be understood with care. If a *bandish* is to be a true aesthetic form, it must appear to be not merely placed in a *rāga-tāla* setting, like some clothes in a box which necessarily remains external to (and separable from) them, but as including, *and* appearing to being formed, by the *rāga-tāla* duo in question. *Within* the *bandish* the *rāga* should be visible all along *and so should the chosen rhythm too*,[6] either through a steady and simple relation of one-one correspondence between the segments of the vocal flow and rhythm (as is the case with *dhrupad* compositions generally), or by way of a skilful, yet intelligible *displacement* of some segments or key moments of the *bandish* (as sung) from the corresponding beats of the *ṭhekā*. In the latter case, because of

→ has been emphasized as the key aesthetic concept. The reference here is to L.A. Reid's, *Meaning in the Arts*, George Allen & Unwin, London, 1969.

5. For a clear account of what a *zarab* is and how exactly it differs from a *mātrā*, please see chapter 10.

6. This requirement cannot be easily met by a *sthāyī* that is sung *very* slowly. In such singing, the form of the *ṭhekā* is not visible to the singer himself, and he depends entirely on the drummer, *not on the structure of the sthāyī itself*. On the other hand, the relatively (or not too) *vilambit* compositions of the late Ustād Aman Ali Khan do *not* suffer from this defect.

the palpably intentional quality of the act, what is avoided at once looks related, if indirectly, to that which deviates — but, of course only to those who are authentic *rasika*s.

What I have just said should make it clear, a little later, why I interpret *āmad* as I do. Literally, the word *āmad* means "arriving at", "entry" or "appearance". In the context of music, I repeat, its minimal meaning, if not its full aesthetic significance, simply is: arriving at the *Sama*. But, in live music — say, in the act of actually singing a *sthāyī* — the *Sama* can be reached in (at least) two clearly distinguishable ways:

a. First, the *sthāyī* may be made to move steadily along with, and as parallel to, the set distinctions within the *ṭhekā*. Here, when (one *āvṛtti* of) the *sthāyī* is completed, *the singer reaches the Sama* effortlessly, and with requisite accuracy, and may then begin the line anew.

   This gives us one meaning of *āmad*: *āmad* as *our* attaining to the *Sama* immediately at the completion of one round of the *sthāyī*. Here, the *Sama* appears more as the target *of the singer at work, than as the inwardly suggested goal of the sthāyī itself.* It sure looks as a point that is duly reached; but it does not appear integral to *sthāyī*'s own inner design. It only comes at the end of the *sthāyī;* but (I repeat) it does not appear to consummate it. Rhythm here just envelops or accompanies, but does not look like directing the singing.

   So, if a *sthāyī* is required *to have* (*or to be*) a form, and if — as is only proper — artistic form be taken to stand for a deep inner cohesion of elements, such a simple arrival at the *Sama* as presents it merely as the immediate sequel to — and not as the direct consummation of — a process, cannot be regarded as the true (aesthetic) meaning of *āmad*.

b. Alternatively, and this is its second meaning which I aim at emphasizing in this essay, *āmad* may be understood as:

   that *identifiable section* of the flowing form of a *sthāyī* (or

> *gat*), in and through which the flow seems to *activate or regulate itself perceptibly at a particular point of the rhythm-cycle*, and therefrom *to move towards*, and *attain the Sama in a well-designed way*, which attainment at once seems to be a *self*-completion of the entire *bandish* as a dynamic design.

If it is understood in this comprehensive sense, *āmad* cannot be translated (I insist) as mere "resolution of tension".[7] Nor do I know of any work which has already discussed *āmad as I have here defined it*. My *argument* at this point here would simply be that the meaning of a word depends on, and changes with conditions at a particular period of time; and that, in so far as our ancient Sanskrit texts had nothing to do with discourse relating to *khyāl* singing and Kathak dance, the two areas in which the word *āmad* is mainly used today, they (the ancient works) could not possibly be concerned with *āmad* as I now understand it, and *in the light of our arts* as they are practised today. Words like *ateet* and *anāgat* refer only to the relation that obtains between the normal rhythmic ending of some rhythmic patterns and their creatively displaced final emphasis. They say nothing about what I am going to speak of, a little later, as "clear emanation", "self-activation" and "clear orientation".

But I hasten to add that though it is surely identifiable as a distinct passage, we cannot isolate an *āmad* from the complete *bandish* in which it appears, without losing sight of its true artistic significance. *Aesthetically, the āmad* not only determines, but is itself determined by its structural embedding in the *bandish*.

To facilitate understanding I may now break up what I

7. This is a phrase to which my attention was invited by Prof. Lobo after the discussion on the paper as presented. I also recall that, on this occasion, the late Shri K.K. Varma rightly pointed out that though my emphasis on the attributes of a good *āmad* was throughout clear, I did not lay enough *positive* stress on the view — which I so far regard unchallengeable — that we just cannot have *an uncommonly good bandish* without a properly structured *āmad*.

have said on the subject into individual points. I regard the following as the essential[8] features of a good *āmad*:

1. It should:

   a. Appear to begin distinctly; and

   b. *Continue to appear* distinct, say, even when it follows the execution of the *antarā* or a rhythmic pattern. (*Clear emanation*).

2. Also appear *to activate or upgather itself* for onward movement. (Self-activation).

3. Seem clearly to *move towards*[9] the *Sama* (*distinct orientation*). This is possible only if the *āmad* is not too brief or overly quick.

4. This movement, moreover, should seem striking and well designed,

   a. either by employing some distinct formal device of singing,

   b. or by virtue of a deft manipulation of rhythm. (*Beauty of rhythmic design*).[10]

   In the absence of any one of these four features, an *āmad* cannot appear as moving towards its goal — that is, the *Sama* — well before the latter (the focal beat) is actually attained. This is, in fact, the translation of a remark which, I gratefully recall, was actually made

8. Essential, to be sure, but not the only features.

9. "*Moving* towards" calls for *āroha* and *avaroha*: hence *their* importance for musical structure. Such movement can be easily seen in the *leisurely* flow of *dhamār tāla*; hence, the usually striking character of the *āmad* of this rhythm-cycle.

10. The fact that Ustād Chand Khan (of Delhi) was an eminent *vocalist* at once answers the protests, made by some during the post-presentation discussion, that *āmad* is heard of only in the context of dance, never in that of vocal music — an objection which surprised me.

and "illustrated" (in terms of actual singing) by Ustād Chand Khan during the course of a talk I had with him, more than fifty years back.

5. Finally, the *āmad* as such should mark — not necessarily stop at — the *Sama* not only (in every case) correctly, but likeably. This demand can be met variously:

    say, by just fondling or caressing, so to say — yet, without eclipsing — the *Sama* with a gentle sway of the voice;

    by including *it* (the *Sama*), as a mere hint in a flowing continuity, so that its second (*unmistakable*) arrival delights us because of the very fact of its having been very lightly shown at the end of the earlier round;

    or, above all, by making the *Sama* appear as the natural culmination of a self-evolving pattern of clearly marked accents; in which case the *Sama* seems to *emerge*, and not *merely* to arrive (terminal propriety).

To sum up, the more important features of a good *āmad*, in my view, are:

Clear emanation

Self-activation

Clear orientation

Beauty of design

Terminal propriety.

In brief, how the *āmad* bestirs itself and takes shape; how it blooms or proceeds and develops itself; and, what is more, *how it consummates itself by embracing (or marking) the Sama* — it is to details such as these that I seek to draw the attention of *rasika*s.

Besides these features that should distinguish an *āmad*, I may also dwell on the following problems that arise in our attempt to understand or design it.

6. How can *āmad* be made to appear (and kept) *distinct* in a rhythm cycle of brief compass, say, *sool tāla* which is

mostly used at *drut* pace. (I answer: by enlivening the point of its origin, or by making it striking because of its contrast, auditory or positional, with its setting).

7. How is the effect of an *āmad* determined by its context, say, by the quality of the *bols* or patterns that precede or follow it immediately?

8. How does an *āmad* determine, by virtue of the *way* it touches the *Sama* — say, as the end of an open *akāra* and vigorous vocal run, *or* with the sharpness of a pointer — the character or disposition of what follows it?

9. Above all, how is *āmad* related to the text of the song?

   This, again, may be considered as the relation of *āmad*:

   a. either to the euphonic or merely auditory character of language,

   b. or to the *meaning* of words.

As for "illustration", we may use *tarānās* liberally; and this because of some clear reasons. In so far as they make only a sparing use of language, they provide a fine field for studying matters of *mere* structure. What is more, they permit a very easy view of the contrast and interplay of such formal features of music as continuity and flow; discreteness and successiveness; or buoyancy and artistic abandon. Above all, their relation to the fabric of rhythm is throughout clearly perceivable largely because of their occasional employment of *bols* as *ẓarabs* or emphases.

For sheer *stateliness* of *āmad,* however, one has to turn to *dhamārs* of the right variety. Nor can *dhruvapads* be wholly ignored. In fact, to consider the question as to how the presence and working of *āmad* can at all be made visible in a *ṭhekā* of brief compass, we have to refer to such compositions as *dhruvapads*[11] in *sool tāla*.

---

11. For my familiarity with the structure and imagery of *dhruvapads* and *dhamārs*, I am deeply indebted to the late Padma Bhushan Ustād A. Rahimuddin Khan Dagar. *Āmad* is, however, →

However, I yet openly admit the possibility of many inadequacies in my entire discussion. Some of these I now see myself quite clearly. For instance, I have *not* distinguished *āmad* from what is called *pakaḍ kī taan*. Nor have I said anything about the delightful possibility of incorporating within the *bandish* a *subsidiary* movement, itself resembling an *āmad*, which ends immediately before the beginning of the main *āmad*.[12] The *Sama* too, *which completes and caps the āmad*, should have been dealt with not only as the destiny of the *sthāyī*, but also as a stimulus to further creation. The idea of *Sama as stimulus* is clearly different to that of *Sama as destiny*.

Let me add however that, in spite of these limitations, I do hope that this brief essay has realised two clear ends, if but incompletely:

> first, to show how detailed aesthetical thinking is both possible and necessary — without much dependence on the hoary works on *sangeet* — with regard to our music *today*; and
>
> secondly, to suggest that Hindustani music — which alone I happen to be familiar with — is quite systematic, without of course being pent up within any closed or final system.

---

→ just as essential for, and possible in *khyāl*-singing as in the case of *tarānās*. The fact that, during illustrative singing, I did not produce any *khyāl* was a clear deficiency of the presentation. But I still believe in the validity of the reason, here advanced, as to why I prefer *tarānās* to *khyāls* in speaking of the details of musical *structure*.

12. I did, however, produce an instance of this detail *while singing*, by way of "illustration", a *dhamār* in *rāga Hindol*.

# 9

# Rhythm in Kathak Dance[1]

I ASSUME that the reader has a fair knowledge of Kathak dance and Hindustani rhythm. My attempt here is only to help him in vivifying this knowledge by means of piecemeal, analytic thinking. I propose to adopt a threefold approach — grammatical, psychological and aesthetic. The object of my analysis is rhythm as a specific constituent of Kathak dance. However, insofar as the primary subject of this whole book is rhythm as an independent art, and also because the creation of ever newer *rhythmic* collocations is an explicit objective of this form of dance, this chapter will be unavoidably brief. At the same time, however, I expect it to reveal to Kathak lovers some rareties of both analysis and composition.

Now, to turn to the subject straight away, rhythm in Kathak is essentially a matter of collocation of some select *bol*s on the basis of the beats, pace, and extent of the rhythm-cycle chosen, without confining itself all along to these basic details. But, just as essentially, it is also a regulated accordance *of bodily movements* with the flow of rhythm as marked by the feet; *and* with the meaning of the text of the song where the dancing is *nṛtya*.

Considered as *tāla,* as distinguished from the more inclusive concept of rhythm as overall accordance of the

1. This chapter is a substantially modified presentation of the essay, "The Role of Rhythm in Kathak Dance", which was first published in *Marg* (Bombay, September 1959, pp. 48-53); and I gratefully recall that the then editor, the late Dr. Mulk Raj Anand, hailed it as "the first breath of fresh air from the Kathak world".

various elements of a total (dance) number, rhythm may be spoken of quite simply as *laya* as measured. That which makes this measurement possible is the unitary being of a *mātrā*. But its being 1/16th, say, of *tritāla* is only the grammatical, not the entire significance of a *mātrā* in this timing-cycle. As experienced, the *mātrā* has a distinct psycho-aesthetic setting which gives it the value it possesses. First, it signifies a distinction which thought everywhere needs. To think of something clearly is at once to hold on to, or to interject, some distinctions therein. In the context of *sangeet* taken generally, a *mātrā* is the recognition of precisely this basic need of thought where it has to deal with a flow. It gives the mind a foothold, as it were, in the run of *laya*. Secondly, the *experience* of a *mātrā* in ongoing music or dance may at once be regarded as one of beauty (as unity in variety) — say, of a properly put accent along with other *mātrā*s in a seamless yet regulated flow, and not that of a mere singleness in a random aggregate of separate units. Correspondingly, the basic idiom of *our entire experience of layakārī*, be it merely grammatical or also aesthetically, is that of a flow that runs over emphases which it cannot do without, and which are all along distinct or distinguish*able*. The numberless forms of rhythmic figuration are all *alike* rooted in this running experience — of *matrā*s that occur as evenly placed accents within a seamless flow. A *mātrā* (or beat) asserting its singleness (not separateness) from the *flow* of the rhythmic pattern being danced, say, by means of an emphatic stroke of the dancer's feet; or the listener's holding on to the *flow* of *laya* imaginatively in spite of the *mātrā*'s own singleness; and the run of the pattern providing such mini tufts of *bols at or between* the *mātrā*s as are not normally played on the *tablā* — of all this variform beauty of rhythm the basic condition is the running flow of *laya* articulated all along by the evenly placed *mātrā*s. And this total fact — the running *laya*, the *mātrā*s it embraces but nowhere quite bedims, and the *bol*s which make for *laya*'s own figuration — has to be heeded all along by the *rasika*; or else he will not be able to register the multiple charm of *layakārī*.

## The Nature of Layakārī

The various remarks I have just made may now all be integrated to make for a succinct account of what they all relate to, that is, *layakārī* or the evermore creative handling of rhythm. *Layakārī is the aesthetic presentation of quite a few mātrās as distinguishing, vivifying and variegating, but by no means disrupting or using up the creative potential of the chosen basic laya-flow which remains (and is visualised as remaining) seamless and steadfast all along, until a change is expressly desired by the (main) performing musician.* And considering that the basic creative source here is the mind as interjecting distinctions (that is, *mātrās* and other emphases) into ideally apprehended motion, the more one organizes rhythm in numberless ways, the more deeply is he (or she) likely to be imbued — *at times visibly to the point of a little awe* — with a sense of the limitlessness of *laya* as the locus of rhythmic charm. It is not without reason that when he resorts to the recitation of a really subtle pattern, the *paḍant* of a veteran Kathak assumes a touch of slight, yet perceptible wonderment which may even appear in his look. The *inward relish of layakārī* — not the merely overt and grammatically correct *articulation* of a subtle pattern — calls for the mind's utter oneness with the rhythmic run — and it is (in secular life) perhaps one of the most obvious experiences of a *passage* from the *realm of* the merely perceptual to that of the utterly, but blissfully non-sensuous. The moment we leave out the subjective element — that is, the mind's self-identification with the *laya*-flow and its experience of contemplative delight — *layakārī* dwindles into a merely calculative activity, and the possibility of a little deepening of (an aspect of our) being through an experience of the exhaustless riches in the *temporal* aspect of Kathak dance collapses forthwith.

Rhythm seasons and sublimates the sensuous, presentative details of Kathak dance with a touch of ideality, rarefying the merely heard (and seen) with the fineness of contemplative following and imaginative sympathy. Two specific rhythmic patterns (both set in *tritāla*) are yet to be analysed later in this chapter; but, by way of anticipating for the reader one of my ultimate conclusions, I may here point out that the really subtle moments of rhythmic play speak largely to the understanding, though definitely they are also perceived, because heard by the ear. And a *rasika* who really enjoys *layakārī* in Kathak dance knows accurately which cycle is being used; flows all along with the otherness, which is no disparity, of the pattern's being woven at delightfully varied angles, across (yet within) the *ṭhekā*'s basic frame, and all this without for a moment forgetting its manner and speed, so that the effect of variety and contrast, of intentional deceleration and raising of pace is never lost sight of. Such sensitive attention is not given to everyone, and *that is why the aesthetic and variform charm of layakārī, which does not lie in mere power or pace of playing, is often missed.*

From such general remarks let me now turn to some specific details. The basic *bol*s of *tatkār* (in *teen tāla*) and their placing are as follows:

| (Tā | thei | thei | tat) | (ā | thei | thei | tat) | (Sama) |
|---|---|---|---|---|---|---|---|---|
| 1-2 | 3-4 | 5-6 | 7-8 | 9-10 | 11-12 | 13-14 | 15-16 | (X) |
| (ता-आ | थेई | थेई | तत /) | (आ | थेई | थेई | तत) | (सम) |
| (1-2) | (3-4) | (5-6) | (7-8) | (9-10) | (11-12) | (13-14) | (15-16) | X |

Here, the only difference between the two (bracketed) segments, which are to be gently distinguished (not jerkily divided) by means of a meandering bodily turn, is between ता at the first-second beats and आ at the 9$^{th}$-10$^{th}$ beats. Between the other *bol*s (3-8; 11-14) there is no difference at all. Now, this overall similarity facilitates steadiness for one who has just begun learning to dance. But there are two other details relating to this simple beginning, one of which is not generally given the attention it deserves.

First, the dancer here quietly learns to see the difference between a sound which is open and appears vertical (ता, आ) and one which appears to turn upon itself midway, so to say, that is, थेई. This is, we may note, a simple but quite educative beginning for a tyro. It prepares him (or her) to notice differences even between those sounds which we are not very careful about, just because they do not make any regular language. If this very first step is not given the attention it deserves, how will the pupil be able to distinguish (later, as the training progresses) the easy-going तक, say, in 'चलो यहाँ से वहां *तक* घूम आएँ' from the emphatic <u>*तक*</u> in 'त<u>क</u> घलांग धधिकत' or from daintily danced तक् in तक् घलांग धधिकत, as also from the slightly upheaving का in तकिटत*का* ? And if the inability endures, it will be a very great handicap; for proper Kathak dancing calls for a meticulous accordance of footfalls (पदचाप) and bodily movements not only in respect of their timing, but in that of their lightness or power. Otherwise, the erring pupil will get (as he actually does) the following admonition from a maestro like Birju Maharaj: 'तुम नाच नहीं रहे हो; नाच रगड़ रहे हो'! It is surely essential to remember that, for an authentic *rasika*, the rhythmic charm of Kathak consists not only in the manner of movement, pace, and length of its *whole* collocations of *bol*s (that is, *toḍā*s, *tukḍā*s) but in exactly how much time *the individual bol*s occupy in actual dancing or in *paḍant* (recitation).

Second, a close look at the basic *tatkār bol*s makes it clear that, in the way they are recited *and followed*, an element of imagination (as make-believe) is actually involved. The dancing feet do not actually produce the slightly drawn out थेई; they only produce an open sharp (and short) sound (like ता), not a sound like थेई which (I repeat) is seen to last for a little while. If the brief sound here actually produced by the feet is yet taken as थेई, it is clearly a case of make-believe. A little later, I hope, the role of imagination in dancing *and* following Kathak patterns will become quite clear.

But, turning to the beginner anew, he (or she) has also to be made to see how the order of *bol*s can be gently shuffled to produce a little look of artistic abandon, that is, regulated variation within an overall order. Thus, see the following simple variant of the basic *tatkār bol*s:

<u>ता थेई तत थेई</u>, <u>आ थेई तत थेई</u>, <u>थेइतथेई ततत</u> <u>थेई थेई तत तत ता</u>

1 4 5 8 9 12 13 14 15 16 सम

An actual dance recital of the traditional manner, however, begins with a ठाट to which I may now turn.

## 2. Some Kathak numbers from the viewpoint of Rhythm

a. *ṬHĀṬ:* This opening number, *ṭhāṭ* (ठाट) is, in the main, a posutre of beauty, but it yet provides a breath of gently burgeoning *pace*, and the very first makeover. so to say, of the merely physical into an eye-catching look. This look, however, is not one of mere quietude. It is rather a live emblem of that reposeful, opening *laya* which is soon to quicken gently into variform movements of rhythmic charm. These little initial movements which the dancer here presents, with requisite restraint and all quite unobtrusively, bear the following five-letter names: *kasak, masak, duran, muran.* They all alike present the opening breath of *laya* as it heralds the easy or multiple movements of dance that are to follow presently. By and large, a *ṭhāṭ* seeks to bring out the running seamlessness of *laya* rather than the singleness of *mātrā*s that here appears rarely, through it is surely quite manifest as the emphasis of *Sama* which itself is indicated by a slight, yet perceptible turn of the neck or the eyes, or by an accordant footfall. If the *tablā* player here presents, as he is expected to, just a sweet and simple *ṭhekā,* the net aesthetic impression produced on us by the lissome wrists (and other movements) of the Kathak doing *ṭhāṭ*, will be mainly one of the basic *laya*-flow as enlivening and regulating the *mātrā*s all along.

However, if the overall uniqueness of a Kathak recital is kept in mind — that is, not only its use of rhythm, *bols*, and the body as its material, but its being *impressively occurrent* as an art — it may well be said to begin not with a simple *āmad* but with *a paran āmad*, to which I will turn a little later.

b. *Āmad*, incidentally, is an Urdu word which means advent or first appearance. But, one may wonder — appearance of what? This is precisely the question which remains to be univocally answered by the interpreters of Kathak dance. Some are of the opinion that the pattern called *āmad* is really to be played on the *tablā;* and that, as accompaniment, this *tablā*-playing heralds the advent *of the dancer*. But such a view tells us nothing about the aesthetic character or the rhythmic design of *the āmad itself*. Our understanding of *āmad* should, on the one hand, mark it off clearly from *ṭhāṭ* (ठाट) and other numbers of Kathak dance; and, on the other, give us a clear idea of the *āmad*'s own form and impact. Now, following the way I have (elsewhere) spoken of it in the context of *sthāyī*s in vocal music, I may say that in Kathak dance too an *āmad* is a rhythmic pattern which *emphasizes the manner of gaining access to the Sama*. Its net overall look is that of a flow's gathering itself (so to say) specially in its final segment, for a final attainment of the *Sama*, by way of a quick collocation of *bol*s that are all along clear and emphatic; and the orientation of approach at once makes the *Sama* appear as the target of the whole rhythmic run.

**Sama : How Central?**

In respect of this cardinal appearance — and from the aesthetic point of view — a little more may be said. The *ṭhekā*, as the ground of all *layakārī*, must have a character of its own. It has to appear organized, say, as a singleness with a clear centre. That centre is the *Sama*. But, I hasten to add, the aesthetically central is a fount of value; and therefore the *Sama* has to appear as determining the beauty of that which encompasses or precedes it, and not merely as occupying a particular place in the rhythm-cycle. Now, if this requirement is to be met — that is, if the *Sama* is to reveal its true character as an aesthetic centre — it must appear distinctive in two ways:

> First, it should have about it an unmistakable sharpness or at least definiteness, conveyed by a stroke of the feet or through a sharp turn of the neck. Further, in so far as it is intended to mark the (relative) cessation of the *laya*-flow as marked by the *ṭhekā* (or as embraced in a rhythmic pattern), on attaining to the *Sama* the danseuse must grow a little statuesque, if very briefly. Otherwise the pattern would look not really completed, but only as overreaching itself into the subsequent one, whereupon the dancing, as a whole, would look a bit too flowing, deficient in inner clarity — a blurring or interfusion, more or less, not a winsome sequence of distinct and self-complete numbers.
>
> Secondly, the *Sama* should appear not merely as the last stroke or *mātrā* of the *ṭhekā* or the pattern, *but (I repeat) as the obvious culmination of a self-evolving movement*. Putting the two together, we may say that the *Sama* should not merely appear to *arrive*, but to *emerge*.

This is indeed what actually happens when the following popular *paran-āmad* is properly danced.

I. (*धातक* *थुंगा*) (*धागेधिंगता*) (*धाधिन्ता*) (*धित्ताकिड़्धा* *तक्काथुंगा*) *तकिटतका* *तिटकतागदिगिन*)

1 3 4 6 7 8 (9 12) 13 14 15 16

II. (*ता* *थेई* *ततथेई* *आथेईततथेई* *थेईतथेततत* *थेईथेई* *तत* *तताता*)

1 2 3 4 5 8 9 12 13 14 15 16 (सम)

The segmentation of this pattern, indicating the *mātrā*s covered by each segment, has been done by me strictly from the viewpoint of *paḍant*, that is, bearing in mind the usual and proper way of its recitation which is done at moderate (*tritāla*) pace and is at no point hectic. What, however, I wish to emphasize here is something quite different. The fact that the first 16 *bol*s all relate to *pakhāwaj* playing is of course obvious; and this indeed is why it is not a simple *āmad*, but a *paran āmad*. But what we have to *try* to see here is the fact that the first four segments all open with the *heavy dhā* ध (or its variant धि) sound — an *akshara* (letter) which occurs 6 times; that they also build on some *bol*s which are just not there in a simple *āmad* employing only the basic *takār bols* — say, *akshara*s like क, थुं, गा; and that all this makes a *paran āmad* not merely different from, but clearly more variegated *and impressive* than an *āmad* without *pakhāwaj bol*s. Whereas the latter (that is, a simple *āmad*) may be said merely to *open* a recital, with a *paran āmad* (on the other hand) the dance may be said to *herald its own advent*, because of the more impressive sounds it builds on. It is true that the first half (I) which ends at गिन (16th beat) freely uses the letter त (which, of course, figures prominently in the basic *tatkār* too) more than eight times, though not in identical ways. Yet, in so far as here it is nowhere used with थेई, its difference from the second half (II) which uses त with थेई very freely remains unmistakable. I conclude, therefore, that the names which Kathak numbers bear have not been chosen without due thinking, effortless though it might have been.

Roughly the same may be said in respect of the following (*tritāla*) pattern, of *anāgat* variety, which takes off from the tenth beat and ends, as is requisite for all such rhythmic collocations in *teen tāla*, at the 16th *mātrā*, that is, just a little before the focal beat or the *Sama*.

*(घिननन नागेतिट) (क्ड़ैधातिट) (घेघेतिट) (घेघेनातिट) (गद्दीघिड़ान) (नागेतिट किड़ान)*

10 13 14 16 1 2 3 5 6 9 10 12

*(तकिटतकिटधा) (तिटघिन तिरान) (धा तिटघिटतिरान) धातिट घिट तिरान*

13 16 1 4 5½ 10 11½ 16 (सम)

To facilitate understanding, as also for the sake of indicating their temporal length in terms of *mātrā*s, the different segments of this pattern have been bracketed. What makes it aesthetically noteworthy is, however, some features of its inner ordering. First, the first four bracketed segments all end at an identical *bol*, namely तिट (*tiṭ*). Second, the 5th and 6th brackets also provide a kind of end-rhyme. My reference here is to घिड़ान (*ghiḍān*) and किड़ान (*kiḍān*). In other words, the Gestalt law which emphasizes our innate liking for similar objects of attention has been duly (if perhaps unknowingly) heeded. On the other hand (thirdly), the 7th bracket provides a syllabic bunch which, if taken as a whole, looks quite unlike the other tufts of *bols*; and so provides some relief from too much of similarity; or, say, satisfies our need for a breath of perceptual contrast. But, because of its manifest otherness, it also looks like heralding the start of a clearly ordered, because *tiyā*-like, approach to the beat (16th) which here occurs very close to the focal beat and therefore forces attention.

However, attention to such rareties of rhythm, though certainly needful,[2] does nothing to compensate for the overall inadequacy of this chapter. It has missed very much more about Kathak than it has taken note of. Luckily, as part compensation for this inadequacy, and if only at the end, I find it possible to say something which may well gladden the hearts of those who prefer to look at Kathak also from the viewpoint of current aesthetic theory; and I put it thus straight away:

Aesthetics in the West has for long been dominated by the view that beauty in art is essentially a matter of unity in variety. Now, in the entire region of art with all its multifariousness, one may not be able to find a more convincing and readier vindication of this view than in a seasoned Kathak's *tatkār* with which he may choose to close his recital. Here, it is all a lovely criss-cross of orderly rhythmic *variants* within the embrace of a *single*, and generally easy-to-follow cycle of rhythm.

---

2. Needful, because dance is essentially an occurrent art. This is why its occasional recourse to beautiful postures keeps it distinct from sculpture.

# 10

# Towards an Aesthetics of Hindustani Rhythm[1]

THE foregoing essays are all aesthetical, though in varying degree. But they hardly show the way to a systematic aesthetics of Hindustani rhythm. It is this need that I here seek to remedy, if but incompletely. It is easy to see why the venture is necessary. Rhythm is an important part of all that is there in *sangeet*. Yet an aesthetic study of it does not get due emphasis in our present music syllabi. Now, aesthetics today aims at two major goals. On the one hand, it tries to fix the meaning of words that we commonly use about objects of art and beauty. On the other hand, it invites close attention to art as it appears when contemplated, or to our actual experience of art. Keeping these two basic approaches in mind, I suggest that a systematic aesthetics of Hindustani rhythm could take the following lines.

### The Basic Concepts

Here, the task will be to ascertain what exactly we mean when we use the key words in our talk about *laya, tāla* and *rhythmic* patterns — such as *vilambit, madhya, drut, ārh, kuvārh, ateet, anāgat, chakkardār, tripalli,* or *gāopuchhā*.

---

1. This essay is a modified version of the Paper "Towards an Aesthetics of Hindustani Rhythm" written for the Seminar on "Curriculum Development and Design for Evaluation of Post-graduate Studies in Music" held at Music College of the M.S. University, Baroda from 31 October to 2 November 1977.

## Aesthetic Analysis

This is required not only by our concern with the meaning of concepts, but by the need to *understand why* a particular detail or device of the art in question appears to us as it actually does.

To illustrate the first of these requirements, the meaning of words like *daab-gāṅs* (दाब-गांस) is not fully explained if we merely say that the word दाब means "press", though this is surely a correct translation of the word. We have further to realise how *daab-gāṅs,* as actually heard, differs — because of its slightly resonant quality — from merely skimming the surface, say, in the execution of *bol*s like *dir, dir.*

The second aspect of the matter requires us to deal with questions of the following kind:

> When we follow a rhythmic recital — that is, in our actual experience of rhythm — when (or why) does a *bol* appear to be skipping, or, as we say, उछलता हुआ? Or, how does one produce the suggestion of a little added fluency without in fact increasing the pace?

Or, in our concern with patterns of *ateet* and *anāgat* variety a relevant question could be easily put thus:

> Does the appeal of such collocations of *bol*s depend only on *their* inner structure or also on *our* imaginative, and not merely auditory involvement?

## Our Rhythm and Criticism

Aesthetics today is also regarded as a kind of meta-criticism that is, as a basic study of problems relating to criticism itself. So, under this head, we may well try to deal with quite a few specific questions.

What are the criteria to be adopted in evaluating, say, a solo *tablā* recital? Is mere fluency the sole requirement here? Are we not to take into account the character and organization of the *bol*s being played? Further, is not a knowledge of the drummer's *intention* (इरादा) here relevant? The value of this question, in our concern with rhythm, is heightened if we look at it against the background of the present-day controversy around the so-called "intentional fallacy". Today it *is* a hotly debated question as to whether or not it is needful to reckon with the artist's intention in assessing the aesthetic worth of what he is able to create. Both sides of the controversy have been argued reasonably. No work of art appears wholly by itself. It is always the creation of a particular artist, and it signifies what it has been made to say or suggest *by that one individual*. So it appears sensible to say that we cannot react to a work properly without determining what exactly the artist in question has intended to do in creating the work. But, the other side argues, what really matters for us, as *rasika*s, is what we actually find, here and now, *in* the work as it faces us. What appears as accomplished, and not what was merely aimed at, should be our only concern. And, in any case, it is quite often impossible to determine a bygone artist's intentions in creating his works. His own declarations relating to the matter may not be available at present. Luckily, however, the matter is not so difficult to deal with in the context of our rhythm. Here, an authentic *rasika* (of *tablā* rhythm) is often found to be conversant with the full form and requisite aesthetic look of the pattern that the drummer has set out to play at a fluent pace, and so he (the *rasika*) may well be able to see where exactly the heightened fluency of *laya* prevents the drummer from playing a particular rhythmic turn with the needful measure of fineness.

## Rhythm and Aesthetic Theory

Here we have to look at our rhythm from the viewpoint of some problems concerning all art. Some of these that have already been discussed in the preceding chapters are as follows:

How can we distinguish the "content" of rhythm from its "form"? Is our rhythm an independent art at all? What are the marks of an art that is truly autonomous? Does the view that art is a kind of symbolic expression apply to our rhythm as well? If not, how exactly is this particular art significant?

I may add that we never admire our drumming by saying that it is meaningful. Instead, a word that is freely used by the knowledgeable in this context is ख़ुशख़ात (*khuśkhat*) which covers quite a few English expressions, such as neatly executed, clear, shapely, *beautiful*. It indeed appears that if it pays due heed to the evidence of our rhythm, contemporary aesthetic theory may well have to temper its (probably) overmuch emphasis on *meaning* in opposition to *beauty* as the central aesthetic concept.

## Sangeet, Our Rhythm and Research

Finally, the aesthetics I am talking about has to analyze not only the inner knitwork of rhythm as such, but its linkages with other components of *sangeet*, say, *laya*, music and dance. This aspect of the matter needs much fuller attention than I have given it so far; and, by way of indicating the limits of my earlier essays — and also the possible lines of further enquiry — I think it essential to make some additional remarks on each one of the constituents of *sangeet* just listed.

### LAYA

The most fundamental concept in our talk about rhythm is *laya*. What is *laya*? What does the word mean in the context of our time-honoured view of *sangeet?*[2] I now offer a quite new answer:

*Laya* is musical duration as actively regulated for the sake of effect or expression, or for explicating some artistic form. But I must explain what I hereby mean:

> First, I speak of *laya* not as merely regular, but *as actively regulated* duration. Our quite common ways of speaking here are: लय क़ायम की जाती है; और क़ायम रखी जाती है। A man's breathing *is* (generally) regular. So is the ticking of a clock. In neither case

---

2. Obviously, we are not here concerned with such metaphysical uses of the word *laya* as signify the merger of a liberated soul in God.

> any effort is (generally) needed to keep the pace regular. It is not regulat*ed*. So, *laya* in *Sangeet* is something quite distinctive.

Here, however, a slight protest may well be made. Once the chosen *laya* has been truly established by a performing musician or dancer, does it not appear to proceed wholly on its own, and quite without effort? What is here the element of active regulation? To questions such as these my ready answer is that though, in the situation visualized, *laya* does seem to move on its own,[3] and appears quite effortless to those who attend to the rhythm (but are not creating it), on the part of the musician himself "keeping" the right *laya* is always some effort, if no actual discomfort; and it even involves a real, though very slight feeling of tension that goes with wariness, which is precisely why even the faintest suggestion of an unwanted increase or slowing of pace by the accompanist — or the *lahrā* player — is not only noticed by the musician, but disturbs or even upsets him. Further, whereas any change of pace in the ticking of a clock is necessarily a defect, in a recital of rhythm (on the other hand) *laya*, for a brief while, can be slackened intentionally — and duly upraised thereafter with a quick, yet gentle spurt — so elegantly that it may elicit admiration at once.

This brings us to the key idea that *laya* is duration not only *as controlled, but as serving an aesthetic purpose*. Often it makes for a distinct but likeable effect, as (I repeat) when we are moved to applaud the sudden, but intended deceleration or upsweep of a brief rhythmic phrase without impairing the overall duration of the total pattern. But it can also be made to conduce to the expression of a (general feature of) feeling. Thus, in *ālāpa* which precedes a *dhruvapad*, a slow upward passage of voice from one *svara* to another — helped by a due regulation of vocal volume — can easily evoke the suggestion of a slight, but perceptible rise of feeling say, as a slight, indeterminate yearning.

---

3. My word here is "automotive".

In passing, it may here be noted once again that *laya* in *ālāpa* (of the kind referred to) is not a matter of beats or even mere movement. Consistently, of course, with the grammatical requirments of the *rāga* chosen, any *svara* or tonal passage may be projected or dwelt upon by the singer for the sake of effect or expressiveness. This again shows how it is better to speak of *laya* as "regulat*ed*" than as "regul*ar*" duration. A key meaning of "regular" is: constant or unchanging. In *ālāpa*, on the other hand, pace is often changed intentionally, though never randomly. In fact, it is all along quietly controlled by the singer. So, if we speak of *laya* only as regular duration, the overall manner of its flow *in ālāpa* will be merely missed.

Finally, and this is vital for what is called a *bandish, laya* is that precise pace (of singing or playing) which helps to bring out the distinctive character of a composition, be it a *sthāyī, a gat or* a *ṭhekā*. It is common knowledge that a (vocal) *bandish* "blooms", as we say, only at its requisite pace; and that it is not always easy to determine this particular pace.

## TĀLA

*Tāla* (we have seen) is our popular word for rhythm in music. The way it is sometimes described — that is, as something which is marked and measured by clapping — hardly tells us anything about what it is and what it does in music, just as we do nothing to *explain* the nature of fever by saying that it is something that we measure with a thermometer. Yet, we *are* here given a basic idea. A clap is an emphasis occupying a moment, not a process; and clapping — where it moves along with the rhythmic flow of music — is at once the act of attending to or holding on to a flow by means of regular strokes which are clear and successive. Likewise, *tāla* in our music is a series of beats or *mātrās*. This distinguishes the rhythm of music very clearly from rhythm in painting or in any other art. Yet, the full meaning of *tāla*, cannot be had without attending to some other allied concepts to which I turn presently.

## MĀTRĀ

What is a *mātrā*? A simple meaning of the word is a measured quantity, as when we speak of the *mātrā* or the precise quantity of a medicine in its single dose. Now, it is known that in a cycle every *mātrā* is numbered, say, as the first or the fourth beat. But how is it *also itself* a measured extent? The answer is that *a mātrā (as recited) itself occupies a measured portion of time;* that, just the same length of time is to be taken in uttering every other *mātrā* in the cycle; and that a *mātrā* — where we indicate the extent of a cycle — is therefore not a mere number, but a number as spoken at a particular pace, as a drawl or very quickly, that is, as itself occupying more or less of time. When a boy is asked to do counting — that is, reciting numbers in ascending order — by his arithmetic teacher, the requirement only is that every number should come at its proper place — say, 3, before *not after* 4 — and that no intervening number is left out. Here, changes in speed are not objected to. But when we indicate the extent of, say, *tritāla* by merely reciting the *mātrās*, the 16 beats have not only to come in due numerical sequence, but at an even pace. Thus, if (as an aberration) in indicating the pace and compass of *vilambit tritāla* the first beat is uttered *quickly*, taking but a mere instant, and then the succeeding beats in a *leisurely* way, the first beat will be *a mere mark, not a mātrā,* because it will not be an index of the pace of what is to follow.

A *mātrā* marks a basic and *equal* subdivision of *laya; so it is both a mark and a measure.* But it is a measure, I repeat, because it is itself a measured occupancy of time which, in turn, is manifest only if the *mātrā* is *recited.* This recitation may be overt or merely ideal, that is, implicit speech, as a psychologist may put it. But, be it overt or merely implicit, the utterance of the *mātrā* has got to be there. Otherwise, the *mātrā* would not be a measured (and measuring) unit at all. The relation between *mātrā* and *bol* (as speech) may therefore be said to be natural.

## ZARAB

A *zarab* has to be carefully distinguished from a mere *mātrā.*

As a unitary measure of the run of a rhythm-cycle, a *mātrā*'s location cannot be changed. A *zarab*, on the other hand, is any such emphasis of the drummer's playing hands as can be put anywhere in the rhythmic run, partly by way of playfully beguiling the listener who may be trying to follow the run, and partly by way of indicating that, in spite of the (intentionally) wayward placing of the *zarab* (stroke), he has not lost his hold over the proper run of the rhythm, because the deviation is his (drummer's) own doing.

## SAMA

It is in this context interesting to note that — as opposed to its extent as a *mātrā* — the location of *Sama as a kind of zarab* may well be changed, and with distinct aesthetic gain.

This does not happen very freely. Commonly, the *Sama* is regarded as a (kind of) checkpoint, and it indeed is so for both the musician and the listener (or the critic). When, after executing a *taan*, the singer attains to the *Sama*, he gets a moment of respite; is free to have another look at the *ṭhekā*; and so is able to adapt himself anew to the basic flow. The listeners too are helped; they get a chance to check if the singer is really possessed of a proper sense of *tāla*.

But its being thus useful is quite different from what the *Sama* can do *to the patterns*. It often helps them acquire their aesthetic character. Consider, for instance, the patterns classed as *ateet*. To say that an *ateet* pattern is one which ends a little after the actual *Sama* is of course right as grammar; but it tells us nothing as to how the pattern here "looks" in drumming of the right kind. I would say it seems ebullient, overflowing; and it does so (partly) because the *Sama* as a *mātrā* is duly remembered, and the *Sama-zarab of the pattern* as it is made to end with creative abandon is judged in relation to *Sama* as the (grammatically) basic checkpoint.

The *Sama,* however, is not the only factor which makes for the creative appearance in question. The other vital requisite is the pattern's own *inner shapeliness*. If an *ateet* pattern is not properly structured it will lack inner dynamics, and would only seem to *end* (tamely) after the *Sama*, instead of appearing to *overflow* the cycle. I must add that an important element of the structuring here needed is the close-knit appearance of the *bol*s that fill up the pattern. Where the disposition of *bol*s is sparse, even the most accurate ending of an *ateet* pattern will not make it seem *to overflow* the cycle. The orderly filling of *bol*s — or बोल भराव (*bol bharāva*) is indeed a vital aid to how a pattern "looks".

## II

Turning to aesthetic analysis, only a single question may be posed and answered. When and why does a *bol* appear to skip (उछलता हुआ)? I may here answer as follows:

(a) When it falls *between* two adjacent beats, not *at* any beat;

(b) further, if its own perceptual character is quite different from that of the preceding *bol*; and,

(c) finally, when its deviation from a *mātrā* occurs at a rather unexpected moment.

Let me explain. Consider the *bol tā* (ता) in the rhythm-cycle called *mughlai*, discussed in chapter 7. It is a quite "open" *bol*, and therefore very different from the relatively "closed" *kat* (कत) which here marks the *Sama*. Further, it not only falls a little *between* two beats — the second and the third — but occurs quite soon after the *Sama*, and therefore a little unexpectedly, because (during a cycle's own simple run) the *Sama* is a beat which generally leaves us engaged for a while. Therefore it appears clearly more jumpy than the *bol tin* (तिन) in the following 15-*mātrā* cycle, a variant of the standard *sawārī tāla*:

धिऽन    धागेतिरकिट    धिनधिन    धातिरकिट/तिन
1 2   3   4   5   6   7   8½
तातिरकिट    धागेतिरकिट    धिनकधा    तिरकिट
9   10   11   12   13   14½   15

It is true that the *tin* (तिन) in the bigger cycle (just cited above) comes *between* the eighth and ninth beats; and that if, as a beat that marks a subtly located *khālī*, it is spoken a little more loudly than the other beats, it may well appear noticeably frisky. But this phenomenal character here is not *so* pronounced as in the case of the *tā* (ता) in *mughlai*; and the reasons that explain the difference are as follows:

> First, the bigger cycle is a leisurely one; the 8½ beat (where *tin* occurs) is quite far removed from the *Sama*; and therefore, because of the absence of contrast with the *Sama*'s steadying quality, the *bol* in question here does not wear that look of suddenness which distinguishes *tā* (ता) in the (smaller) *mughlai* cycle.
>
> Secondly, in respect of its auditory quality, the *tin* (तिन) is by no means opposed to the immediately preceding तिरकिट (*tirkit*). In fact, both are इकार (*ekāra*) *bol*s, and therefore similar, the difference between the two being only one of length.

Here it may at once be noted that even as relating to the choice of the right word for how exactly a particular *bol* affects the ear, aesthetic analysis is by no means irrelevant. We have to mark off the *beaded* rapidity of a pattern packed with articulate *bol*s, such as तिटकतागदिगिन, from the merely *tremulous* fluency of the one which may build largely upon *dir dir*. Otherwise, it would not be possible to pick, collocate, and recite the *bols* with requisite sensitiveness.

## III

In respect of rhythm considered in relation to aesthetics *as* metacriticism, I will just make a few quick points:

> First, here the critic has *got* to take into account the इरादा or intention of the drummer. For, if he does not know which particular *bol*s or patterns the drummer intends and is trying to play, how can he at all determine whether the execution is right or wrong? And if one does not care for the right निकास (or execution) of *bol*s, a vital part of the "critical" task will be just left out. Nor is access to the artist's intention here as difficult as,

say, in the case of poetry. Knowledgeable listeners are often quite conversant with our stock rhythmic patterns; and it is common to find them complaining that, at the pace being attempted, the drummer's specific intention is failing to "go".[4] For the critic, in particular, it is necessary to know which particular *bol*s the drummer intends, and is able to play. Otherwise, his write-ups will begin and end with such glib compliments as *fluent, mellow, steady* or *brilliant*. Penetrating seizure of details will here be missing.

Secondly, it is needful to reflect on the question of criteria also in respect of *sangat*.[5] The literal meaning of the word is "giving company to", or "being along with". In the context of music, however, it is playing along with *the main performer:* and this may be done by a drummer, or by a *sāraṅgī* or harmonium player. Accompanists of the last two kinds aim, as a rule, at duplicating the music either along with or very quickly after the main performer has sung (or played) a phrase or pattern. The drummer, on the other hand is (as a rule) not *so* prompt. What is, however, important to remember is that such duplication is not the *basic* function of the drummer. What distinguishes him from the other accompanists is the fact that he has to play the *ṭhekā* clearly and steadily; and this as long as the main performer continues his (/her) recital. This is his primary duty; and, I insist, even where he duplicates a pattern in a way that may seem to go along with the playing of the main performer, the "accompanying" is to be so done that the *andāz* (rhythmic idiom) and main divisions of the cycle — or at least the off beat and the *Sama* — may be never eclipsed.

Where the *drummer* is an accompanist, the ideal meaning of *saṅgat* truly is; playing the *ṭhekā* and reproducing patterns. We in fact mean all this when, for instance, we ask: "इस सितार के आइटम के साथ कौन संगत कर रहा है?" Yet, even of this overall function (I may add) the crux is *ṭhekā*-playing. However, in so

4. In Hindustani, the complaint here is: 'इरादा जा नहीं रहा है'।

5. From here to the end of the present section, I have used material from my Paper: "An Essay in Understanding Man in relation to Music" presented to the Seminar on "The Concept of Man in Music" (IIAS, Simla 3-8 October 1977).

far as the drummer too is an artist, he is expected not merely to facilitate the main musician's work, but *to add to its beauty*. This aesthetic purpose, I believe, is served ideally when the drummer duplicates the manner of *the musician's patterns* almost *along with them* — without of course causing any disturbance (to the musician) — and is thereby able to heighten the overall beauty of the music through the formal devices of contiguity and similarity, as the Gestalt psychologist would put it. Reproducing the pattern clearly *after* it has been played by the main performer — and only when the latter has begun to play the basic *gat* so simply that it appears to be a *lahrā* — is only. अनुगमन, a kind of coming after, not the *confluence* which *saṅgat* really demands; and, in relation to what the (main) musician *now* does, it seems closer to solo playing than to *saṅgat*. In respect of patterns indeed, the ideal kind of *saṅgat* is a ready intertwining (लिपटना). Where the drummer is permitted leisurely playing *after* the musician has done his bit, the "accompaniment" does *not* really make for the *spell-binding* quality which a good recital is expected to have.

Here, as an additional sample of doing aesthetics *as metacriticism* in relation to rhythm, some thought may be given to dancing as well. Consider the case of a drummer providing accompaniment to a Kathak danseuse with whom he has never played before. Is the fact that he is not already familiar with the patterns (being danced) — and has therefore to improvise the *saṅgat,* so to say, on the spur of the moment — to be taken as an *extra* ground of critical acclaim? I would say "yes", provided the drumming has the requisite measure of clarity, and also duly follows (by and large) the extent and *andāz* or *chalan* of the dancer's patterns, even if the individual character of the (constituent) *bols* is not — as (in such cases) it can hardly be — truly reproduced. And my argument here may be put as follows:

> If rhythm is an art, and I am convinced it is, it must be creative too. It is so when a composer of rhythm produces a new pattern; when a drummer elongates or compresses the flow of some

*bols* in a pattern, without really losing hold of its overall extent, in a way which differs from their set embedment in the fixed form of the pattern as taught by the teacher; or, finally, when improvised and well-nigh simultaneous *tablā-saṅgat* is provided to a (new) dancer or musician. In respect of a drummer who is playing before us we rarely know what he has composed himself. Nor are we actually generally aware of the precise way he has been taught. So, the common and easy way to determine whether he is creative or not is to attend to the kind of *saṅgat* he provides to a new musician or dancer. Here, the fact that he does not know beforehand the patterns being presented is clear from his failure to reproduce syllables of exactly the same *individual character*; and his creative ability is (yet) admired because he is quite able to adopt the *manner and range* of his "accompanying" patterns to those of the main performer.

## IV

I may now say something about the way we can relate rhythm to some basic aesthetic concepts and *problems*. One key problem (we have seen) concerns the nature of *form* in art. Here, is it quite enough to say that it is *articulate*, that is, a unity of *distinct* sounds? Why our music (vocal and instrumental) does not here admit of a categorically affirmative answer has been already brought out in the first chapter. But now I think it necessary to put the matter in a duly qualified way. We may speak thus:

Where the *dānā* or singularity of a note is at all *required to be manifest*, it has to be clearly so; this is how the norm of articulation applies to our vocal and instrumental music. No slurring of details is permitted here. In a *meend* (or glide), I know, the *dānā* is not there at all. But this is no slurring of detail, for here the *dānā* is *not required to be* manifest; and so a *meend* is no real exception to the norm as I have put it. In rhythm, on the other hand, distinctness of details is always a key requirement; and so (in principle) form is here articulate *all along*. Even in the playing of very quick patterns — say, a *relā* or a *rau* — fluency is not allowed to level off its *undulating* run.

By way of closing this section, I also think it advisable to add a remark to what in the opening essay I specified as "the primary creation" of rhythm — that is, "the automotive and articulate *symmetry* of pure pace." "Symmetry" is here to be taken simply as shapeliness, and not in the sense of *symmetrical balance*; for, as in widely known, we have quite a few *a*symmetrical cycles as well in the region of our rhythm.

## V

In spite of all these additions, I am by no means satisfied with our present understanding of the aesthetics of rhythm. Nor is this book of essays anything more than a mere start in the field. Within the region of rhythm itself such basic distinctions have yet to be clearly thought out (and put in words) as the one between a *quāyedā* and a *tukḍā*,[6] though both these kinds of patterns are quite commonly played. And in respect of its relations with both music and dance, our study of rhythm has perhaps not taken a single step beyond the simple question as to what specific *tāla* (or *laya*) is demanded by a particular composition, though such awareness is surely essential. A *bandish* which incorporates words of such serious significance as 'करीम नाम तेरो' or 'जगत सपना री, आली; काहे करत गुमान' cannot be sung in *drut teen tāla*. And it is easy to list — say, as follows — many little details of actual drumming which are readily enjoyed, but not understood as to what it really is which makes them fascinate us. The facts that the displacement of a single *zarab* (vocal emphasis) by even half a *mātrā* may at once make a *bandish* appear "coming to life", so to say; that whether a cycle *appears* serious or flirtatious depends not so much on the number of *mātrā*s it comprises as on pace at which it is played; and that the compression of

---

6. I hasten to add, however, that significant thinking of this kind has already been done by the late Sri Sudhir Kumar Saxena (Baroda) in some of his talks prepared for AIR. But it admits of development in many directions, chief of them being phenomenological study.

the second half of the penultimate word of a *dhamār* may appear to accelerate our run to the *Sama* — truths such as these are yet to be isolated as objects of analytic understanding.

The West, I may add, has already done quite a good bit of serious thinking on rhythm; and, as our next chapter may be able to show, some details of this thinking could with profit be checked from the viewpoint of Hindustani rhythm.

# 11

# Our Rhythm vis-à-vis Susanne Langer's View

ONE of the few modern aestheticians who are regarded as being "systematic" — because they have tried to give us an orderly, unified understanding of all the major arts — is Susanne K. Langer. Her work is noteworthy also because she has written on rhythm as fair length. But the reason why *I* think her views on rhythm deserve serious notice simply is that so far they have never been tested at the anvil of Hindustani rhythm. It is precisely this academic blank which the present chapter tries to fill.

Langer's explicit view is that, like every other art, rhythm too is *a symbolic projection of life as felt*. But this is very likely to look odd to many; for, specially in India where solo expositions of rhythm by seasoned drummers are still welcome to trained audiences, this art is ordinarily taken to be appealing *in itself*, and not by virtue of any relatedness to objects or happenings in the everyday world or to contents of inner, personal life. Yet, because she nowhere speaks of rhythm as an *imitation* of some detail of life — and distinguishes *symbolic projection*, her own preferred concept for relating art to feeling, pretty sharply from direct representation — Langer's entire thinking on the subject calls for a careful study before any judgement is passed on its net value. One may even say that her view of rhythm is distinctive not only because of its positive emphases, but also by virtue of the way she opposes the commonly accepted notions of this art. However, the angle from which I propose to consider her account cannot be very wide; it has to be specific, or that of *Hindustani* (or north Indian) rhythm; for only with this genre of rhythm I can claim to be truly familiar and still actively concerned.[1] This is going to be a clear limitation of this chapter; but it is luckily set off, if in part, by the fact that quite a few concepts and general features of Hindustani rhythm are also to be found in the way the art is understood and practised in south India.

I also feel encouraged by the fact that — though, of course, in its own way — Hindustani rhythm utilizes almost all the individual appearances of rhythm in the various arts; and that this is easy to illustrate. In music, in its basic form of virtual time, rhythm appears as regulation of abidance at some chosen notes, as also by way of a quick or leisurely passage across more or less regular sequences of stressed/unstressed or long and short syllables; and in painting, sculpture and architecture, in the following diverse ways: harmonious or balanced employment of lines, colours, figures and volumes; interactive sequences of masses and voids; and adroit alternation of light with shade. Now, temporal analogues of these devices are all clearly seen in our art of rhythm. Variations of pace and accent; alternation of brief and crisp segments of syllables with those that seem to elongate themselves majestically; and a deft punctuation of close-knit *bols* with *pauses* that do not divide the pattern, but only make it partly an object of contemplation by prompting the *rasika* (and the drummer himself) to visualize where exactly the

1. I say so because on 26 and 27 November 1996, I recorded a fairly analytic discussion on, and exposition of the art of *tablā*-rhythm for our national archives, and on behalf of Sangeet Natak Akademi, New Delhi. The *tablā* maestro who played and was "interviewed" on this occasion was Sudhir Kumar Saxena, a retired Professor of *tablā* from the College of Performing Arts, Baroda University. He was ably assisted by his leading pupil, Madhukar N. Gurav, who provided longer pieces of illustrative playing. And, of course, the present chapter bears some testimony to my own familiarity with Hindustani rhythm.

(sounding) playing is to resume, — these are all common features of our experience of listening to a recital of rhythm. But the *overriding* features that determine our rhythm as its norms are not the ones that Langer emphasizes, namely "mutual conditioning" and the build-up and release of tension. I would rather pick *articulate form, regulated pace, adroit segmentation,* and timely *accentuation* as the main determinants of creative work in our rhythm. By "articulate", I here mean "relatedness of syllables which yet retain a measure of clear self-existence"; and by "regulated", not all along changeless, but only "actively controlled with an eye to fitness and clarity of both form and flow".

However, before I turn to bring out the differences that separate Langer's view of rhythm from the way this art is practised in the field of Hindustani music, it would obviously help if the essentials of Hindustani rhythm were outlined anew and quite simply. Incidentally, if it be taken to mean a measured and organised number of *mātrā*s (or beats) — (that is, a *tāla*) — *rhythm* is not really *the fundamental* temporal concept of Indian music; that place can be given (I repeat) only to *laya*. *Laya* is aesthetic pace or duration which may either be regulated (measured and identified) with the help of beats including some accented ones; or, as in the case of *ālāpa* by a *dhruvapad*-singer, only by his individual aesthetic sense, and with an eye to some specific effect or proper unfoldment of the *rāga* chosen for treatment. So to speak of *laya is*, however, a bit too succinct; and I think it needful to clarify what I have just said.

First, *laya* signifies not only the pace at which the musician moves from one note or bunch of rhythmic syllables (or segments) to another, but the length of time (or duration) he invests in singing just a single *svara*, or melodic phrase, or in playing a collocation of *bol*s (or syllables) of rhythm. As sheer pace, *laya* has to keep itself steadfast, unwavering. In other words, unless the drummer himself intends to quicken or decelerate it, the present tempo should not wobble or undergo any change. Expressly, however, it can surely be made to move leisurely (*vilambit* or adagio), nimbly (*drut* or allegro), or very fast (that is, *atidrut*). Yet, once any one of these paces has been taken, it has to be kept as such, quite without wavering for some time, that is, until a further change is wilfully desired. So, to use a concept suggested by Langer, *vilambit*, *drut*, and *atidrut* are *'phases'* in the flowing fabric of *laya*, not mere steps to be climbed without a break and in an ever upward motion, as we do while negotiating a staircase.

As duration in the form of *abidance*, rather than as pace of *passage*, *laya* contributes to the quality of music in quite a few striking ways. If the singer just marks the *taar ṣaḍja* (upper tonic) gently and tunefully, but for a *mere moment*, the note may seem to twinkle as a star; and if he lets his voice tarry at the note in question majestically in a sweet, steadfast and full-throated *akāra*, it may look like a column of radiance. Further, how long the singer dwells at a particular note is, in general, also a vital determinant of the grammatical rightness of the *rāga* being sung. A prolonged utterance of the note *re* in *rāga puriyā* and a mere touch at the same note (in *taar saptak*) in *rāga sohnī* would both be violations of the set character of the two *rāga*s.

If it be contended, here, that whatever I have just said about *laya* does not relate to rhythm as such, and so is irrelevant to the subject of this chapter, my answer would be threefold. First, even if it is taken in the familiar sense of regular recurrence of beats, rhythm would not be itself if the beats it comprises do not follow one another at *even* pace. In other words, *laya* is the requisite underrunning evenness of rhythm; and, therefore, to talk of *laya* is in no way to abjure rhythm, but only to refer to its very essence. Second, in *dhruvapad*-singing which is a venerable, if not very popular form of classical Hindustani music today, the traditionally accepted forms of *rhythmic* variations, such as *ārh, kuvārh* which do not (in principle) cause any violence to the verbal meaning of the composition, are called types of *laya*, not of *tāla* or rhythm. Thirdly, *laya* not only signifies something which is the very essence of rhythm (that is, as evenness of pace) but relates to a distinct and important temporal idiom to which the word rhythm (as *tāla)* is generally not applied. My reference, here, is to *jāti*. We commonly speak *of jāti*s of *laya*, not *of* rhythm or *tāla*.

A *jāti* is simply a distinct kind of *flow*, distinguished by the number of beats it comprises and the location of its emphases. *Tāla* or rhythm, on the other hand, is (in Hindustani music) necessarily a *cycle* with a focal beat, called the *Sama*. It sets out from and lapses back to the first beat, making this beat appear central and itself as completing a round. No such focus or cyclic quality is to be seen in a *jāti* as such.

But there is one other important difference too between *laya* and *tāla* (or rhythm). The *stroke*s that make the regular patterns played across and ultimately within a rhythm cycle, are all roughly similar in sound to the *bol*s — or utterable syllables, may be a single letter or bunch of letters, but all alike meaningless — that may be said to name the elements of drumming. This is why whatever is played at the drums, be it a cycle or a rhythmic pattern, is foreknown to the drummer and can be recited by him. The only exception to this parity of playing and openness to recitation is provided by those improvised flourishes with which a seasoned drummer may choose to relieve his set playing. Now, all this relates only to rhythm, not to *laya* as such. However, the point to be noted here is that Hindustani rhythm as actually played (as a solo recital) is subject to a double orientation. It has to arrive at the *Sama* recurringly, and with split second accuracy; *and* it has to conform to the design and details of the pattern (or the cycle) as remembered and recitable. In other words, it is all along an intentional blend of overt act and parallel ideation.

To conclude, the role of rhythm in Hindustani music is multiple. It makes for determinateness of the pace of singing or playing, and for variety in the look of notes or phrases as they relate to rhythm and appear to contemplation; helps in accuracy of *rāga*-rendering through *laya* as extent of abidance at some specific notes; makes the basic composition appear self-complet*ing*; and serves (in its cyclic form) as the ground of numberless collocations of *svara* and changes of pace, thereby making them appear orderly or patterns, and not mere variations. *Rhythm in Indian music is surely not a mere paving of the way for what is to come*; and because the way it may well be regarded as an independent art has already been argued in our very opening chapter, we may now turn to see, at some length, what Langer's own views on the subject are.

## Negative Emphases

To begin with her negative emphases in respect of rhythm, they may be briefly put as follows, along with some argument from my side:

> It is commonly believed in scientific thinking that the essential character of rhythm is the repetition of any distinct, recognisable event at equal intervals of time, i.e., rhythm is periodic repetition. But, in fact, not all rhythmic repetitions are strictly periodic. There may even be rhythmic sequences of events which are not really repetitive; for instance, a performer of "modern dance" rarely repeats a movement, yet every least motion of the dance has to be rhythmic,[2] in the sense, we may add, that in the economy of the whole number every step or bestirring of the limbs leads to, or makes for the one that follows.[3]

Recurrence of identical units at equal intervals is, of course, what we commonly understand by rhythm — at least in the case of drumming which builds on beats or *mātrā*s. But such

---

2. Langer, *Mind: An Essay on Human Feeling*, vol. I, The John Hopkins University Press, Baltimore and London, 2nd Printing, PS, 1975, p. 323.

3. "Rhythmic concatenation . . . [is] a sequence wherein the subsiding phase, or cadence, of one act (or similar element) is the up-take for its successor" Langer, Ibid., p. 323.

periodic repetition cannot be taken as the *essence* of rhythmicity taken generally, though it may well be regarded as a key structural principle of music. Consider, for instance, the ticking of a clock. It is repetitious and regular; and the ticks are mostly identical. But it cannot be regarded as rhythmic in itself. Why *I* say so (supporting Langer) can be brought out with the help of two simple examples. If fifty stone slabs, all similar in shape and size, are put up on the roadside at equal distance from one another, we may well be struck by the appearance of order and similarity, but nobody will call the entire arrangement rhythmic. Even regularity of succession *in time* may not be said to be the essence of rhythm. Day and night follow each other with unfailing regularity, but nobody takes this alternation as a case of creative rhythm. The point really is that in cases of mere regularity of succession — that is, where there is no dynamic interplay of elements or processes — the mind must enter into, and do some active ordering in respect of *what is presented to it* before the presentation can come to appear and be regarded as rhythmic. Thus, if in the process of counting, one chooses to group every four adjacent numbers ideally as one, and then utters the opening number of every segment a little emphatically, the process will at once come to wear the look of rhythm. So there *is* truth in Langer's remark that the ticks of a clock come to appear rhythmic only when "the human mind organises them into a temporal form".[4] By themselves, indeed, features like similarity and repetition are not enough to produce the appearance of rhythmicity.

Nor are these features *always* there in what seems to be rhythmic. Consider, for example, the case of a talk that impresses the listeners with its rhythmic quality. Obviously, it cannot be a succession of segments of equal extent, all comprising words of similar sounds. In such cases, even the pace is not uniform all along. Nor are the sounds, extent,

---

4. Langer, *Feeling and Form*, Routledge & Kegan Paul, 3rd Impression, 1963, p. 126.

and meaning of the words used similar. The truth here rather is that phrases, emphases, and even single pauses are all so organized that the present utterance (or pause) makes us look forward to *what is to come next*; and that the complex of succeeding words satisfies the expectation.

Take, again, a matter that relates to rhythm as it permeates the "pure" patterns of Kathak dance. In collocations of *bol*s that begin, thus: तक्थरि। तक्थरि। कुकुथरि। कुकुथरि। तक्धलांग। तक्धलांग (in *tritāla*) we sure have both identity of syllables and equality of extent (of rhythmic phrases), but neither of them is so visibly there in patterns that run thus (again, in *tritāla*):

*घिनननागेतिट    क्ड़धेतधातिट    घेघेतिटघेघे(ना) तिट    गद्दीघिड़ान    नागेतिटकिड़ान*

9  12  13  15  16  4  5  8  9  12

*तकिटतकिटघा    तिटघिटतिरान    ऽ    धातिटघिटतिरान    ऽ    धातिटघिटतिरान*    (सम)

13  16  1  4  5  6  10  11  12  16  1

Here the syllables क्ड़धेतधातिट, which serve as a kind of wedge between the adjoining bunches of *bol*s, appear to move quicker than the rest, because of the touch of alacrity provided by क्ड़; and the bracketed ना before तिट seems a whit more restful in pace because of the *mātrā*. Nor is the order of syllables conspicuously similar or repetitive, the opening घिननन occurring only once in the entire pattern. But what is invariably present in every rhythmic pattern is that, by virtue of its own pace, *the very opening syllable* generates in our minds the expectation that, by and large, a definite tempo will be kept, and that occasional (and intentional) increase or deceleration of pace will be duly redeemed, so as to save such deviations from appearing as wanton infringements of the basic, overall requirement of unrelenting hold over *laya* or aesthetic pace. Where the reparation is not duly done, rhythm disappears forthwith.

**Langer's Positive Views**

The way is now paved to consider Langer's positive account

of rhythm. Here, perhaps the most striking detail in her thesis is that rhythm is "related to *function* rather than to time".[5] Function, as we know, is a (potential) activity appropriate to a person or thing. An activity is a happening or an event. As a process in time, it has a beginning and an end; and a "rhythmic pattern arises whenever the completion of one distinct event appears as the beginning of another".[6] Langer is indeed emphatic on this point. In *Feeling and Form* she openly declares that the *essence* of rhythm is the preparation of a new event by the ending of a previous one.[7] Can we illustrate this emphasis? Langer is convinced, we can; and she here lists quite a few instances:

> The classic example is the swinging of a pendulum. The momentum of its drop drives the weight upward in the opposite direction, and builds up the potential energy that will bring it down again; so the first swing prepares the second; the second swing was actually begun in the first one; and similarly, after that, each swing is prepared by the one before. The result is a rhythmic series.
>
> Or, consider the breaking of waves in a steady surf on a beach; the momentum of the water drives it up the beach, until that momentum is spent, and the slant of the shore causes the water to run seaward again; but the piling of the second, incoming wave is also sucking back the spent water, and making its return a downward rush that stops the bottom part of the new wave and causes it to break over itself. Here, again, is a rhythmic pattern. The completion of each breaker's history is already the beginning of the next one's.
>
> In a living organism . . . the most obvious rhythmic processes are, of course, heartbeat and breath. In the heart, every systole starts a diastole, and vice versa. . . . In breathing, . . . as the oxygen of a breath is used up, it builds up the imperative need of oxygen that is really the beginning of the new breath. This sort of mutual conditioning is the law of organic function. . . . In

5. Langer, *Problems of Art*, Routledge and Kegan Paul, 1957, p. 50.
6. Ibid., p. 51.
7. Langer, *Feeling and Form*, p. 126.

> every cell, the very process of its oxidation — its burning away, breaking down — is the condition that has already started the chemical change which builds up its characteristic substance again . . . [Rhythm is really] a functional involvement of successive events . . . [and] periodic rhythms [are only] a special sort [of rhythm].[8]

Now, I have nothing to say about the first two examples. But, in the third extract, Langer's account of instances from *organic* life appears to contain some clear errors. Where she characterizes the swinging of a pendulum and of "the breaking of waves in a steady surf on a beach" as rhythmic, her meaning professedly is that each movement is not only prepared by the one before, but makes for the one that follows. This is also why, in her view, heart beat is a rhythmic process; "every systole starts a diastole, and vice versa". But, we may note, though the two physiological events are definitely cyclic in recurrence, so that the one necessarily starts after (or before) the other, neither can be said to give rise to the other *straight away*. Systole and diastole are quite disparate haemodynamic events; the former is a positive action brought about by the pacemaker and the latter is a rather passive, relaxed state of the heart. Each one of them *ends* before the other one begins; so neither can be said to start the other directly. What is more, according to clinical pathology of the heart, there may even be a very brief interval between systole and diastole of auricles and ventricles — a kind of refractory period during which the heart remains quite still. If this period is prolonged beyond a certain point, the stillness can even be felt as a sinking sensation of the heart.

Again, it is *not* the consumption (or being "used up") of the oxygen *of a breath* that "builds up the imperative need of oxygen that is really the beginning of a new breath". The need in question relates rather to the metabolic requirements of the body cells and tissues; and, though it is undeniably

8. Langer, *Problems of Art*, pp. 51-52.

imperative, the need varies from time to time. Langer's explanation of the way the two breaths are related is further invalidated by a simple, verifiable fact. As in a heart attack or cerebral stroke, a dying tissue may simply perish *after consuming* the last available amount of oxygen *without* creating any need for a fresh supply of the life-giving gas.

It is also wrong to speak of the oxidation or "burning away, breaking down" *of cells*. Only the nutrients in a cell — such as carbohydrates, fats, and protein — are burnt out, the first two completely, and the third one partly, to yield energy for cellular activity. Cells and their structural contents (organelles) certainly age and eventually die, but they are never oxidised or burnt away in the sense of getting metabolised. Incidentally, the term *oxidation* is used only for chemicals (and biochemicals). Finally, it is too sweeping to speak of "*mutual* conditioning [as] *the law* of organic function". A major process like secretion of enzymes (and hormones) operates only as a *one-sided response*, so to say, to a need. Unlike the heartbeat, it does not work ceaselessly. The sight or smell of food may well bring about a secretion of saliva containing an enzyme, but the secretion in question does not obviously bring about the presence of food. Again, there is nothing rhythmic — in the sense of "mutual conditioning" — about the working of brain and organs of sense-perception. When a person wishes to raise his hand, a motor impulse from the brain/spinal cord may readily bring about the desired movement; but all this is occasional, not periodic in a regular way. And, to be sure, the raised hand may not directly cause any further motor impulse. Barring, of course, the heart, most of the bodily organs — like the liver, stomach and kidney — work by way of unidirectional response to some need or stimulus, and not as a mutual conditioning of stimulus and response.[9]

---

9. Here, in pointing out all these inaccuracies in Langer's view, I have been helped by my son, Dr. P. Kumar, an Associate Professor in the Deptt. of Zoology, Hans Raj College, University of Delhi.

However, inaccuracies such as these need not disturb us; for what Langer here wishes to emphasize — namely the point that rhythm is importantly, if not exclusively, "a functional involvement of successive events"[10] — is surely relevant to a considerable amount of art; and so we cannot ignore it. Even in drumming, practised in India (I repeat) also as an independent art, the completion of one rhythmic phrase is freely seen to make for what follows, quite directly. Langer's overall writing on rhythm, however, makes some other points as well; and to make our study of the matter adequate to her total view, we may discuss them all individually, along with some recall, where necessary, of what we have already noted.

I. (a) Rhythm is essentially a matter of function, not of time. In organic life, as also in nature, rhythm is to be found as the "mutual conditioning"[11] of processes, movements, or events; *or* as (b) "the preparation of a new event by the ending of a previous one".[12] The mind too, "even in its highest operations . . . follows the organic rhythm which is the source of vital unity: the building up of a new dynamic *Gestalt* in the very process of a former one's passing away".[13]

Now, the reason why rhythm cannot be regarded as, in essence, a matter of periodic succession has already been discussed earlier. But a little clarification is surely demanded by some other points in (a part of) Langer's view just stated. Is (a) the *mutual* conditioning of processes exactly the same thing as (b) "the preparation of a new event by the ending of a previous one"? We can hardly say, yes. For, whereas (a) may well be regarded as signifying a kind of cyclic rhythm — a clear instance, here, being the twosome of inhalation and

10. Langer, *Problems of Art*, p. 52.

11. Ibid.

12. Langer, *Feeling and Form*, p. 126.

13. Ibid., p. 128.

exhalation which determine *each other* — (b) can be merely serial and ever onward, that is, quite without a determination of the antecedent by the successor. Which of the two may be said to be Langer's overtopping emphasis? I cannot say, *mutual* conditioning, specially if we look at the matter from the viewpoint of rhythm as it appears *in the arts*. Langer, I believe, opts for the "serial" view where she says that everything that *prepares a future* creates rhythm",[14] that the rhythm of destiny is the feeling or appearance that the future is already an entity "embryonic in the present"[15] — which is obviously quite different from the thought that the future too *determines* the present; and that the tragic rhythm is "*the deathward advance of* . . . [our] individual lives . . . which has a series of stations that are *not repeated*: growth, maturity, decline". Tragedy, she adds, "is a cadential [not cyclic] form. Its crisis is always the turn towards an absolute close".[16] In all such cases the rhythm involved is clearly not cyclic. The difference is heightened by what Langer has to say on rhythm as dialectic. Where, as in the case of repetitive playing of a rhythm-cycle, the successor is "a replica of the predecessor", which is "often" [but not necessarily] the case;[17] and where "*each* element in spending itself prepares and initiates its own converse", such as a rise making for a fall, or suction pressing for expulsion — rhythm may be said to be a dialectic.[18] This means that, according to Langer, cyclic or dialectic rhythm represents only a form of rhythm, and not its very essence.

But, to turn anew to the opening formulation (in I, a) of the points being discussed, how can *the higher workings of mind* be said to bear out Langer's basic thesis in respect of rhythm? I may answer the question thus, largely following Langer's own line of thinking:

14. Langer, *Feeling and Form*, p. 129.

15. Ibid., p. 311.

16. Ibid., p. 351.

17. Langer, *Mind: An Essay on Human Feeling*, vol. I, p. 204.

18. Ibid.

Suppose, after a look at works of art which are commonly admired because they seem to move us readily — to tears or laughter, or to open acclamation — we arrive at the unifying view that art is the powerful expression or transmission *and evocation of emotions*. Suppose, further, that thereafter our attention is invited to acknowledged works of art which are *non*-representational in character and which, like the whole of our classical instrumental music, charm us essentially by virtue of their formal organisation or some other striking quality — such as sparkling fluency, clarity of utterance or steadfastness in *vilambit* playing or observance of *laya* (or even pace) generally. Attention to such cases may well impel us to reject our first generalisation about art. But in the very dissolution of this *Gestalt* (or whole-view) we may be moving towards an alternative view, say, the view that art is "expressive" in the sense of giving utterance not only to the commonly recognised emotions of joy and sorrow, fear and jealousy, but even to such details of felt life as excitement, vitality, languor, and repose; or to a third simpler view that, quite without any essential relatedness to human emotions, art is just the creative aesthetic embodiment of some meaning which emerges only when the work is completed.

It must, however, be added that transition to "alternative views" will actually take place not automatically, but only if *we* try to remove, by means of more careful thinking, our dissatisfaction with the first view. The "highest symbolic operations" of which Langer speaks in this context have all to be kept up *by us*; but, of course, because of its very felt quality, the (unsatisfactory) *Gestalt* of the first view may also be said to press for its own transcendence by a more adequate view, and so to generate a kind of tension, as Langer would like us to say.

(b) Rhythms like the one of self-correction, evermore embracive thinking that we just visualized are, however, not the "fundamental" ones. The latter, according to Langer, are those processes of mutual conditioning that regulate organic function; they may be called "fundamental" or "major" because if they are "greatly disturbed, or suspended for more than a few seconds, the organism collapses, life stops".[19] It is because of the ceaseless operation of these basic rhythms that life, as the process of remaining active and suffering diverse experiences, feels one and undivided.[20] This unity does not stand in need of any proof; for it is felt, and feeling is "the sense of life itself . . . the realisation in direct [experience] of what sets organic nature apart from inorganic".[21] But in the higher organisms, "secondary rhythms [also] develop; [these are] specialised responses to the surrounding world, tensions and their resolutions within the system; emotions, desires, attentive perception, and action".[22] In organic life at the lower level, three of the many *subsidiary* rhythms that Langer takes pains to distinguish are those of (1) *successive individuations,*[23] (2) *contraction and expansion*, and (3) *induction and inhibition.*[24] She points to these three kinds of rhythm where she speaks of some cases of colonies of coelenterates, mutilated organisms, and organs or cell types. But in so far as her ultimate aim in citing such instances is to show that it is the symbolic projection of these very rhythms of life that makes *art* significant, it would be quite proper if, instead of dwelling upon details of the cases referred to, we straight away turned to see if *the three rhythms we have just spoken of* are to be found in the region of art as well.

---

19. Langer, *Problems of Art*, pp. 52-53.
20. Ibid., p. 50.
21. Langer, *Feeling and Form*, pp. 327-28.
22. Langer, *Problems of Art*, p. 53.
23. Langer, *Mind: An Essay on Human Feeling*, vol. I, p. 341.
24. Abridged edition of Langer's works by H.V.D. Heuvel, p. 125.

Now, I see it clearly that they all operate in rhythm considered as a distinct art in itself. But the rhythm of successive individuations — which, in the case of some coelenterates, is *necessary to preserve the life of the stock*[25] — is important quite differently in the art of drumming. Here it often brings out the room that the ambit of a single rhythm-cycle offers for endless creative work, so impressively indeed in the case of a top-class drummer that he is himself awestruck, at times, by the illimitableness in question; and, therefore, generally prefers to focus, in his solo playing, essentially on *one tāla throughout his career!*.[26] The patterns woven across the rhythm-cycle — and also (in a way) *within* it, for they have (as a rule) to end at *its* focal beat — are all "individual" in the sense that they appear to be *self-complete and indeed are no mere fragments;* and in case the form of the cycle has been properly established at the very outset, they strike us as its own individuations, and not as only imposed on it, because they all appear to *rasika*s as welling up from within its intrinsic, determinate pace and compass. Here, however, I may also refer to a detail of Hindustani rhythm which may seem to — but does not really — counteract what I have just said about the individuality or wholeness of patterns. What is called a *tukḍā* in the region of *tablā*-playing may well be an extraction (as a rule) from some elaborate collocation of *pakhāwaj*[27] *bol*s; but here it is yet saved from appearing fragmentary by adding to it, as a

25. Langer, *Mind: An Essay on Human Feeling*, vol. I, p. 341.

26. Roughly the same infiniteness of aesthetic potential may be seen by a great vocalist in the ambit of a single major *rāga*.

27. *Pakhāwaj* is a big, *one*-piece drum; so quite different from the *tablā*. It produces deeper sonant effects than the latter, and is the right kind of drum to provide rhythmic accompaniment to the *dhruvapad-dhamār* forms of Hindustani classical vocal music.

suffix, a *tiyā* or threefold rhythmic phrase which generally suggests completion.[28]

The rhythm of contraction and expansion is also freely seen in the practice of Hindustani rhythm. To illustrate, I may turn again to the following *anāgat* pattern which begins from the off beat, ends a little before the *Sama*, which is why it is called *anāgat*; and which has already been used earlier, though for a different purpose:

*घिनननगेतिट    क्ड़धेतधातिट    घेघेतिटघेघे(ना)तिट    गद्दीघिड़ान    नागेतिटकिड़ान*

9    12    13    15    16    4    5    8    9    12

*तकिटतकिटघा    तिटघिटतिरान    ऽ    धातिटघिटतिरान    ऽ    धातिटघिटतिरान*    (सम)

13    16    1    4    5    6    10    11    12    16    1

Here the *bols*: क्ड़धेतधातिट show a little contraction; for, धातिट comes after क्ड़धेत very quickly. On the other hand, the relatively sedate नातिट, घिड़ान and किड़ान (the bracketed ना, in particular) show a little distension of syllabic filling.

To turn, in the end, to the rhythm of induction and inhibition, it may be said to be intrinsic to the very basic form and run of a rhythm-cycle, say, as follows: The *ṭhekā* (or the cycle as played) *induces* the settlement of the basic pace by virtue of the duration of its own first beat. But, at the same time, it may also be said to inhibit, first, its own run by coming back to that particular beat, the *Sama*; and secondly, the course of the patterns too, in a measure, because they are all generally required to end (ultimately) at *its* focal beat, failing which they fall into immediate error.

(c) Such (secondary) rhythms are quite various, and are often the explicit objects of attention as we

28. That is, in the way of a correct arrival at the *Sama*, the focal beat of the rhythm-cycle.

contemplate art. But, according to Langer, reflection on art itself requires us to pay due heed to rhythms in *life* as well; for it is, she believes, only by projecting these rhythms that art (quite generally) acquires its distinctive significance. Now, "life" may be taken in two basic senses: first as "the characteristic functioning of organisms", or as what is "opposed to death"; and, secondly, as what happens, or as "what the organism encounters and has to contend with".[29] In both these senses, life may be said to be characterized by rhythm. Indeed, besides the fundamental rhythms of organic function that we have already spoken of, the rhythm that may be regarded as basic to man's *existence* as an animal is *the strain of maintaining a vital balance* amid the alien and impartial chances of the world, complicated and heightened by passional desires. The pure sense of life springs from this basic rhythm, and varies from the composed well-being of sleep to the intensity of spasm, rage, or ecstasy. . . .[30] As comedy presents the vital rhythm of self-consummation . . . [The tragic rhythm is] the deathward advance of . . . [our] individual lives . . . [a passage] towards an absolute close. This form reflects the basic structure of personal life, and therewith of feeling as non-analytic, and immediate, but not quite characterless awareness when life is viewed (detachedly) as a whole.[31]

(d) Now, what really concerns us here, in respect of Langer's views as outlined above, is not the validity of the way she relates tragedy and comedy to human life, but how exactly the diverse instances she cites of organic function, man's existence, and the literary genres of tragedy and comedy can all be said to be cases of rhythm. This, in turn, demands that we

29. Langer, *Feeling and Form*, p. 214.

30. Ibid., p. 330.

31. Ibid., p. 351.

reconsider the basic question. What exactly is rhythm, in life and in art? Here, two of Langer's unambiguous answers that we have already touched upon are as follows:

(*a*) The essence of rhythm is the preparation of a new event by the ending of a previous one.[32]

(*b*) The essence of rhythm is the alternation of tensions building up to a new crisis, and ebbing away in a graduated course of relaxation whereby a new build-up of tension is prepared and driven to the next crisis, which necessitates the next cadence.[33]

Now, either definition assumes that rhythm is a matter of function (see: "building up", "preparation of" in the two definitions just cited). This is, in fact, a view which Langer freely repeats in her works. But if this emphasis is agreed to, how can one speak of the (literally, moveless) rhythm of colours in a painting? This, however, is not the only point that I wish to press against the definitions. My protest is fuller, and I put it thus:

The first definition, claiming (like the second) to seize the essence of rhythm, does not use the word *tension* at all. Therefore, it may be said to be quite relevant to the cases of rhythm as *mutual conditioning* which Langer cites in *Problems of Art* — say, "the swinging of a pendulum" and "the breaking of waves in a steady surf on a beach" — in respect of which she herself uses the word *momentum*, not *tension*. And the preference is warranted; for, *none* of the more widely acknowledged meanings of *tension*, namely the following:

> stretching, a pulling strain, stretched or strained state, strain generally, (or, formerly, pressure in gases or vapour), a state of barely suppressed emotion, as excitement, suspense, anxiety or hostility,

32. Langer, *Feeling and Form*, p. 126.

33. Langer, *Mind: An Essay on Human Feeling*, vol. I, p. 324.

is really applicable to the cases of mutual conditioning just listed. But, if this is so, if no tension may be said to be there in instances of rhythm which Langer here cites, how can (*b′*) which defines rhythm explicitly in terms of *tension* be said to hold?

Further, if as (*b*) requires us to do, rhythm be defined as a *cycle* (see "alternation") of "tension-crisis-ebbing away (or cadence) and another tension-crisis-cadence", and so on, how can the deathward (or towards a *final* or *"absolute* close")[34] advance of individual lives be regarded as making for tragic *rhythm*? The second definition (*b*) is indeed not true to the practice of Hindustani rhythm. Here, so far as the *ṭhekā* is concerned, there is (ordinarily) no building up of a tension, nor any "ebbing away in a graduated course of relaxation. . . ." Artistic form is here secured only by an evenness of pace and clear and "blended" execution (on the two drums) of the constituent syllables of the *ṭhekā*, besides, of course, a consistently accurate marking of the *Sama*. The language in which a well-played *ṭhekā* is commonly acclaimed is roughly as follows:

वाह! क्या ठेका क़ायम किया है! दायें बायें का वज़न भी बराबर है!

In the first segment of such applause, the reference is to evenness of pace; and in the second, to a skilfully balanced employment of the two drums. And, to turn to the various *patterns* in which a solo exposition of rhythm abounds, though some kind of tension may well seem to be built up, at times, in the manner of their gaining access to the *Sama*, what follows the attainment of *Sama* or completion of the patterns — is surely no "ebbing away in a *graduated* course of relaxation", but a prompt return to the *ṭhekā* as it was before the pattern took off.

A few more details are suspect in Langer's view of rhythm, if we look at it all from the viewpoint of Hindustani rhythm. Traces of tension, I admit again, are surely to be found at

34. Langer, *Feeling and Form*, p. 351.

places in our rhythm as practised and contemplated. In fact, one important feature of our rhythmic system is that (as pointed out earlier) if we are used to contemplating rhythm as art, the pace at which the very first *bol* is played or uttered, makes us expect — may be, a little tensely, say, where the pace suggested is markedly slow — that the subsequent pace too will be leisurely, in accordance with the way the first *bol* has been projected. Further, though evenness of pace (or *laya*) is admittedly a basic requirement, what is admired as a mark of *special* technical excellence is not this steadiness in itself, but the ability to keep it even when the *sitār* or *sarod* player executes patterns of "wanton heed and giddy cunning"; or when the drummer himself plays a pattern which does not go haywire in *laya*, in spite of the incorporation of a phrase or syllable that deviates purposely from the basic *laya*. In either case, we may note, a kind of gentle *pull* is created, and even felt as such, between the normal tempo and the moments of wilful deviation. Yet it seems to me that the emphasis that Langer puts on the build-up and release of *tension* is a little overdone. When a *ṭhekā*, which is the ground of all our rhythm, has been properly established as a measured extent of even and articulate pace, it seems to move on effortlessly — of its own impulse, so to say. Nor does the *rasika* here see (or experience) any tension. Rather, in an *easy* exercise of imaginative sympathy, he just feels swayed and lulled into sweet acquiescence by the self-completing rhythmic flow. Our experience, here, is one of effortless following, not of any strain or pressure at all.

Consider, next, a detail of Langer's protest against the commonly held view that rhythm is a matter of periodic succession. As a rebuttal of this view, she points to a matter of fact. A tennis player's motions may well "impress one as rhythmic — [even though] he does not repeat a single action"; and, what is more, he may well be less metrical in his step than "a drunkard walking".[35] Langer would like us to believe

35. Langer, *Problems of Art*, p. 50.

that in such cases we see rhythm only because every movement of the player at once paves the way to the next. But I do not think her reasoning here is supported by the evidence of fact. The most easily identified locus of rhythm in tennis is a long rally comprising (seemingly) effortless and flowing strokes unruffled by jerky movements. If a movement prepares the way to the next, *but with sudden and manifest effort* — say, by way of a leap to counter a lob, or as a dive for scooping a drop shot — the playing is likely to seem acrobatic rather than rhythmic, and if some may yet prefer to call it *rhythmic* it will only be if the return turns out to be a winner, in which case the appellation will relate to the adequacy of effort *as a whole* to attainment, and not really to the conduciveness of just *one step* to another.

And in the context of architecture and painting, the inaptness of Langer's view is perhaps even *more manifest*. No one can deny the presence of rhythm in every art. As Otto Baensch points out,

> rhythm not only dominates music and poetry, but also, in a wider sense, architecture, sculpture, and painting: the bigger part of a space is heavier than the smaller; one spatial form, whether linear or plane, weightier, more striking, or stronger in character than another; colours, also, are distinguished from various points of view by their greatly varied impressiveness. . . . If, therefore, we want to define rhythm in general, we have to say: rhythm is the alternation between heavy (stressed) and light (unstressed or less stressed) parts, in so far as it follows certain rules.[36]

Now, there is no doubt that we freely speak of the rhythm *of colours*. But, by and large, our meaning here simply is that they seem to go well together; and it would be very odd if, using Langer's language, someone chose to say that in the case in question every colour (as perceived) is *an event that paves the way to the next*.

---

36. Langer (ed.), *Reflections on Art*, The John Hopkins Press, Baltemore, 1958, p. 26.

I hasten to add, however, that the generalization on rhythm by Otto Baensch (which I have just cited) itself seems questionable. It cannot be said to cover *every* instance of rhythm; and my argument here is as follows:

> The basis of north Indian rhythm, we have seen, is the *ṭhekā* or the rhythm-cycle. The structure of this cycle is admittedly a blend of *khālī* and *bharī*, or the unstressed and stressed beats, the *Sama* being always the focal point of emphasis. But though this structure is, of course, the foundation on which the entire edifice of our rhythm stands, it is not aesthetically the most satisfying feature of the practice of this art. Much more admirable is the infinite variety of patterned ways in which a good drummer can gain the requisite access to the *Sama*-point. Such access surely heightens the look of the *Sama*-beat too, partly because it is reached with split second accuracy; but our delight here, we may note, relates to the whole manner of gaining access to the pivotal beat, instead of being confined to this beat as played; and the distribution of delight over that complete segment of the pattern where it appears to take a look at, and (so to say) to move towards the *Sama* noticeably, is precisely what *is not* covered by the conception of rhythm as a mere balancing of stressed and unstressed beats. The same may be said of those brief passages where the pattern is made to *deviate* purposely, though for a very brief while, from the basic pace of the *ṭhekā* — only to repair to that pace unfalteringly.

### What is Rhythm: A Proposal

To cover *every* instance of what strikes us as rhythmic in the creation and contemplation of art, *and* in everyday life, I think *we* could perhaps put forth the following definition of rhythm:

> Rhythm is such an ordered (or order*ly*) disposition of elements, acts, processes, events, or stages that, because of some specific factors, the mind feels (on the whole) happy — or in some way enlightened — in traversing it as an object of contemplation. The factors in question are mainly the following: regular recurrence, contrast and balance, mutual complementariness, directed attainment of an end, or the mind's own expectations generated by habituation, past training, or present interest.

We may now see if this definition covers our experience of rhythm and rhythmic quality in diverse areas of life and activity.

To begin with, notice may be taken of a possible distinction between the order*ed* and the order*ly* or between that which has been put in some order *by* human effort — as in the creation of a work of art — and that which is *originally given to us in an order*, like the sequence of seasons or the alternation of systole and diastole. The word *disposition*, as meaning arrangement, may be taken to signify not only sequence and juxtaposition but interplay; and so to cover not only the occurrent arts of music and dance, but literature, sculpture, painting and architecture. As for *contemplation*, it obviously stands for both *looking at* and *considering* attentively. "Enlightenment", again, is to be taken in its usual senses of "imparting knowledge or information to" and "elevating by knowledge". Discriminating awareness of the regular and repeated sequence of the various stages of human life not only informs us, but may even elevate us into a philosophical acceptance, of the inevitability of decay and death. These stages may be said to provide a kind of rhythm not only because of the constancy of the order in which they occur, but because, as Langer would say, the very tapering of one stage is at once a making for the emergence of the next.

How our definition may be said to cover every feature of our practice *of rhythm as a distinct art* may be brought out next — at some length, say, as follows:

> The shapely passage of a pattern towards the *Sama* of the *ṭhekā* is covered by "directed attainment of an end"; and the momentary passages of wilful straying from — and prompt reparatory return to — the basic pace, by the following words in our definition: *mutual complementariness*. And, of course, we feel gratified in either case, as we follow the turns and passages of rhythm.

The *felt agreeableness* as the mind traverses details of the object contemplated is, indeed, the essence of the matter here;

otherwise they are not likely to appear as making a *rhythmic* whole or sequence. Where we speak of the rhythm of events, actual or as projected in a novel or film, our reference is to such likeable chains of events as are, on the whole, satisfying and/*or* in some way enlightening. A good instance of such a chain *in actual life* is provided by the following:

> the long incarceration of Nelson Mandela as the champion of South Africa's struggle for freedom from *apartheid*; his eventual release; repeated meetings with the country's President F.W. de Klerk; the holding of non-discriminatory, democratic elections; the president's magnanimous admission of defeat; the election of Mandela as the country's first black president; therefore, the establishment of black majority rule through negotiation; and a graceful acceptance of the right of the majority Black by the minority White.

Where the chain comprises events that are merely virtual, as is to be found in the unfoldment of plot in a novel or a play, it may put an edge on our awareness of a good deal of what we surely encounter in real life, but do not contemplate enough: say, the diversity of human nature, the interplay of situation and character, the havoc that may be caused by petty human foibles, and the (possible) ominousness of a present situation. The chain of *actual* events we have referred to (in the preceding para) is of course good warrant for Langer's view too; but, just as clearly, it does not elude the grasp of the definition *we* have put forth. It is, in fact, duly covered by the following words in our definition: "*directed attainment* of an end".

As for the "several factors" that lend a little charm to the mind's passage across concatenated details or elements, and make them appear rhythmic, they are all at least as clearly at work in the practice of our rhythm as in the region of any other art. Thus, regular recurrence is visibly there in the beats that occur at equal intervals; and in being actually played on the drum (that is, as *bharī*) or as quietly affirmed in the mind (*khālī*), they not only provide a kind of balance by opposing each other, and so prevent an overplay of sound or silence, but necessitate attention to both overt playing and ideal attunement, again by virtue of their very opposition. It is also a noteworthy feature of the practice of Hindustani rhythm that whole bunches of mnemonic syllables (*bol*s) often seem to be mutual complements in the sense that the later bunch provides what the earlier one *lacks*, say, syllables having a subdued sound. Thus, in the following sequence: तकिटतका, तिटकतागदिगिन whereas the first phrase has only one *bol* of closed sound (किट), the second has as many as three: तिट, गदि, गिन.

The *effective* working of all these factors, however, depends on the past training, habits of attention, and present interest of the contemplator. No detail of the practice of rhythm as a *flowing*, yet articulate form can be rightly perceived unless one is able to hold on to the basic pace of the *ṭhekā*; and this ability is not an instant acquisition, but the product of long training or habituation. It works necessarily, if subduedly, where what is contemplated is not merely the *ṭhekā* as such, but a full pattern that runs across and, on the whole, within the ambit of the *ṭhekā*. And where the pattern in question is exceptionally intricate — may be because of some moments of intentional deviation from the basic pace — intenseness of concurrent attention is an indispensable requirement.

### Three Critical Questions

But these explanatory comments on *our* definition of rhythm do not throw any direct light on some questions which are debated by aestheticians today, and some of which relate directly to Susanne Langer's aesthetics. I may put these questions as follows:

(1) Is the time (or its semblance) that we find in rhythm similar to, or different from time as we experience it in daily life?

(2) How does Langer avail of the concept of rhythm in defending her thesis that all art is a *symbolic projection of felt life*?

(3) And, finally, how does the concept in question (2) facilitate interrelation of the other concepts in her aesthetics of music and of art in general — concepts like "forms of feeling", composition and organic unity.

Of all these questions the second one may be taken up first, because of its greater relevance to an assessment of the crux of Langer's aesthetics. It calls for some critical attention to all the major arts. But, to keep our discussion within manageable limits — and also because it is *literature* which is commonly regarded as *related to life* essentially — we may here focus on drama, ignoring non-dramatic poetry for the sake of brevity.

Now, turning to the two key concepts that figure in (2), namely *rhythm,* and *felt life* — I find it necessary to give a clear, if brief, account of what Langer has to say about them, though it is bound to involve some repetition of the thinking we have already done. Rhythm, we have seen, can be easily cyclic — that is, a matter of mutual conditioning — *or* merely serial. A distinct form of the latter is what Langer, would like us to call, *cadential* rhythm. The word *cadence* admits of at least three clear meanings: the beat or measure of something rhythmic, a *fall* in the pitch of the voice at the end of a sentence, and the *close* of a musical phrase or section. Langer seems to take the word, quite generally, in the sense of a fall or close. I say so in view of her following remark:

> Unlike the simple metabolic process [which may be said to be cyclic], the deathward advance of . . . [our] individual lives has a series of stations that are *not repeated*; growth, maturity, decline. That is the tragic rhythm. Tragedy is a *cadential* form. Its crisis is always the turn toward *an absolute close*. This form reflects the basic structure of personal life. . . .[37]

Now, a mere close as such cannot be said to be rhythmic. But where it comes as the end of a series of events or stages, each of which appears to prepare the way to the next one, it may

37. Langer, *Feeling and Form,* p. 351. Italics added.

well be said to culminate a cadential rhythm. What is necessarily present in every kind of rhythm is (a) change, process, flow and succession — besides, of course, (b) determination of that which follows by that which precedes. Strictly speaking, the "stations" that Langer distinguishes in our individual lives are not fixed positions, but phases, that is, stages in growth or development. But, be that as it may, in Langer's view the two essentials we have distinguished (as *a* and *b*) hold of every instance of rhythmicity. Where a process *is* rhythmic, "the consummation of one phase is the preparation for another, which in its consummation prepares its successor. . . ."[38]

Some attention may now be given to the other concept, *life*, as Langer understands it. Here, for the sake of clarity, our treatment may be divided under two distinct heads:

1. Life as featuring rhythms
2. The pure sense of life

1. Now, the rhythms that distinguish life are organic, emotional, mental. The rhythm of attention is an interesting link between them; and, taken together, they compose the dynamic pattern of feeling,[39] or how it actually feels to be alive. As mutual conditioning, we have seen, rhythm "is the law of *organic* function".[40] On the outside, the daily life of an individual shows the rhythm of vigorous activity and consequent languor, followed (as naturally) by sleep which, in turn, generally prepares one for another day of vigorous activity. *Emotional* rhythms are provided, say, by the dualities of excitement and depression, joy and sorrow, elation and frustration.

38. Langer, *Mind: An Essay on Human Feeling*, p. 204.

39. "Dynamic" *and very complex*, because "all sorts of processes may culminate in feeling with or without direct relation to each other . . ." Ibid., p. 67.

40. Langer, *Problems of Art*, p. 52. Italics added.

These are all cases of mutual conditioning in the sense that the more we yield to any one of the pair, the more liable we become to experience the other, if not quite readily. Attention connects them all in the sense that one is always more or less clearly aware of their character when they occur; but, we may note, attention is itself rhythmic in nature in so far as every act of intense concentration of attention presses for, and is followed by a state of felt relaxation which, however, may or may not be incidental to the attainment of a desired end.

2. By "the *pure* sense of life" Langer means sensation, awareness, and expectation. These may be called "pure" because they belong "to *all* higher creatures". The *personal* sense of life — that is, the realisation that one is a distinct self and is possessed of a life that has a "beginning, efflorescence, and end" — "probably belongs only to human beings, and to them in varying measure".[41] It is "more elaborate and more integrated" than the pure sense of life. Yet both are alike "fundamental forms of consciousness" that drama may be said to abstract from reality as its building material; and, speaking quite generally, they may be taken as one to make "the sense of life". This (total) sense is infinitely complex and "variable in its possible expressions". But it is by no means the feeling of a chaotic series of indeterminate elements; for, as that which distinguishes the animate from the inanimate, life is teleological, — a characteristic which manifests itself as "self-preservation, self-restoration, functional tendency, purpose". And, what is specially germane to our present concern, all these manifestations involve rhythm as determination of what follows by that which comes earlier, often in

41. Langer, *Feeling and Form*, p. 327.

the way of a need as itself pressing for a specific fulfilment. To illustrate,

> A tree . . . that is bereft of the sunshine it needs by the encroachment of other trees, tends to grow tall and thin until it can spread its own branches in the light. A fish that has most of its tail bitten off partly overcomes the disturbance of its locomotion patterns by growing new tissue, replacing some of the tail; and partly adapts to its new condition by modifying the normal uses of its fins, swimming effectively without trying to correct the list of its whole body in the water, as it did at first.[42]

In a much more complex and integrated way, human beings too manage to survive by regulating their efforts and attitudes to changing circumstances. This is the rhythm of adaptation. The challenge of new situations elicits new responses, because of the pressure of the instinct of self-preservation.

**Rhythm in Drama**

Now that Langer's basic views on both rhythm and life have been brought out, in order to see how (according to her) rhythm serves as a link between art and life, we may first state, in brief, how exactly she traces the presence of rhythm in one form of literary art, say, drama.

An important, if general remark that she makes in this context is that

> a dramatic act is a commitment. It creates a situation in which the agent or agents must necessarily make a further move; that is, it motivates a subsequent act (or acts). The situation, which is the completion of a given act, is already the impetus to another — as, in running, the footfall that catches our weight at the end of one bound already sends us forward to land on the other foot.[43]

---

42. Langer, *Feeling and Form*, p. 328.

43. Ibid., p. 355.

So, as determination of what is to come next by the present event, act or stage, rhythm may be said to be necessarily there in the art of drama. But here some critical comments are necessary. The word *act* in the extract cited is to be taken as something done or as a doing, *not* as a distinct (main) section of a play; for there are one-act plays too, and *such* a play cannot obviously be said to make for something to follow. But then, if *act* is to be taken as a *doing*, what shall we say of those *speeches*, as by the Fool in Shakespeare's tragedies, which only throw into bolder relief the gloom or ominousness of the situational context in the play, instead of directly suggesting any further move?

## Rhythm as a Paving-the-Way-to

Langer could possibly rejoin by suggesting that the very deepening of the character of the situation makes the reader *expect* something catastrophic to happen; and that, therefore, the speeches in question could well be said to create a rhythm. I make this suggestion because of her following emphatic utterance:

> (a) Everything that prepares a future creates rhythm; (b) everything that begets or intensifies expectation, including the expectation of sheer continuity prepares the future; (c) and everything that fulfils the promised future, in ways foreseen or unforeseen, articulates the symbol of feeling.[44]

But one of the three points just listed by me as [(a), (b), (c),] is clearly questionable; and another, not readily clear. What (a) says is clearly too sweeping. Where excessive bleeding on his surgeon's table is seen to *lead* a patient straight to his death, no one will profess to see any rhythm in the situation, in spite of the fact that the flow in question is very likely to cause alarm, and apprehensive expectation of what is *to come*. So it is too much to say that *everything* that prepares a future

44. Langer, *Feeling and Form*, p. 129.

creates rhythm. Further, the emphasis does not show any awareness of the truth that, speaking quite generally, rhythm involves *recurrence*. What (b) says may be allowed to pass; for to *expect* is necessarily to look forward to some future happening. But, to turn now to (c), what does it mean to say *that everything that fulfils the promised future . . . articulates the symbol of feeling*? To answer this question we have, first, to remind ourselves that by "feeling" Langer means "whatever is felt" — may be, the sheer passage of "lived time"; and, second, to consider the italicized words along with the following that the make their immediate sequel:

> Whatever the special mood of the [musical] piece, or its emotional import, the vital rhythm of subjective time (the lived time that Bergson adjures us to find in pure experience) permeates the complex, multi-dimensional, musical symbol as its internal logic, which relates music intimately and self-evidently to life.[45]

Now, looking at all these cited words as one — they, in fact, occur in the same para — "the symbol of feeling" may be equated with "the musical piece", also because *all art* (according to Langer) is a symbolic projection of the forms of feeling. "The vital rhythm of *subjective* time", of which she speaks here, may be taken to mean the rhythm or complementariness of need, expectation or effort, and fulfilment or attainment. This is indeed what lived (or felt) time really is. Clock time is unchangingly periodic; the ticks occur at equal intervals. But lived time, or time as experienced in actual life, seems to move slowly or quickly according as one's life is soured with anguished waiting or enlivened with a series of happy events. As for the word "articulates" (in "articulates the symbol of feeling"), it may be taken to mean "gives a clear appearance of elements that are distinct, though related in an orderly way". Here I take my stand on Langer's explicit view that the *form* of music is *articulate* in so far as the

45. Langer, *Feeling and Form*, p. 129.

elements which are here held as one retain a measure of self-existence in spite of the interlacement.[46]

The net meaning of the extracts I have picked for reflection could now be put thus. (a) Every *individual* phrase, accent or change of aesthetic pace (*laya*) which makes a *distinct* contribution to the emergence of the music's final form at once invests the piece with an *articulate* form. (b) Such a *form*, however, is no mere juxtaposition of parts, but an organic unity; and this is so because the whole is permeate with a rhythm in the sense that every part prepares the way, and makes us look forward, to what is to come next. Both these points, I may add, are clearly borne out by even a casual look at the practice of Hindustani rhythm. Generally speaking, every beat, as marking and maintaining the even flow of aesthetic pace, makes us look forward to the next one at an equal interval of time; the next one, as it comes expectedly, not only relieves the gentle tension of looking-forward-to, but paves the way to yet another beat; and, what is more, far from disrupting the unity of the *laya*-flow, the plurality of beats only lends a look of articulate form to the total playing which, in turn, makes them all appear as gentle accents, and no protuberant wedges in the *laya*-flow.

## Rhythm and "Life" in Drama

To turn again to literature, we may now briefly outline Langer's views as to how it is rhythm which enables tragedy and comedy to project a semblance of life. As forms of the art of drama, both of course show the rhythm that has already been referred to, namely the rhythm of an act as creating a situation which presses for "a further move",[47] and so on,

46. "Music, like language, is an articulate form. Its parts not only fuse together to yield a greater entity, but in doing so they maintain some degree of separate existence, and the sensuous character of each element is affected by its function in the complex whole." Langer, *Feeling and Form*, p. 31.

47. Ibid., p. 355.

throughout the play. In life, on the other hand, if an individual's career is considered in relation to the totality of situations and happenings that fill it, two distinct kinds of rhythm may be distinguished: the rhythm of destiny and the rhythm of fortune. As rhythms, both signify a kind of dynamic relatedness; but whereas the rhythm of destiny or fate is the "appearance that the future is already an entity, embryonic in (or determined by) the present",[48] "the rhythm of fortune is that of "vital continuity",[49] that is, the open and episodic rhythm of challenges or obstacles as making for appropriate, remedial action. Now, according to Langer, "tragedy is the image of Fate, as comedy is of Fortune".[50] Tragedy shows the largely inevitable rhythm of growth, efflorescence, and exhaustion. This is obviously quite similar to the rhythm of stages (of ageing) in real life. But comedy too may be said to project the motion and rhythm of daily living — the rhythm of confronting and dealing with situations as they arise, off and on. But in neither case does the dramatist merely copy life; he has to organize and articulate a symbol for the "sense of life".[51] This, however, calls for some explanation.

Take tragedy, to begin with. Whereas in actual life (as a rule) something *singular* and menacing must happen *a little before* we become apprehensive as to what is imminent — as when the doctor's definitive diagnosis that the only earning head of the family is suffering from cancer at once makes us think of the ruin that awaits them all — in a play we are quickly presented with "the whole [complex] set-up of human relationships and conflicting interests *long before* any abnormal event has occurred",[52] though in such an integrated and suggestive manner that we *readily* perceive "an ominous

48. Langer, *Feeling and Form*, p. 311.

49. Ibid., p. 335.

50. Ibid., p. 333.

51. Ibid., p. 363.

52. Ibid., p. 311.

situation", and visualize that some far-reaching action must develop out of it. This creates the peculiar tension between the given present and its yet unrealised consequent, [or] form in suspense, [which is] the essential dramatic illusion . . . [This *tension* is the *rhythm* of destiny. It does not imitate anything in life, but it surely resembles] "an aspect of real experience . . . [something] which distinguishes human life from animal existence; the sense of past and future as parts of one continuum, and therefore of life as a single reality".[53]

## Art and the Character of Life

This should not however make us believe that, as a dynamic relation, rhythm brings about a perceptible resemblance between life and the art of drama *alone*. According to Langer, every work of art betrays this similitude. See, her following emphatic utterance:

> . . . All art has the character of *life*, because every work must have *organic* character and it usually makes sense to speak of its *fundamental rhythm*.[54]

Now, partly because "fundamental rhythm" is here taken to be present not only in *life* but in art, and partly because Langer also introduces — elsewhere, but again in relation to art — the concept of *commanding form*, I think it necessary to make some explanatory remarks on the extract cited.

To begin with, "life" is here to be taken *not* in the "social" sense — that is, as "what happens, (or) what the organism . . . encounters and has to contend with" but as "the characteristic functioning of organism" or as what is "opposed to death". With this specific meaning in mind, we may say that all art is organic in character — or is similar to life — because, very much like life, no work can be regarded as a mere summation of elements of determinate individual values. Langer's following remark is here very pertinent:

53. Langer, *Feeling and Form*, p. 311.

54. Ibid., p. 214.

> Who could say *how much* of a natural organism's life is in the lungs, how much in the legs, or how much more life would be added to us if we were given a lively tail to wave?[55]

The task here visualized is impossible; and, similarly, "although it is possible to analyse *what* [or *how* the elements of a work of art] . . . contribute to the . . . [work], it is not possible to assign them any of its import *apart from the whole*".[56] What a line contributes to a painting, a look of tension or of tranquillity, or of mere flow, can be determined only by noticing its position *in* the whole work; and, of course, the question, *how much* it contributes, would be quite out of order. "The essence of all composition . . . even purely percussive . . . is the semblance of organic movement [that is] the illusion of an indivisible whole."[57] Now, this is surely true of composition in the region of Hindustani rhythm. Like any vital, organic process — such as digestion or circulation of blood — the run of a rhythmic pattern is inseparable from, and is determined by many other factors or processes. Here, indeed, a pattern has to be so composed that (a) the *bol*s it integrates may, in fact, be *playable* in the same order in which they have been put together; (b) that the whole pattern may bear a determinate and identifiable relation to the basic pace as set and marked by the *ṭhekā;* (c) that the various segments of the pattern may appear to demand each other; and (d) finally, that the whole form may strike the knowledgeable listener as moving towards the focal beat as its destiny.

But though we may agree that, as a dynamic interplay of elements or processes, rhythm is to be found (generally) in works of art as well, before we finally accept the thesis that art projects the rhythms *of life*, we have to settle an important question of general significance. Can the analogues of a rhythm which has its locus is in a particular region of reality

---

55. Langer, *Problems of Art*, p. 135.

56. Ibid.

57. Ibid., p. 126.

or experience be effectively projected in a quite different setting? Here, following Langer, we may at once say *yes*, and with due reason. When, for instance, we speak of the rise and fall of a stately life, we create *in language* an analogue of the rhythm which we often come across in inorganic nature — say, in the run of an undulating billow; and which may also be said to resemble the rhythm of the gentle swell and easing off of the chest in normal breathing. But if a brief linkage of words, which are admittedly symbols, can create an analogue of the rhythm of life, why should the elaborate structure of an art symbol be denied the power to project analogues of the complex rhythms of life?[58] The artist achieves this by exercising a common capacity with which he is very well equipped. Langer calls this capacity "logical intuition". This type of intuition makes for the immediate recognition of such relational factors in experience as "distinctness, similarity, congruence, relevance".[59] It is this capacity which enables the artist to seize the equivalence between forms of felt life and certain artistic structures.

But does an artist actually do this, or are we merely supposing that he does so? Now, so far as I know, and I speak in the light of my close personal relations with them, our *tablā* or *pakhāwaj* drummers would simply feel bewildered if they were told that what they really do (when they play at their drums) is projection of some forms of feeling. They would hasten to add, in one voice, that they only try to play the *ṭhekā* and the various patterns according to established norms; and that their playing is determined not at all by the thought of expressing any feeling or its "form", but rather by such basic requirements as are valued by all those who practise the art of rhythm, namely the following: crystal clear 'cutting' of syllables that make the various patterns; due accentuation of some of the constituent *bols*; correct attainment of the *Sama*, preferably in a well-designed way;

58. Langer, *Problems of Art*, pp. 132-33.

59. Ibid., p. 166.

methodical sequencing of patterns as they make a whole recital; and, of course, the ability to keep the basic *laya* from wobbling.[60]

To conclude, a close look at the art of Hindustani rhythm does not bear out Langer's basic thesis in respect of art taken generally.

---

60. I may here cite the following from my write-up, "Ustāds pay brilliant homage to Dagars", already referred to: "Most of those who provided 'accompaniment' (to the musicians) on the *pakhāwaj* . . . impressed one and all, by virtue of their fluency, clarity and steadfastness of playing".

# 12

# Laya, Tāla, Rhythm and a Contemporary Debate

How aesthetics of Hindustani rhythm may be done has been already indicated, if only cursorily. We have also seen how a careful look at our rhythm can be of help in removing a few obscurities in the avowed views of some eminent philosophers of art, as also in estimating, with due reason, their emphasis on certain concepts as being fundamentally relevant to all art. So it would only be filling a gap, so to say, if we now tried to see how some analytic attention to our rhythm could be relevant to a specific ongoing aesthetic debate relating to time as it may be said to permeate rhythm in music.

Let it not be protested that much more vigorous debates are raging today in respect of music as a whole, and that rhythm is only one of its elements; for, in the way of regulated duration, pace, pauses and emphases, rhythm is the very life-breath of the art it enlivens. The formal relations without which music cannot exist are first of all rhythmic. Taken wholly by itself, a single sound can surely be musical, but it cannot be regarded as the *art* of music, just as the most meaningful word — say, one of intense profound symbolic significance, like *Cross* or *Resurrection* — cannot be regarded as a sermon. Indeed, for a succession of sounds to be heard properly as music, they must be connected by *a perceptible temporal pattern of duration, pace and stress* — in other words, by a rhythmic form. Be it noted that the meaning of the italicized words is not confined to repeated patterns of *regular beats*, or to what we speak of as *tāla*; and that, in so far as our *ālāpa* (of the *dhrupad* genre) too is not merely a matter of temporally regulated abidance at, and passage across individual *svaras*, but also of due emphasis on some key notes — it is duly covered by the words cited above. Therefore, a careful look at what we call *laya* in *ālāpa* will be quite germane to our discussion of the debate to which we may turn after paying a little more attention to *laya* than we have done so far in the earlier chapters.

What is *laya*? It is with an eye to better understanding of this basic concept that I address the question anew. Some acknowledged (dictionary) meanings of the word are: melting, dissolution, absorption-in, rest, and repose. None of these meanings, however, is categorically or *uniquely* relevant to rhythm. One may well feel utterly absorbed for a while also in contemplating a beautiful landscape, and so at rest. Therefore, though one *can become engrossed in following* (say,) *the run of a sweetly played drut tritāla ṭhekā* too, we have to look for another meaning of *laya* which may be relevant to rhythm alone. Now, there is only one way to do this. Following what is one of the most acceptable dictums of twentieth century philosophy, we may try to determine the meaning of *laya* by considering the different ways in which the word is commonly used in our talk about *gāyan* or *vādan* (vocal or instrumental music) whether or not it is "accompanied" by a drummer whose basic task is to go on playing a rhythm-cycle *steadily* as long as the recital lasts. Commonly, of course, it is with reference to a *rhythm-cycle* as played or to rhythmically organised music that we talk of *laya*. How such talk can be variform is known to all those who love our music. What yet remains to be emphasized only is that though steadiness of flow or pace is admittedly an important meaning of the word, it cannot be regarded as an equally *basic,* objectively determined *and pervasive* feature of *both ālāpa* and rhythmic singing; for,

first, specially in the case of *ālāpa*, evenness of speed is itself the

> result (entirely) of the vocalist's own active willing, instead of being determined by *mātrās*;
>
> and secondly, though never randomly, the *ālāpiyā* is free to sing two adjacent *svaras* or tufts of notes *at inequal speed*, either for the sake of evoking a specific effect or by way of meeting the objectively pre-fixed, grammatical requirements of the *rāga* being sung.
>
> So, if such a charactization of *laya* is demanded as could cover both *ālāpa* and beat-measured singing, *and* also suggest how *laya* is related to what we commonly speak of as *time*, I may venture to answer simply as follows:
>
> Going by the way the word is used *today*, *laya* may be taken to mean *time* as it is sensed in *sangeet* in the form of pace and duration.

As I speak thus, I at once pave the way to a treatment of the controversy which I have in mind, and which I propose to discuss a little later. But let me first draw attention to a matter of detail. Those who are engaged in the controversy in question speak all along of *time* (in music and in daily life), not of *laya, tāla* or rhythm, I have, on the other hand, spoken of *laya, tāla*, and rhythm, not of time. But a little close thinking will make it clear that a reference to time is surely implicit in the way I have gone about the subject. The point is easy to see. While doing *ālāpa*, how long one stays at a particular *svara* is *duration*; and how we traverse different *svaras*, nimbly or leisurely, is a matter of *pace* or *speed*. In either case, a reference to time (*as we commonly regard it*) is implicit; for, pace and duration are surely the two basic ways in which we commonly relate to time all that is there and happens around us in real life. We speak of things and relations as impermanent or abiding; and of a task as accomplished quickly or by slow degrees. Therefore, when I speak of *laya* in *ālāpa*, duly bearing in mind its moments of tonal abidance — as also the shifts in its run — an implicit reference to time is all along there. As for *tāla*, it is nothing but *laya*, or the flow of time in *sangeet*, as organized and made articulate and measurable with the help of beats, *bols*, and *vibhāgs*. And the two, *laya* and *tāla*, taken together is all that we mean by *rhythm* in the context of *sangeet*. But one note of caution is yet here needed. Merely to talk of *laya, tāla* and rhythmicity is one thing; to experience all this in the actual contemplation of ongoing music is quite another. Here, in immediate listening, *time* as implicit in *laya and* (*tāla-baddh*) *rhythm* is only *sensed as fused with*, not as distinguished from the two. This is precisely why in listening to music absorbedly we easily lose sense of the passage of actual time.

Now, I may quickly outline the controversy I propose to look at from the viewpoint of Hindustani rhythm. The reference all along will be to the views of Susanne K. Langer and Philip Alperson.

To turn first to Langer, she believes that the (semblance of) time that we find in music is virtual. What exactly she means by speaking thus, and how exactly she argues this view — both these questions admit of a definite answer which I may put as follows, at places with some comments of my own, with an eye to greater clarity.

Ordinarily, we experience time as a sequence or passage of states or happenings. It is only rarely — may be in a moment of *stunning* grief — that time seems to come to a stop. Otherwise, *is going on, has just been* and *is yet to come* — such are the words that we use ordinarily in respect of time. More or less similarly, what enables music to present an auditory apparition of time is the (apparent) movement that we see in it. "Music flows; a melody moves; a succession of tones is heard as a progression."[1] But this movement of music, Langer insists, is simply *virtual*. It is quite different from the *actual* vibrations that cause the sounds that we hear. The motions of strings are "extremely small, rapid, and repetitious". Surely,

> we do not hear vibratory motions in music, but large linear movements . . . rhythms that are not at all like physical oscillations. We hear marching, flowing, or . . . progressive

1. Langer, *Problems of Art*, Routledge and Kegan Paul, 1957, p. 36.

> motion. Yet in a musical progression there is nothing that is displaced, that has gone from somewhere to somewhere else.[2]

Frets and keys which produce music are, of course, laid out in space; but *the music* which they produce cannot be said to occupy space. One cannot put any *thing* between two accents *of music*, as one easily can between any two points in actual space; and, in respect of vocal music, it would be clearly silly to say that the notes are spread out all over the vocal chords. Indeed, in a musical ascent or descent no actual thing is seen to traverse a moveless path. "The listener (only) hears musical figures that move through a definite tonal range, from points of origin to points of relative rest."[3] Musical movement may therefore be said to be illusory — in the sense of being different from movement of things in actual life, quite like "volumes in pictorial space" which surely do not fill a room as chairs and tables do. Another very clear index of the difference between what (and how) we hear and follow, as movement in music and the motion that is actually there is provided by the fact that "when a figure ascends to a resting tone", and we hear "sustained rest" or "a changeless continuity in time" — "the *actual motion* of the air is faster on that resting tone than anywhere else in the passage".[4]

So, as an evocation of this virtual movement, the *time* that we see in music may also be said to be *virtual* — not only because of its patent otherness from clock-time, but because it is a *created analogue of time as lived and felt*. Here, to begin with, two differences have to be noted clearly: first, between clock-time and experienced time; and second, between the latter (or lived time) and musical time. Clock-time — that is, the time by which we regulate our daily work and appointments — is "a simple one-dimensional trickle of successive moments". It regulates our lives, to be sure; but it has no

2. Langer, *Problems of Art*, p. 37.

3. Ibid., p. 38.

4. Ibid., p. 39.

content of its own, and is rigidly set in its abstract, unvarying course. Lived time is very different. To read in a watch the exact moment of one's arrival is surely not the same thing as the felt moment of relief on having made it at last, say, without delay and after a long and arduous journey. Indeed, our direct experience of time has a felt quality,

> a sort of voluminousness and complexity and variability that makes it utterly unlike metrical time. That is because . . . (it is) the passage of vital functions — somatic, emotional, and mental tensions, which have a characteristic pattern.[5]

When we notice the changing positions of the hands of a clock we do not experience, but only infer the actual passage of time. And this passage (as experienced), "involves more properties than 'length', or interval between selected moments"; it involves what may be called bulk or *volume*, a sense of being full on the inside. The suggestion is warranted by such familiar turns of speech as "a moment of destiny", "a memorable occasion", or "a hectic day at the office". In such temporal experiences of daily life the "volume" as felt is by no means simple, but is full of "*tensions* — physical, emotional, or intellectual", tensions which may appear as impatience to do diverse jobs quickly; as subdued anxiety (maybe) in respect of challenges that a new responsibility brings to light; or as the dawning of a pregnant insight which, so to say, insists on being worked out straight away.

This "lived" time, however, differs not only from clock-time, but from the time that we sense *in music* — or, as *I* would prefer to say, in the autonomous art of rhythm. Virtual time, or the time in which musical forms or rhythmic patterns appear to move, is not a part of our actual, everyday time; *it rather tends to obliterate our sense of the time that regulates our daily lives*, at least for the duration of the music contemplated, provided the music heard has the requisite measure of aesthetic appeal. Again, what fills actual time is a shifting mass of everyday

5. Langer, *Problems of Art*, p. 37.

situations and activities. The content of musical time, contrarily, is provided by orderly collocations of tones and rhythmic turns. Actual time (a) is measured by clocks and watches; virtual time (b, in music), through *sensibilities, tensions, emotions*. The former fact is common knowledge; but the latter (b) too is quite easy to illustrate by making a simple reference to Hindustani music. If, in spite of its manifest tunefulness, the singing of the *tāra sā* does not satisfy him, a *rasika* — that is, a person, of trained aesthetic *sensibility* — may well tend to *complain* that the note has not been sung long enough, *without of course looking at his watch at all*. Again, in the case of *ālāpa* (say) in *rāga pūriyā*, the note, *ni* (in the middle register) is said to have been given its due occupancy in time *only after* it has created in our minds a *tense* expectancy for the requisite supplement of a touch of *r̥̥ṣabh* followed by *sā*, both in the *tāra saptak*. Finally, a *sthāyī* deserves to be called *vilambit* (or adagio) only if it *feels* duly tranquil to *rasika*s. In all such experiencing no one goes by the ticks of a clock.

There is at least one other way to distinguish actual time from virtual time. The latter, which is (according to Langer) the primary illusion of music, is entirely perceptible through hearing alone; we sense it *only* in relations of (heard) tones to one another. The perception of actual time, on the other hand, depends on such motley objective factors as a clock, delay in the arrival of a friend, or a satisfying run of the day, so to say, over a quick succession of pleasing engagements. This is the point in Langer's following words:

> Inward tensions and outward change, . . . clocks, daylight and routines and weariness furnish various incoherent temporal data, which we coordinate for practical purposes by letting the clock predominate.[6]

Yet, though she does not in any way identify the two (in *Feeling and Form*, p. 113), Langer openly speaks of our everyday

6. Langer, *Feeling and Form*, Routledge & Kegan Paul, 3rd Impression, 1963, pp. 109-10.

experience of the passage of time as providing a model for the virtual time created in music:

> The direct experience of passage, as it occurs in each individual life is, of course, something *actual (not virtual) . . . yet it is the model for the virtual time created in music*. There we have its image, completely articulated and pure; every kind of tension *transformed* into musical tension, every qualitative content into musical quality, every extraneous factor replaced by musical elements.

Now, this is a significant utterance, and I think it necessary to say something way of clarifying it, partly because it is likely to appear a little rhetorical to casual attention:

All that Langer here says by way of pointing (if *implicitly*) to the *difference* between actual time and the virtual time of music admits of supportive illustration. Time in the art of rhythm — I prefer to speak of rhythm (I repeat) as an independent art, not of rhythm *in music* because, as a mere element of music, rhythm is not able to manifest its full aesthetic potential — is surely "pure" and "completely articulated". It is pure in the sense that it is quite free from the admixture of everyday happenings which variegates our experience of time in real life; and it is fully articulated in the sense that not only the syllables which make the *patterns* of rhythm, but the beats and segments (*vibhāg*s) which the basic *ṭhekā* comprises present a picture of (*laya*-) flow as *the underrunning unity of quite distinct accents*. The tensions which appear in configurations of rhythm are freely seen to assume the following diverse forms: a seemingly compulsive orientation of a patterned flow towards the *Sama*; the aesthetic strain of having to hold on (inwardly) to the basic pace, even where the (overt) playing is made to stray for a while purposely, say, as a mark of wilful abandon; and where the drummer has to provide accurate "accompaniment" to a *sitār* (or *sarod*) player, including moments of conscious endeavour to replicate the latter's patterns faithfully, again without loosening his grip on the basic pace of the matrix (or the *ṭhekā*). All these "tensions" in rhythm, I may add, have their rough parallels in daily life, say, in the form of unremitting endeavour towards a goal; intentional abstention from indulgence in a friendly gathering of revellers; and meticulous description of the details of a complicated situation. Nor is it difficult to show how rhythm — or rhythm in music — transforms every qualitative content of everyday experience into rhythmic (musical) quality, or replaces every extraneous factor of everyday experience with a rhythmic (musical) element. We freely distinguish the course of daily living as leisurely *or* crowded with happenings. This is something that is known to all. What is not so commonly and clearly realized is that the distinction in question can be just as easily made in the flowing form of music or of rhythm as patterned. Further, as approximate aesthetic parallels of leisureliness in everyday experience — such as the *protracted* waiting for the outcome of a long, but promising surgical operation — rhythm may project expansive, winsome patterns which are richly inlaid with syllables; which wind their way majestically, say, through three segments of equal extent; and which ultimately complete themselves immaculately at the *Sama*, which itself may be all along foreshadowed by the determinate relation which the patterns appear to bear, as they flow, to the underrunning basic pace. But all these rough parallels, it is obvious, do nothing to bedim the *difference* between "virtual" time (or rhythm in music) and time as experienced in daily life. The sense that a very busy day appears to have passed very quickly is one thing; the notice of a long and nimble rhythmic pattern, comprising a bevy of multifarious *bols*, which has just completed its run by pecking the *Sama* immaculately, is quite another.

In spite of all these clear differences, Langer's view that time as sensed in music (or as rhythm) is *virtual* has been vigorously questioned by Philip Alperson. It is a reasoned protest, and so I think it necessary to consider, at some length, if it could be fairly met by Langer. How Alperson formulates Langer's view and how he criticizes it may both be put as follows:

1. According to Langer, (a) all music creates an order of virtual time, in which its sonorous forms move in relation to each other — always and only to each other, for nothing else exists there . . . and (b) music makes time audible, and its form and continuity sensible.

2. Further, Langer adds, musical or virtual time is quite different from *clock-time* in two clear ways. First, whereas clock-time is a clear "abstraction" (of "pure sequence") from the "direct experiences of time" — and so is a mere *concept* — musical time is *perceptible*. Second, whereas *clock-time* is but a one-dimensional continuum — say, of "before" and "after" — musical time may well be said to have more than one dimension, for it has form and variform organization, volume, and units and segments which are all clearly distinct.

3. At the same time, Langer (yet) continues, no such clear differences may be said to separate musical time from *actual* (or lived) *time*. The truth rather is that — musical duration is an image of what might be called "lived" or "experienced" time — the passage of life that we feel as expectations become "now", and "now" turns into unalterable fact. Such passage is measurable only in terms of sensibilities, tensions and emotions.

4. But, and now Alperson turns to criticism, if this is so, if the resemblance between the model and its image is so complete, wherein lies the difference? Langer does not specify . . . [any] difference. . . . [Could it not, then, be said that] the temporality of musical perception is simply another example of our direct, intuitive experience of all things temporal [?]. . . . As an occurrence, . . . a piece of music is of a piece with all phenomena that occur in time: it has a determinate period of duration; an objective and irreversible time-order . . . [;] it calls upon the same faculties [that] we

> employ in all time perception . . . [namely] attention, memory . . . . apperception . . . [and] anticipation. [Indeed . . . Alperson concludes] the truth . . . seems to be that the temporal dimension of musical experience is *not* [*sui generis* or] fundamentally different from that of any other sort of temporal experience. [So] why say [at all] that "music creates an order of virtual time"?

The crux of Alperson's *protest*, it is clear, occurs in No. 4. But, I believe, the critical points it tries to make can all be met by Langer, squarely. To begin with, it is incorrect to say that Langer does not specify the difference between "lived time" (or the "model") and its image, that is, musical time. In fact, if No. 1 is taken along with some (other) utterances of Langer, at least two differences between the two orders of time would seem to be suggested by her quite clearly. Here are some such utterances:

A. The direct experience of passage [or lived or actual time] . . . is . . . like all actuality . . . *only in part* perceived, and its fragmentary data are supplemented by practical knowledge and ideas from other realms of thought altogether. *Yet* it is the model for the virtual time created in music. [But] here we have its image, completely articulated and pure . . . [only] the sonorous image of passage, abstracted from actuality to become free and plastic and *entirely* perceptible.

B. Virtual time [which music creates] is entirely perceptible, through the agency of a single sense, that is, hearing. There is no supplementing of one sort of experience by another. . . . Music spreads out time for our direct and complete apprehension by letting our hearing monopolize it — organize, fill, and shape it — all alone.

Now, a look at B (and at no. 1 in Alperson's formulation and criticism of Langer's view) makes it clear that, according to Langer, the virtual time which music creates is experienced only *through* the sense of hearing or just by attending to the sounding (sonorous) forms. But this at once suggests a clear difference between virtual time *and lived time which is* freely marked by a "supplementing of one sort of experience by another". To illustrate, my experience of the present moment is a "heterogeneous" mix of some thinking incidental to writing, visual perception of the words being written, hearing of the birds' chirping from outside the window of my room, and some bodily sensations arising from being seated in a chair, as also from a shuffling of the forearm across the sheet of paper being used. One's experience of attending to music, on the other hand, comes mainly — and indeed quite clearly — through just listening to tones and passages as they rest or move up and down the scale. It is true, of course, that musical listening is *not merely* a matter of hearing; and that, for example, the evenness of pace between two adjacent beats has to be kept and followed *in idea*. But unless the beats are *drummed* the requirement of keeping to the pace and sensing that it is being properly done just cannot be met.

Here, however, I feel compelled to qualify what I have just said, from the viewpoint of our rhythm *as an independent art*. In respect of *our* rhythm it is indeed very true that whole collocations of syllables — even the most intricate and elaborate patterns — can be rehearsed merely in the mind. Such quiet recitation may be well be said to involve only some implicit speech, where there is no question of hearing at all, because no sound is produced. But the point is that Langer and Alperson do not discuss rhythm as an independent art; and of rhythm or time as sensed *in music,* it is certainly true that the sole agency of its experience is hearing which (I repeat) at once distinguishes it from lived time.

The second distinction that Langer draws between the two temporal orders is also quite clear in A. I may put it as follows:

Whereas the direct experience of the lapse or passage of time

> — or of lived time — is only *partly* provided by perception, music presents the passage in question in an *entirely* perceptible *form*. Perception may here be taken to signify immediate experience; and the net meaning of the distinction suggested could be put quite simply. The passage of time is, of course, ceaseless; but, because we generally remain occupied in life's diverse activities, it is only dimly or fitfully that we remain or become conscious of the passage. Occasions that make it a distinct object of direct awareness, like a prolonged waiting for the delayed arrival of a friend, are infrequent; otherwise, in general, some practical awareness — as of the fact that, when I keep working at the table in the morning, the milkman rings the door-bell at a particular time — may make me only vaguely conscious, say, of how long I have been busy in writing. Similar awareness may also be provided by ideas from some altogether different "realms of thought", as when a look at the many reports of his pathological tests makes a person aware of *the long course* of the disease he has been suffering from. On the other hand, when we listen to music, temporal features like the *meteoric* ascent of a *taan*, the *leisurely flow* of a *dagar* passage, or the sweet and reposeful *abidance* of voice at the upper tonic are all *directly* presented to us.

Nor is it proper to argue that the two temporal orders, rhythmic and everyday, cannot be regarded as *dis*similar because the *same* mental acts or attitudes are involved in the way we experience them. Would it make sense to deny the distinctness of sweet from salted food on the ground that they are both relished by tasting? It is, I would say, not *how* we experience them, but *what* exactly we experience *in* them that makes the two orders of time *quite* unlike each other.

The point becomes very clear if we consider it in the context of rhythm as an independent art. A *tablā* or *pakhāwaj* maestro dwells in the unique world of rhythm — comprising beats, *bols*, and their variform collocations — with as perfect a sense of encompassment as a mathematician in the company of symbols and formulae. And "happenings" in the drummer's world can be quite out of the ordinary. Where, for instance, in the ordinary world do we produce beauty, as our drummers occasionally do, by deviating designedly from a set course of flow, with meaningless letters (or *bols*) alone as the instruments of charm? Even generally, the time that *we* regulate and beautify cannot be the same as the one which is only *given to* us *and is so often the locus of wayward and unforeseen happenings.*

# Bibliography


Alexander, *Beauty and Other Forms of Value*, MacMillan, London, 1933.

Barfield, Owen, *What Coleridge Thought*, O.U.P., London, 1972, 78.

Barlingay, S.S. (ed.), *Indian Philosophical Quarterly*, Poona, vol. I, no. 2, January 1974.

Beardsley, M.C., "The Aesthetic Point of View", *Metaphilosophy*, vol. I, no. 1. January 1970, 46.

Bossart, W.H., "Form and Meaning in the Visual Arts", included in *Aesthetics and the Arts*, ed. L.A. Jacobus, McGraw Hill Book Co., 1968.

Coleman, F.J., *Contemporary Studies in Aesthetics*, McGraw Hill Book Co., 1968 (PB).

Croce, B., *Aesthetic: As Science of Expression and General Linguistic*, Vision Press, London, 1962 rpt.

Dewey, John, *Art as Experience*, Capricorn Books, New York, 1958 (7th impression).

Frye, N., *Anatomy of Criticism*, Princeton University Press, 1957 (PB).

Gatt, Giuseppe, *Turner*, A Dolphin Art Book, Thames and Hudson, 1968.

Heuvel, G.V.D.: *S.K. Langer: Abridged edition*, The John Hopkins University Press, Baltimore (PB), 1988.

Langer, S.K., *Feeling and Form*, Routledge and Kegan Paul Ltd., London, 1963, 3rd impression.

———, *Mind: An Essay on Human Feeling*, vol. I, The John Hopkins University Press, Baltimore and London, 2nd Printing, PS, 1975.

———, *Problems of Art*, Routledge and Kegan Paul, London, 1957.

——— (ed.), *Reflections on Art*, The John Hopkins Press, Baltemore, 1958.

———, "The Dynamic Image: Some Philosophical Reflections on Dance" included in *Aesthetics and the Arts*, ed. L.A. Jacobus, McGraw Hill Book Co., 1968.

Pepper, S.C., "Aesthetic Design", in *Introductory Readings in Aesthetics*, ed. John Hospers, The Free Press, 1969, p. 69.

Read, Herbert, "A Definition of Art", in *Aesthetics and the Arts*, ed. L.A. Jacobus, McGraw Hill Book Co., 1968.

Reid, L.A., *Meaning in the Arts*, George Allen and Unwin, London, 1969.

Saxena, Sushil Kumar, "Aesthetic Character of Some Asymmetrical Rhythms" *Sangeet Natak*, Journal of Sangeet Natak Akademi, no. 34, October-December 1974.

———, "Aesthetic Theory and Hindustani Rhythm" *The British Journal of Aesthetics*, vol. 16 no. 3.

———, "Embodiment and the Quest for Key Aesthetic Concepts" in *Contemporary Indian Philosophy* (ed. Margaret Chatterji), George Allen & Unwin Ltd., London (1974), pp. 321-52.

———, "Essentials of Hindustani Music", in *Diogenes*, Spring 64, no. 45.

———, "Phenomenology of Sama in Hindustani Rhythm" in *Indian Philosophical Quarterly*, Poona, vol. IV, no. 3, April 1977.

———, "*Sama* in Hindustani Rhythm: A Psycho-Aesthetic Study" presented to the Conference on *Psychology and Music* organized by Sangeet Natak Akademi (New Delhi) at Poona, on 12 January 1975.

———, "The Role of Rhythm in Kathak Dance", *Marg* (Bombay, September 1959, pp. 48-53).

———, "The Fabric of Āmad: A Study of Form and Flow in Hindustani Music", in *Sangeet Natak*, Journal of Sangeet Natak Akademi, no. 16, April-June 1970.

Sparshott *The Structure of Aesthetics*, Routledge and Kegan Paul, 1963.

Stephen, Spender, *World within World*, Hamilton, London.

Tovey D.F., "Handel as Composer", in *Encyclopaedia Britannica*, 11th edn., vol. XII (1910).

# Index